Right to Kill

* * *

A Brooklyn Tale

Jim McGinty

iUniverse, Inc.
Bloomington

Right to Kill
A Brooklyn Tale

iUniverse books may be ordered through booksellers or by contacting:

iUniverse
1663 Liberty Drive
Bloomington, IN 47403
www.iuniverse.com
1-800-Authors (1-800-288-4677)

ISBN: 978-1-4759-5953-6 (sc)
ISBN: 978-1-4759-5955-0 (hc)

Library of Congress Control Number: 2012921234

Printed in the United States of America

iUniverse rev. date: 11/29/2012

Acknowledgments

They say writing is a lonely task. That's true. But rarely is writing done alone. A writer, especially a rookie, generally needs help—lots of it. My heartfelt thanks to my wife, Pat, my sons, my daughters-in-law, and several friends who suffered through early drafts of this work. They provided constructive advice on plot, scenes, and characters. Most of all, they encouraged me to keep going.

Family and friends are usually very kind—too kind, in fact. Writing help must come via professional editors. I had three very professional editors during the years this book took shape. Barbara DeSantis (DeSantis and Associates, Los Angeles, California) helped me with her critique and revision of my first several chapters. She got me in tune with the basics of story construction. Tammy Greenwood (Writers Center, Bethesda, Maryland) reviewed an early draft focusing on a revision effort and provided a score of useful suggestions. The real heavy lifting was provided by the book's editor, Susan Malone (Malone Editorial Services, Ennis, Texas). Susan provided a chapter-by-chapter, scene-by-scene critique covering all aspects of creating a work of fiction. She labored with me through several revisions. I doubt the final work could ever do justice to her editorial talent, but I guess that's a cross all great editors must bear.

A significant degree of help came from an unconventional source. Through the good graces of my friend Delores Snowden, her Silver Spring, Maryland, book club agreed to review an early draft. Not only did these ten avid readers forsake reading and discussing a known title, but they actually agreed to meet with me and provide a critique. It was humbling but extraordinarily helpful. Fortunately, the book was in early stages of revision, and many comments and suggestions from these literary stalwarts were incorporated in the final draft. I am in their debt.

A final mention of thanks to my many instructors at the Bethesda Writing Center, especially Ann McLaughlin and Jim Mathews. These accomplished authors, along with my classmates, not only provided critique and technical guidance but constantly fostered the all-too-necessary motivation to keep writing.

Author's Comments

The primary purpose of this novel is to entertain. It's also meant to help better understand the late sixties, perhaps laugh a little, maybe cry, and hopefully gain a new perspective about those who lived through these tough times.

Right to Kill is a work of fiction; all the characters and most of the events are products of the author's imagination. As in much historical fiction, some events did transpire, and some places and organizations actually did exist. There was nothing fictional about the Vietnam War, the Que Son Valley, Hue City and Khe Sanh, or the Marines who fought, bled, and died in those places during 1967 and 1968. In fact, units of the First and Fifth Marine Regiments fought in those locations, but there was never a Fifth Battalion of the Fifth Marines and no Alpha Company of Five/Five. The Seventh Marine Regiment actually occupied Hill 55, but for reasons connected to the fictional plot, the Fifth Marines were used.

Battle scenes described in this story, with a few exceptions, are fictional composites developed from what the author experienced, listened to (he was a Marine communications officer), or had relayed to him by other Marines. Official unit after-action reports and a vast body of literature including *ProQuest Historical Newspaper Archive* databases covering the period of 1967–68 also informed this novel.

In terms of the home front during this era, there were hundreds of antiwar demonstrations and thousands of antiwar activists. All those depicted in this book are fictional. The Brooklyn neighborhood of Gravesend existed then as it does today. While all neighborhood characters are fictional, the character of the people living in that neighborhood at that time, especially the way they embraced and supported those of us who fought in Vietnam, was anything but fictional. It was one of the motivating forces behind this novel.

Prologue

On a cool, dreary morning, two young men hurried down a street flanked by a decades-old brick wall forming the north side of Washington Cemetery. They reached the partially gated entrance of the burial ground and joined a group of mourners filing behind two slow-moving black limos and a hearse.

The procession made its way through the rows of tombstones and crypts to a tent housing a dozen folding chairs. A few feet away, a mahogany coffin sat suspended over an unseen hole rimmed by mounds of fresh dirt. The gatherers parted for a burly man, ashen with tears, who guided a woman sobbing quietly behind her lace veil. They sat in the first row, the man covering his head with a black silk yarmulke.

The two young men stood in the rear and stared at the tent. Frankie Ryan, clad in a black woolen coat covering most of his lanky frame, would have blended in well with the group of mourners were it not for his ponytail, neatly tied behind his wavy black hair with a thin red ribbon. He motioned to his friend. "Sal, let's get over to the far side of the tent. I see Frank Cercone with Sean's mom. She looks in a bad way."

Sal Lente adjusted his thin, black tie and pulled up the collar of his trench coat. "Yeah, take a look at Grandma Rosa over there." He nodded toward a frail old woman in the last row, hands at her breast, brown rosary beads laced through her fingers. "I'm not sure Rosa's gonna get through this." He shook his head. "We got to get whoever did this, Frankie."

Frankie nodded, his jaw tightening. "We're gonna get whoever did this. And we're gonna kill 'em."

Book I

Chapter 1

A Year Earlier
Gravesend, Brooklyn
Late October 1966

The Culver Line subway train caused a deafening roar as it snaked through Brooklyn on an elevated steel platform that disfigured the otherwise tranquil neighborhood of Gravesend. The shrill of iron wheels on steel tracks drowned out conversation within a couple of hundred feet of the El. The McDonald Avenue Park ran parallel to the Culver Line El, and a silent mode went into effect whenever the boxlike train roared past on its way from Coney Island through Brooklyn to its terminus in a remote part of the Bronx.

As soon as the train was out of earshot, Sean barked at the guys. He hated it when they executed a sloppy play. "Come on, pick it up, Gremlins, pick it up. You're sleepwalking. Frankie, cut sharper—eight yards, not twelve. It's a quick hit. Timing's gotta be right." Waving his arm past his ear, Sean cried, "Mickey, take the snap. Quick look left and zing it. It's timing, all timing. Come on, do it again."

Eight men moved into a formation. Joe D'Angelo, muscled arms protruding from his dirty gray undershirt, led them to an imaginary line, and five men assumed a three-point football stance. Two others positioned themselves a few feet apart behind the five down linemen. The last of the group, Frankie Ryan, tall and lanky with wavy black hair pulled back in a ponytail, placed himself slightly behind and ten feet to the left of the five linemen.

Sean and his gang considered touch football serious business, in contrast to the touch football shown in TV documentaries depicting the recently slain president and his brothers frolicking on a manicured lawn in Hyannis Port. Touch in Brooklyn was a brutal game, played much the same as regular football except that there was no protective equipment and the playing field was concrete.

Six feet tall, lean with an almost too erect posture, Sean Cercone differed from the others. He had clean-cut good looks, dark brown hair cropped short with a slight part, and a tan complexion accenting his gray-green eyes. A newly commissioned second lieutenant on weekend leave from the Marine Corps Basic School in Quantico, Virginia, Sean was on his first leave since officer candidate school in midsummer. He was happy to be home again, helping his old teammates prepare for their next battle.

"Hey, Sean, did the damn Marines make you Vince Lombardi or what?" chided Mario, an interior lineman.

"Shut your mouth, you 4-F prick," grunted Joey D'Angelo, a rookie cop, former Army paratrooper, and captain of the Gravesend Gremlins. "Have some respect. He's the only officer we got in the crowd. Besides, he's right. We gotta get sharper."

Sean smiled at the retort from D'Angelo, who, like most of the neighborhood guys, had done peacetime military service after high school. He knew Joey and the guys were proud of his recent enlistment in the Marines, since Vietnam was fast becoming a real war and most college guys were not exactly storming the recruiting centers. *That's right, Joey. Probably the most difficult decision of my life. Now I'm on a different team in a different ball game—playing for keeps. Hope I can hack it.*

A smallish man with a ruggedly handsome face and jet-black hair dressed in a dark business suit strolled up the sideline. "Sean, how them Marines treating you?"

"Hey, Jimmy. I'm good! How's the best detective in Brooklyn South doing? Not here on official business, I hope."

Detective First Grade Jimmy Napoli glanced toward the field. "Maybe! Keeping an eye on your wide receiver. The one with the ponytail."

"Who? Frankie? Hey, Nap, known him all my life. He's like a brother to me. And knowing him the way I do, doubt if you could get anything on Frankie."

"Yeah, maybe. Just wanted to give you a heads-up. Friend, buddy, or neighborhood good guy, don't give a shit. If he crosses the line, I'll lock him up."

Sean smiled. "Jimmy, only had a year of law school, but I know the score. If somebody commits a serious crime and you can prove it, you gotta put 'em away."

Sean crossed his arms over his head, signaling a break in the practice. "See you around, Jimmy. Gotta get some water." He trotted toward a fountain on the far side of the field next to six clay tennis courts.

Looks like Nap had a guilt trip about busting a neighborhood guy—why else would he tip me off about Frankie?

Gulping down the not very cool water, Sean glanced at the game of mixed doubles on the court closest to the fountain. He couldn't help but notice an exquisite pair of bronze legs that ran up the short white skirt of a girl hunched in a tennis stance. After making a quick sliding move, she ambled to the rear court, and he got a full view. She was tall, maybe five-nine, thin but not skinny, with big, dark eyes and a sharp jawline.

He lingered at the fountain, watching her arch her body and launch a powerful serve. For the second her body vertically extended, Sean caught sight of her round, slightly oversized breasts. Her follow-through caused her skirt to flap momentarily, revealing a well-developed butt.

"Hey, Marine, you gonna drown staring at that babe," said Sal "the Scribe" Lente, a defensive back and close friend of Sean's since their altar-boy days.

"Tell you what, Sal," Sean said, never changing his line of sight. "I could drown myself all day looking at her. Who the hell is she?"

"That's Sandra Gold, What's-His-Name's kid sister. You remember the tall guy who lived on Third off the Parkway. He went to Brandeis. An All-City tennis player, couple of years ahead of us at Lincoln."

"Yeah, I remember him. He just graduated from St. John's Law school. Met him last fall. Bob Gold. He was editor of our *Law Review*." Sean laughed. "He interviewed me for *Law Review* last spring. Didn't know he had a sister like that—woulda made him my best friend."

Sal took a quick drink, and the two began jogging back to the practice. Sean glanced over his shoulder, trying to catch one last glimpse of Bob Gold's kid sister. "Woo Sal, you see that? Those two really collided. She took a bad hit. Let's get over there, see if we can help."

A guy with skinny legs, the girl's doubles partner, was on the ground holding his head, moaning. She was flat on her back, hands covering her face, one of her ankles turned in an awkward position.

Sean bent over the sobbing girl. The large bump over her right eye didn't look serious. He moved to her ankle, touching it softly, and she let out a screeching cry. A bad sprain, maybe even a break.

The other players were useless, appearing more in shock than the two casualties. Sean barked at Sal to get some ice from the Gremlins' cooler. Sal bolted off toward the other end of the park.

"Okay, just take it easy," Sean whispered, his face inches from hers. "You got a bad bump—doesn't look too serious. I'm afraid your ankle may be a problem. Just take it easy." He placed one hand behind her head, and she settled down.

Sal returned with the ice in a towel, and Sean wrapped her ankle. The skinny guy and the two others clamored for an ambulance.

"You guys can wait for an ambulance. I'm taking her to Coney Island Hospital. I'll make it in ten minutes."

"Just take me home," she pleaded. "I only live a few blocks away. Just take me home, please."

Sean scooped her up and carried her out of the park toward his car. Despite his firm grip, her leg wobbled, and she screamed. She relented and agreed to go home via the hospital.

Mid-Saturday morning, the emergency room at Coney Island Hospital was clear of the Friday-night frolics, and it was too early for the parade of high school football injuries. They waited only twenty minutes for a doctor, who complimented Sean on his icing. The ankle didn't appear broken, but the doctor wanted X-rays and sent them to the second floor.

Sean introduced himself and tried to make her comfortable in the waiting room, her legs across his lap. "Just take it easy. Keep that leg elevated."

"Sorry about all of this." She pulled herself up on her elbows and grimaced. "I'm Sandy. I can't thank you enough." Her gravelly voice sounded sexy. "You were right about coming here, but you're wasting your Saturday. I'm such a klutz. I can't believe this is happening."

Her voice and the smoothness of her legs rendered him speechless. He grinned, his mind racing for something to say. "It's Sandy Gold, isn't it? I know your brother Bob. Met him last year at St. John's. He helped me to apply for *Law Review*."

"Oh, you're at St. John's Law School. And *Law Review*, that's quite impressive. What year?"

"Was at St. John's, left a few months ago, took a leave of absence, sort of."

She pointed to the small black letters on Sean's gray T-shirt. "What does USMC stand for? Is that a frat?"

Sean jolted upright. "You're kidding, right? You have to be kidding. You really don't know what USMC stands for?"

Sandy's face reddened. "Not really."

"United States Marine Corps," Sean said, almost glaring. "I'm a Marine. That's why I'm not in law school. I enlisted."

She reached for his hand. "Sean, I know nothing about the military. Of course I've heard about the Marine Corps. They're the best; everybody knows that." She squeezed his hand.

"Well, I guess—I don't know." He searched for something to say. "Maybe it's because you're pretty shook up."

Sandy raised her head and opened her wide dark eyes, still clutching his hand. "I'm sorry."

He took a deep breath, exhaled, and spoke slowly. "You didn't do anything. I'm the one who should apologize. I shouldn't be so uptight. It's just that everybody thinks I'm making a mistake—Dean McNight, my professors, my law-school buddies, my family." He shook his head. "The only ones who understand are the neighborhood guys. And some of them say I'm crazy for joining the Marines."

Sandy's brow wrinkled, and her face hardened. After some hesitation, she asked, "Sean, is that war more important than your family, your career? Why the Marines?"

He responded in a determined, almost lecturing tone. "Vietnam is really a part of our protracted conflict with Communism. Not much different than the situation we had in Korea. In some ways, the fate of all Southeast Asia is on the line. Why the Marines? My dad was a Marine; so was my godfather." He shrugged. "Guess it's in the family. Kind of have a moral obligation to serve, just like they did."

He continued as if talking to himself. "Leaving law school to go to Marine Officer Candidates School was a tough decision. Dean McKnight didn't approve but said they would hold my scholarship. I'll get back there after my hitch. This is more important. It's what I want to do. Everybody just has to understand."

Sandy nodded. "What about your girl, what does she think?"

Sean grinned. "Had someone in school a while back, but it didn't work out. Just as well. Probably not a good time for a relationship. Wouldn't be fair."

A green-clad Filipino intern walked up pushing a wheelchair. He told them Sandy had a bad sprain with no sign of a fracture. Placing a soft cast on her now-swollen ankle, he gave instructions to stay off of it and motioned to Sean to get Sandy in the chair.

★   ★   ★

Sean helped Sandy into his backseat and pulled out onto Ocean Parkway. *Been talking nonstop, didn't let her get a word in edgewise, hardly know her.* "So, Sandy, now you know all that heavy stuff about me, what about you? Who's Sandy Gold?"

Sandy tried in vain to get comfortable with her foot extended across the backseat. "I'm a senior at Brooklyn College, an ed. major. Live at home with my folks on Third, off Avenue T. Graduated from Lincoln, where I played a lot of tennis. I love tennis. Played varsity at Brooklyn for the past two seasons. Want to teach, but I'll probably go for my masters first, maybe focus on early childhood."

During the five-minute ride from the hospital to Sandy's house, she didn't get past the basics and the fact her parents were well off—a fact that became apparent when Sean pulled in front of a large, two-story brick house with a Spanish-tile roof. It sat on a double lot surrounded by well-manicured shrubs and huge old oak trees, one of several homes lining Avenue T a few blocks off Ocean Parkway. Sean knew this little enclave of wealth, since his own modest two-story stucco house was only three blocks away.

"Hold it. Let me help you out," Sean said. "Put your arm around my neck and keep that ankle up. When we get to the stoop, let me pick you up." He carried her up four stairs and was startled when the ornate door burst open.

A slim, attractive woman with jet-black hair stood in the foyer. "My God, what happened? Sandy, what did you do to yourself? What's that on your leg? Look at you—your forehead, God!"

"It's okay. I'm all right."

"She's okay—just a sprain," Sean said. "Nothing serious, but she is getting a little heavy. Can I park her somewhere?"

The woman pointed to a room off the foyer. She was in her late forties, perhaps fifty, but looked much younger. Tall, with her black hair pulled tightly in a chignon, long-necked and regal, she was not nearly as dark as Sandy but every bit as beautiful. Her lips were not as full, but she had the same straight, white teeth and the same way of smiling.

She led them to a long, Spanish-style sofa opposite a white brick fireplace in a good-sized room with a twelve-foot ceiling. Sean listened as the two exchanged words about women playing mixed doubles. "Your sister is right, Sandy," Sean said, thinking the situation needed some levity. "Better listen to her and stay away from—"

"I'm her mother!" The women glared at Sean, then smiled slowly. "But thank you just the same." Retaining her smile, she turned to her daughter. "And who might this charming gentleman be?"

Sean laughed, and Sandy blushed. "Mother, this is Sean Cercone. Actually, it's Lieutenant Sean Cercone. He's a Marine."

"I'm Juliana Gold. And I really am her mother. A pleasure to meet you, Lieutenant. A Marine officer, how wonderful." Glancing at her daughter, she raised one eyebrow. "Sean's a lovely name. Irish, isn't it?"

"I'm half Irish, half Italian—tough combination to beat." Sean grinned.

"Tough combination indeed." She fixed a stare at her daughter. "I'm sure my Sam would find it especially tough for his Sephardic Jewish princess. Sean, perhaps you might want something cold to drink, maybe something to eat."

"Thanks, Mrs. Gold, but I have to catch up with some friends." He extended his hand. "Well, Sandy, get better soon. Hope to see you again."

Sandy pulled herself upright, reached for Sean's hand, and gave a half-smile. "Thanks so much for everything, Sean. Good luck at Quantico." She hesitated, her voice faltering. "Please stay in touch."

Juliana escorted Sean to the door and thanked him for helping her daughter.

Sean flashed a sideways smile. "It was my pleasure, Mrs. Gold. Hope to see you again sometime."

Juliana rushed back into the living room. "A Marine! Your father would just love that. Are you really planning to see him again?"

Sandy smiled mischievously. "I hope so."

Chapter 2

Sean stood at the Golds' front door, adjusted his uniform, and rang the doorbell.

When the doorbell chimed on Sunday morning, Mr. Gold was startled. When it chimed again too rapidly for any polite visitor, he was annoyed. Bolting from his chair, he rushed to the door, a cigar clenched in his teeth and the sports section of the *Times* in one hand. He swung open the door to find a young Marine, gold bars on his neatly pressed shirt, clutching a bouquet of flowers.

"Who the hell are you?"

Sean removed his garrison cap and looked into wide dark eyes that dominated a whiskered face. *And a good morning to you too!* He extended his hand. "Name is Sean Cercone. I'm here to see Sandy. I take it you're Mr. Gold."

"Yeah, it's Sam Gold. Come in, come on in. So, ya know my daughter?"

Sean glanced over his shoulder. "Yes, sir. Met Sandy yesterday. How's her leg doing?"

"Juliana, call your daughter!" Sam shouted. "Some guy got flowers for her. Juliana, ya hear me?"

"I'm right here, Sam," Mrs. Gold said with a pained expression. "No need to shout. Oh, Sean, how good to see you again. What beautiful flowers! Let me get them in a vase." She rushed out of the foyer, ignoring her husband, who still held the door, and called through the hallway, "Sandra, you have a caller—it's Lieutenant Cercone."

Sam's dark eyes narrowed. "Well, mister, you the dumb son of a bitch who ran into my daughter on the tennis court?"

Sean slipped through the foyer and glanced back at Sam. "Nah, I'm the one who took Sandy to the hospital after that dumb son of a bitch ran into her."

Sandy hobbled down the hall in tan sweatpants and a red tank top that flattered her athletic figure. "Sean, how nice of you to stop by. Please come in. Sit down." Motioning Sean into the living room, she turned. "Dad, this is the boy—I mean, the young man who took me to the hospital."

Sean stepped down into a room across from the one he had visited the day before. Two sand-colored love seats faced an oversized black leather chair in front of a stone fireplace that ran to the ceiling. He sat on the edge of the leather chair. "I'm afraid I can only stay a few minutes. Have a 3 p.m. shuttle back to DC. Just wanted to check up on your leg."

Sam entered the room and sat on one of the love seats. His wife and daughter ignored his presence and fawned over Sean. He leaned forward and spoke in a loud, staccato voice. "So, when are they shipping you out? You gonna fight in that dumb war? Johnson's an ass to get us in a land war in Asia. Gonna get a lot of people killed."

Mrs. Gold glared, and Sandy stiffened as Sean repositioned himself in the leather chair to face Sam.

"Expect to receive orders next spring," Sean said in a lawyerlike tone. "True, most wars are dumb but have to be fought or dumber things happen." He smirked. "I'm no fan of Johnson; I voted for Goldwater. Don't like a land war in Asia, but sometimes we don't get to pick where aggression starts."

"You ready to see a lot of people die?" Sam growled.

"Not really," Sean shot back, "but I guess that comes with the job."

The burly man stood up, face contorted. "Comes with the job! Is that what you think war is all about—a job? I'll tell you what it's about. It's about people getting killed. It's about—"

Mrs. Gold sprang to her feet, fixing her dark Spanish eyes on her husband. "Sam, that's enough. Enough!" She moved to grasp Sean's arm, almost lifting him out of the chair. "Sandra, I'm afraid we might be keeping Sean. Sean, it's been a pleasure." She hurriedly escorted him to the foyer. "Please, Sean, not a word, please. Sam had a bad time in Warsaw during the war," she whispered. "Do come back. I'm sure Sandy will want that. Just call first. Good luck, Sean, and go with God."

★   ★   ★

Sean ambled down the tree-lined street, trying to understand what had just happened. He had thought Sandy's father a raving fool until Mrs. Gold whispered about Mr. Gold having a tough time in Warsaw during the war. Now he was intrigued, but still angry at having his visit with Sandy cut short.

He walked down the avenue with its stately brick homes on double lots to a street crammed with attached houses and small front yards. He thought of his own father and the price he had paid for his service. How his mother would hold him and dry away his tears when he asked if his father was coming home. How, as a teen, he had scrambled to watch every session of the TV documentary *Victory at Sea* in the hope of catching a glimpse of his Marine father landing on some hostile beach. His mood lifted when he saw two guys perched on his front stoop. He'd forgotten Joey and Frankie (known to his friends as "Brain") had agreed to take him to the airport.

The trio jumped into a red Bonneville and drove down a street made narrow by rows of parked cars. Frankie drove while Joey lounged in the backseat, peppering Sean with questions. "Sally says you took that Gold chick to the hospital yesterday. What happened? Doc Tanzi saw you buy a big bouquet of flowers after Mass. Who they for?" Joey said, reaching forward, his hands gripping the black leather front seats. "And then we come over for breakfast and you ain't home. Got your mom all upset. What's going on? I bet it's that broad."

Frankie cut in, "Hey, Joey, you're a cop less than a year. What are you—practicing to be a fuckin' detective with this third degree? Let the man be. It's okay, Sean. You got a right not to incriminate yourself. It's there in the Fifth Amendment. To say nothing about your right to privacy, which I believe is found in the Fourth Amendment." He glanced over at Sean, waving one finger. "Then again, there's the bond of friendship, which clearly transcends—"

"Shut the fuck up! I'll talk," Sean blurted, "not that I could withhold anything from Sergeant Friday and fuckin' Clarence Darrow."

"Hey, Sean, no cursing—remember, you're an officer and a gentleman," Frankie teased.

"Right, Frankie, and you know all about being a gentleman," Sean said. "Even with straight As, you managed to get kicked out of St. Simon. Got caught mauling Theresa Zenni in a coat closet. Then you got your sterling academic career terminated at Lafayette High with that SAT caper."

"Hey! Who else in this crowd got 740 in Math and 650 in English? Tell me that, Lieutenant."

"Very true, Brain." Sean flashed his sideways smile. "But nobody ever got caught taking the SATs for three other guys."

"That's not what we're talking about, Sean. Tell us about this broad."

Frankie and Joey listened in silence while Sean recounted the incident at the park and his visit to the Golds' house. He finished when they were halfway to the airport.

Frankie looked over at Sean as he eased off the Belt parkway onto the Van Wick expressway. "Know what I think, Sean? Let me tell ya what I think—couple of things." He ran his hand through his wavy black hair and laughed. "One, I think you've fallen for this girl Sandy. Two, I don't think her old man is the asshole you think he is. Three, next time you're in town, I want to meet the mother."

After a moment of silence, which usually followed whenever Frankie offered an opinion on anything, Joey lamented, "Brain, I buy in on point one and point three. But tell me why this guy Gold ain't a couch case after the way he talked to Sean. Showed no respect for the uniform. Matter of fact, I bet he don't like Italians." He tapped Sean on the shoulder. "Ever think of that, Sean? The guy's a Jew, right? Think he wants wops like us calling on his daughter?"

Frankie responded with an air of authority. "It's all about Warsaw. Like the lady said, he saw some bad shit. Warsaw was fuckin' unbelievable. If this guy was a Jew in Warsaw during the war, he's gotta be one of the few who made it out." He gunned the engine and spoke over the roar. "Didn't you read about the Warsaw ghetto uprising? The Jews were butchered after several weeks of resistance. They fought out of cellars and sewers—men, women, kids. And how 'bout this. As the war was ending, the Red Army was supposed to liberate Warsaw. So the Poles staged another uprising to support the invasion. Guess what?" Frankie flashed Sean a hard look. "The fuckin' Russians held up outside the city.

Waited till the Nazis cut the Poles to pieces. So he had to survive that as well. I'm sure he had some family. Good chance a lot of them wound up in those camps—probably died like animals. That's gotta fuck up your mind. Know what I mean, Sean?"

Sean stared out the side window into the graying midafternoon sky. *Wonder if Vietnam is gonna be as bad as Warsaw.*

Minutes later, the big Bonneville pulled curbside at the entrance to the Eastern Airlines Shuttle. Sean opened the door and turned back to his friends. "You're right, Brain. Guess I have to cut old Mr. Gold some slack. Not gonna matter anyway. Can't get involved with anyone now. See you guys in a few weeks when I'm home for Christmas leave. Thanks for the ride."

As he moved through the art deco Eastern Airlines lounge back to his Marine Corps world, Sam Gold's words echoed in his mind. *It's all about people getting killed.*

Chapter 3

Sandy knocked on the glass-partitioned wooden door. A woman with well-coiffed white hair worn off her face peered through one of the panes. She opened the door cautiously.

"Mrs. Cercone, good evening. My name is Sandy Gold. I'm a friend of Sean's." The woman stood in the doorway in silence. "Actually, not a close friend; I mean we just met last week. I was wondering—"

"Please, dear, please come in." She smiled, motioning Sandy through the foyer into a cozy living room with two stuffed armchairs, a coffee table, and a gray-green couch. The wall behind the couch was studded with pictures. "Mrs. Cercone is a little formal, dear. My name is Ann. How about some tea, Sandy?"

Sean's mother darted into the kitchen, returning with two mugs and several pieces of Italian pastries. She had pale blue, tired-looking eyes, yet her creamy skin was taut, without a wrinkle. Sandy thought she might be fifty, though she had the figure of a much younger woman.

Sandy sat erect in the armchair, her black hair pulled to a side twist, expensive-looking clothes tastefully accentuating her athletic build. The two women talked and laughed over the story of how Sandy and Sean had met. "He stopped in to see me last Sunday. Forgot to give me his mailing address at Quantico." Sandy frowned. *That's not exactly true, but it could be the case.*

"Of course, dear, I'll get the address," Ann replied with slight smile that couldn't mask a look of concern.

Sandy gestured to one of the larger framed photos of a Marine in his dress blues. "Is that Sean?"

"No, it's his father," Ann said, her gaze dropping to the floor. She rose and looked toward the cluster of wall-mounted memories. "He was killed on Iwo Jima, February '45. Sean was almost three. So many of them died in that place, thousands of Marines, all young." She motioned to another picture. "Sean never knew his dad. That's Tom holding Sean the day before he left for the Pacific. Sean was just too young to remember. When he was a little boy, Sean would sit and cry in front of these pictures." Her voice cracked. "He desperately wanted to remember something about his dad. He was just too young. Don't think he's ever gotten over not knowing his father. Guess I haven't either."

"I'm so sorry," Sandy whispered. "Sean told me his father was a Marine but never told me he was lost. Is that why Sean …?"

"Joined the Marines?" Ann finished Sandy's thought. "Guess that's part of it. He tried to join when he graduated from high school. His uncle Frank, my Tom's brother, talked him into going to college first. Frank was a Marine too. He was only eighteen when he was wounded in Korea." Her pale blue eyes widened. "Grandma Cercone nearly died when she got word she'd almost lost a second son. Frank was in the hospital for over six months. They gave him several medals."

Ann Cercone returned to the couch and sat across from Sandy, her eyes welling. "Sean respected his uncle Frank. Thank God he listened to him about college. Did very well as an undergrad. Won a full scholarship to St. John's Law School. I'd been working at the school for ten years as a secretary to Dean McKnight. You can't imagine how proud I was when Sean was awarded that scholarship. He had a wonderful first year. They say that's the hardest." She sighed, clutching her hands, and looked away. "Then, just at the end of the semester, last May, Sean made the decision to leave law school to become a Marine officer. Everyone tried to reason with him—his uncle Frank, Dean McKnight, even the Marine Corps recruiter. They wanted him to wait until he got his law degree before going in. Sean wanted none of it."

The widow grasped Sandy's hand and lost her composure. "He's going to get himself killed like his father. My God, I know that's going to happen. Mary, mother of God! Why is this happening? Please bring him home—please."

Sandy embraced the widow's lean frame as if she were a fragile doll, and the two women began to sob. *How could Sean put his mother through this?*

★   ★   ★

The next day, Sandy sat in the student lounge at Brooklyn College thinking about how devastating Sean's decision was on his mother. She'd been trying to write him but didn't know where to begin.

"Hey, hello. How's the ankle?"

Sandy looked up at a boy who appeared older than most students. He was stocky, on the short side, with cropped curly hair and a pleasant smile. She felt she knew him but couldn't place him.

"Guess you don't remember," he said. "You were pretty shook up. I'm Sal Lente. I was with Sean at the park."

"Oh, of course. I remember—you brought the ice," Sandy said. "Thanks, it really helped. Do you go here?"

"Kind of a night student going days. Did a tour in the Navy after high school." He smiled. "Work as an evening copy editor for the *Brooklyn Eagle*. I'm an English writing major, trying to minor in poli-sci. If I can get my course schedule to align with my night job, should get out in two years. How 'bout you?"

"I'm an ed. major. If I manage to get in my entire student-teaching load, should graduate next May." Sandy laughed. "Actually, I'm doing some writing. Trying to write a thank-you to your friend Sean. Afraid I'm not much of a writer."

Lente took a chair next to Sandy. They didn't talk about writing, but to Sandy's delight, Sal talked about Sean and their lifelong friendship—how he and Sean shared the same values and political beliefs, not as much conservative as decidedly antiliberal. He joked about Sean's quick temper, little patience, and caustic sense of humor that sometimes caused him grief. He had just started talking about Sean going to Vietnam when, as if on cue, someone at the far end of the lounge started shouting antiwar slogans.

"Johnson is a pig! Stop the baby killing! Get us out of Vietnam now!"

Three coeds manning a table joined the chant. "Get us out now! Stop the killing now!" A large banner proclaimed their affiliation: *Students for a Democratic Society.* The antiwar group was led by an activist with dirty blond hair who seemed too well dressed for a war protester.

"Know that guy, Jay Delfano," Sal said. "He's been in several of my classes over the years. Really a bright guy and a good debater, but off the wall about Vietnam. Lives in one of those fancy homes in Manhattan Beach. Think his father is some kind of judge." He shook his curly head in disgust. "Smart as he is, Delfano is just another rich liberal. Never been out of Brooklyn but claims to be an authority on foreign policy."

The protest grew louder, so they walked across the pathway bisecting the campus lawn. Sandy asked, "How do you feel about the war? Think we belong in Vietnam?"

Sal gestured to a nearby bench. He opened one of his textbooks, flipping through it until he came to a page-sized map of Indochina. "This place was once part of China. Now it's Laos, Cambodia, and since the midfifties, North and South Vietnam. Lot of history in this place. Early this century, the French were the big players, until the Japs rolled it up along with the rest of Southeast Asia in '42. When we defeated Japan in '45, the Vietnamese weren't real interested in being a French colony. They wanted independence." His brow wrinkled and his lips curled as if he had seen a bad call in a ball game. "The French thought otherwise, and somebody in Washington agreed. That's what started it all. The French got kicked out in the midfifties, and the country split, with the north under Communist control."

Pointing to the map, Sandy rested her finger on a red line labeled DMZ. "Is this the separation point between North and South Vietnam?"

"It was supposed to be," Sal said. "Fair amount of controversy about that line. It was to be a temporary partition until a national election could be held. That election never came to be. But the North Vietnamese never gave up the idea that the entire country should be under one Communist government. They began infiltrating political and military forces in the South. When JFK came in, he made the decision to help the South Vietnamese." Sal shook his head and shrugged. "At the time of his death in '63, Kennedy had sent over fifteen thousand people to South Vietnam, mostly military advisors, including a large Green Beret force. Johnson was of the same mind and upped the ante in '65 when he sent in the Marines."

Sandy frowned. *God, hope he doesn't think I'm a dunce!* "Certainly a complicated situation. Guess it's difficult for people to understand why we should be fighting for a country most people can't find on a map."

"Exactly the problem, Sandy," Sal said, eyebrows rising. "It's gonna be like the war in Korea, with one big exception." He flipped to a page with a map of Korea. "See the 38th parallel? That's where we stopped the North Koreans after three years of a very brutal war. Once we established a solid defense along the thirty-eighth parallel, the bad guys were stopped. We controlled the seas on both flanks. It ended in a stalemate, but at least Communist North Korea was virtually sealed off from the south."

Sandy looked at the map, embarrassed by her lack of knowledge about the Korean War. "Do you think we stop them again? Stop the Communists from taking over South Vietnam?"

Sal flipped back to the map of Vietnam. "Same kind of war, very different geography. Look at South Vietnam. See the difference? One flank of the county is the South China Sea, which we control. That's the good news. Bad news is the other flank of the country is an open border. Runs four hundred miles through Laos and Cambodia. Both politically unstable, plenty of sanctuaries, lots of areas to infiltrate. All dense jungle—not a good military situation." He nodded, his blue eyes fixed on Sandy. "That gets to your question. Given the history, the political situation, and that geography, can we stop the Communists? Can we save South Vietnam?" He threw his hands up. "It's a long shot, a real long shot. I don't know. Nobody knows for sure."

Sal snapped the book shut. "What I do know is guys like Sean are betting their lives on that long shot. Win or lose, another thing I know for sure, a lot of them aren't going to make it back. End of lecture. Come on. I'll give you a ride home."

During the ride through the tranquil Brooklyn streets, little was said. Sandy couldn't stop thinking about Sal's comment. *A lot of them aren't going to make it back home.*

Chapter 4

Sean planned to reserve Sunday night for squaring away his uniform and brushing up on platoon tactics. He wanted to be ready for the upcoming field exercises. But poor weather delayed his flight from LaGuardia and made him three hours late getting back to DC. After driving forty miles south, he exited I-95 onto a narrow, dark road that wound through an isolated part of the massive Marine Corps base at Quantico, Virginia. Ten minutes into the drive, he took a fork in the road following a sign labeled TBS.

The Basic School—or TBS—as it was known to its occupants, was the place where newly commissioned officers, virtually all second lieutenants, were taught to be Marine officers. Unlike other services, the Marine Corps thought it best to have its rookie officers, whether graduates of the ten-week officer-candidate program (OCS), ROTC types, or graduates of the naval academy, attend an intensive five-month course of formal training before ever setting foot in front of a platoon.

The Basic School had the appearance of a college campus, with its three-story dorms, abutting classrooms, and meeting areas. It even had a cozy bar called the Hawkins Room named for a lieutenant killed on Tarawa. The dining room was spartan, not unlike the typical collegiate eatery and with the same boring food.

Bachelor officers were quartered two to a room and shared a head with an adjoining room. To their dismay, most rooms had one or two extra lockers to accommodate the uniforms and gear of married officers who had the privilege of living off base.

The young lieutenants at TBS were gentlemen by an act of Congress and were treated as professionals by the staff instructors, mostly captains and majors recently returned from combat tours in Vietnam. The training was tough, demanding, and relentless. A daily rotation system required each person to serve in various rifle-company billets from fire-team leader through commanding officer. It was especially dicey since each man's performance was graded by his peers.

Sean winced in frustration as he tried to find a parking space in the crowded gravel parking lot reserved for lieutenants. He was anxious about being late for a meeting with his mustang roommate. While most of the young officers at TBS were recent college graduates, about 15 percent of the class were "Mustangs." They were Marines from the enlisted ranks that, because of some outstanding performance, had been sent to Officer Candidate School. If they made the grade at OCS, and most did, they were commissioned and sent to The Basic School. Sean and most of the other college guys realized Mustangs added a dimension of real-world experience to the class. They were sought out frequently for advice.

★   ★   ★

"Well, here he comes, straight from the streets of Brooklyn," Sean's roommate, BW, laughed. Lieutenant Booker Washington Farnsworth sat hunched over a steel-framed bed, his M-14 rifle disassembled for cleaning. "What happened, man? Those mob guys get you involved in a caper? Thought you were supposed to be here early to go over the platoon in the attack problem they're gonna throw at us this week."

Sean grinned, tossing his valpak on his bunk. "Great you're cleaning your weapon, BW, but it would be nice if you used your own rack. Get any oil on my sheets, and I'll place that cleaning rod up your hillbilly ass."

"Nasty people, you Yankees from New York. Reckon it's an Italian mafia thing."

Sean shot back, "If you're good to me and pass on all your Mustang insight about platoon tactics, I'll prevail on my Brooklyn associates to provide you protection—protection you'll need when the local chapter of the Monks Corner South Carolina KKK find out there's a Negro running around disguised as a Marine lieutenant."

"You got that one right," BW muttered. "Okay, here's the deal. We go down to the Hawkins room. You buy. I'll talk. You listen. Before we down three beers, you'll be a platoon tactics jock."

Late in the evening, the Hawkins room bar afforded some privacy. By their second beer, Sean realized just how much BW knew about platoon tactics.

"Was a corporal when we landed at Da Nang in August '65. Had a rifle squad," BW said, his fist raised in a show of pride. "Picked up E-5 real quick, 'bout three months. In late November, we run into a VC bunker complex. Those fuckers were dug in good. Our lieutenant got hit the day before. Staff Sergeant Walters was running the platoon. Moved me up to platoon sergeant. Ten minutes into the shit, don't Walters get two AK-47 rounds in his leg!" BW raised his beer mug in a show of triumph. "There I was, Booker Washington Farnsworth, twenty-one-year-old son of a South Carolina sharecropper, great-grandson of a slave from the Farnsworth plantation, platoon commander, Delta company, Second Battalion, First Marines."

"That where you got that Bronze Star?"

"Yeah, my Purple Heart too. Shoulda had my head examined. Got dinged in the arm but was able to call in some pretty good arty. Then led the assault. Lost some good Marines, but we overran those fuckers." He chugged the beer. "'Course, I got hit again. Through and through shot in my leg. Got evaced. Sent back to Lejeune after a couple of months in the hospital." He threw his hands up and flashed his perfect white teeth. "Guess it changed my life. When I reported in a gunny in the G1 notices I have a year of college and a 125 General Aptitude Test score. Calls me in, says with my GAT score, my six-two lean body, and my handsome black face, I'm a picture poster Marine. Should be a Marine officer. I agreed. Next thing I know, got order to Officer Candidate School with all you college guys. Now here I am at Basic School, sharing my wisdom with a sorry-ass city kid like you."

★   ★   ★

A few hours later, a groggy Sean and BW were rousted from sleep by a sharp command. "Good morning, gentlemen. Might I ask you to get your sorry asses out of bed and prepare yourselves for another great day in the Corps. Let's go, gents. We have thirty minutes to formation."

The greeting came from Lieutenant Mike Slattery, a married officer whose locker was in the room. Dressed in starched utilities and spit-shined boots, Slattery was squared away and ready for work. He expected the same of his roommates.

"Slattery, you probably dressed last night and waited up just so you could come in here and harass our asses," Sean said, stumbling toward the head. "Are all you boat school guys this motivated? How the hell did you wind up in the Corps, anyway? Thought you wanted to be a carrier pilot."

"As cruel fate would have it, my eyes failed the Navy's flight physical," Slattery said. "Much to the consternation of my dad and granddad, both retired Navy captains, I elected the Marine option at the naval academy. So here I am—waking up early, trying to apply a little leadership, and listening to your guff."

"Thought academy guys were supposed to start TBS in August. How'd you wind up in Echo Company?" BW said, peering from behind the door to the head.

"Another cruel twist of fate, an appendix attack. Had to start TBS three months late and wound up in Echo. In your company, so to speak," Slattery said.

"What a lucky break for us." Sean grinned. "Say, Mike, what does Mrs. Slattery think about you wasting all that good sack time making yourself so squared away every night? You best give priority to your young wife's needs."

Slattery stiffened his compact frame. His blue eyes narrowed, and he glared at Sean behind a crooked smile. "So, the budding mob lawyer from Brooklyn is lecturing me about my wife's needs. Well, I am sure those white slaves you refer to as your babes have needs as well. Then again, given your recent leave and your ineptitude with the opposite sex, I suspect vibrator sales are now soaring in Brooklyn." Slattery buffed his already spit-shined boots. "Talking about my young bride, Val's requested your presence for dinner next Saturday evening. We're hosting one of her sorority sisters. Val wants her to meet some Marine officers. Note I said meet—not ravage, not hit on, not get laid by, just meet—some Marine officers. Think you two can accept this offer? You'll receive some excellent booze and a reasonably good steak."

"Val a good cook?" Sean asked.

"Val's Main Line Philadelphia. As such, cooking is not her forté. She is learning. This weekend, however, I'll do the cooking."

"Main Line Philly—that got anything to do with American Bandstand?" Sean mimicked a Brooklyn accent. "You want I should get one of them white slaves from my neighborhood to come down and teach Val a few moves, or how to cook, maybe make a sauce?"

"Just get your ass to my house next Saturday at 1830," Mike said. "Now let's get down to the formation."

★   ★   ★

Monday-morning formation was the start of a long training week. They put in ten-hour days: four hours of classroom instruction followed by four hours of field work culminating in a forced march or organized PT. Later that week, the schedule included a night exercise that kept the training going for twenty straight hours. When night ops concluded Thursday morning at 0330, a driving rainstorm drenched Northern Virginia and, to the pleasure of the staff instructors, soaked the platoons of lieutenants as they pitched canvas two-man tents.

"What's the matter, Sean?" BW cried. "Afraid of getting a little damp? It's good to wallow in the mud, makes you a better Marine."

Sean scowled and tried to clear water from the tent. "You of course know all about wallowing in the mud and practicing at being miserable. With all your experience, maybe you can enlighten me on the lecture yesterday by that JAG captain from headquarters. Kind of strange, a lecture on handling and treatment of POWs right after a two-hour lecture on ambush tactics."

BW tightened his lips, remaining silent for a long moment. "Think it was a cover-your-ass lecture. The brass could point to it if there was ever a messy situation. They don't want some guy saying he was taught to finish them off."

"Wait a minute," Sean said. "Isn't that what we were just taught to do after an ambush? To hose down the kill zone, and use grenades at night?"

"Yeah, you gotta consider anyone in the kill zone fair game," BW said. "But somebody gotta make a call on when to stop. Somebody gotta decide if there's no more threat—when a wounded gook should be treated as a POW. That somebody is the platoon commander, the senior guy on the spot." He paused and pointed. "That's gonna be us,

Sean. Real problem is the troops. Most of them in-country more than a few weeks probably watched some guy get hit, maybe lost a buddy. They're in no mood to play games. They just want the bad guys dead." His eyes seemed focused on something not in the tent. "Things got screwed up when civilians got involved, especially in some of those vills. You never knew who was a VC. Women. Young kids. Old men. Lots of them wound up dead. Didn't happen often, but once it did, it kind of stays with you."

"It's that bad?"

"Yeah, it's bad—real bad. It's all about killing; that's what it's all about, Sean. Now I need some sleep, maybe get three hours before they have us jog back to main side."

Sean curled up in his gray-green rubber poncho, but sleep didn't come. He had never thought about killing, had never seen anyone killed. He had just assumed that was what you did in a war—kill the enemy. His father had killed Japanese, his uncle Frank had killed North Koreans, and now he was being sent to kill Viet Cong. What would it be like to take a life? Tossing on the wet ground, he thought about Sandy Gold's father and his ranting about Sean knowing nothing about war. *Maybe the crazy guy was right.*

Chapter 5

Late Saturday afternoon, Sean drove his racing-green '65 Fairlane along the winding road from Camp Barrett to the town of Triangle. Before reaching the town, he turned on I-95 North toward Washington. Traffic on the major north-south highway was light. In a few minutes, he exited at Occoquan, Virginia, and pulled into the parking lot of the Stafford apartments, home to Mike Slattery and his bride, Val Pruett McGee.

Too bad BW had pulled duty and would miss the dinner. Thoughts of his roommate faded when he saw a tall, smartly dressed young woman with long black hair exit a red Mustang convertible. Despite her good looks, Sean frowned when he spotted a yellow peace symbol on the Mustang's rear bumper.

Twenty minutes early, he stayed in his car to reread a surprise letter he had received from Sandy Gold. She covered a lot in a clear but rambling style. She thanked Sean for his help after her accident and offered an apology for her father's remarks. She told of her father fighting in Warsaw, living in a sewer, and watching his brother die during the ghetto uprising. How her mother had met an emaciated Sam in a displaced-persons camp in Madrid. Frankie was on the money with his assessment of Mr. Gold.

Sean winced and his stomach knotted after reading Sandy's account of her meeting with his mother and discussing the death of his dad. His mood changed as she described speaking with the Scribe at Brooklyn

College. Sal had made an impression. She didn't sound like a hawk but did seem to understand his decision to become a Marine.

> Men like you would give everything for what they believe. I've never met anyone quite like you. I'd very much like to see you again. I'm not certain where it will all lead, but I think it's a place I want to go. Please write.
>
> Sandy

★ ★ ★

"Hey! Are you Sean Cercone, the famous Marine from Brooklyn?" The shout came from a young woman, blonde hair pulled in a side twist, leaning over the wrought-iron railing of a third-floor balcony.

"It's me in the flesh!" Sean shot back. "And you must be the unfortunate creature wed to the sailor trying desperately to become a Marine."

Slattery appeared on the small terrace next to his bride. "Get your ass up here, Jarhead."

Sean took the stairs two at a time. At the front door of apartment 3A stood the petite blonde with a spray of freckles on her nose.

"Hi, Sean. I'm Val. Please come in." She motioned to the woman standing next to her. "This is my big sister from Delta Kappa Delta, Beth Wilenski."

The woman from the red Mustang!

After exchanging greetings, they moved into a tastefully decorated apartment. Sean sat on a large leather sofa, the two women opposite him on muted-green twin side chairs. Behind an expensive-looking teak bar that fit perfectly in the corner of the room, Mike waved at Sean and called for drink requests.

"White wine, dear," Val chimed.

Beth smiled, crossing her long legs and staring straight at Sean. "Scotch on the rocks with just a splash, lemon wedge if you got it."

Sean gave one of his sideways smiles. "Double scotch, neat. Nice to meet you, Beth." He gestured to a portrait of a tall, gray-haired man in a dark suit standing in front of an oversized desk. "Val, who's the distinguished-looking gentleman?"

"My dad. They had that done when he became chairman of the bank."

No wonder the fancy apartment and Slattery and his bride driving new cars. Mike married well.

Mike came from behind the bar and tried to divert the conversation from his well-to-do father-in-law. "Say, Sean, you and Beth have something in common. She's in law school."

Sean nodded. "Where you going?"

"In my last year at Georgetown. I'm interning in Senator Kennedy's office. Hope to work on the Hill when I graduate."

He raised his eyebrows. "Impressive. Where did you and Val meet?"

"Villanova," Beth replied. "The man in the picture, Val's dad, had a lot to do with it. His sister, a nun, was my high school principal. When she found out my folks couldn't afford college, she and her brother, who happened to be on the board of Villanova, got me a scholarship."

"And well you deserved it!" Val said with a giggle. "You were the top graduate at St. Stanislaus, probably had the highest SATs in Wilkes Barre."

"Highest SATs in Wilkes Barre. Now that's impressive." Sean grinned. "That's a coal-mining town; had an uncle from up there. Pretty conservative, blue-collar area. How'd you get mixed up with Kennedy?"

"Didn't exactly get mixed up with Senator Kennedy. I interviewed and got the internship," Beth said, raising her eyebrows. "He liked some of my writing on inner city problems. I'm doing some work with the Kennedy family foundation on housing issues."

"That's good, Beth. For a moment I thought you might be involved with his Foreign Relations committee staff," Sean said. "They've got some radical views about Vietnam."

Beth stiffened. "Radical views? Think that's a poor choice of words, Sean. Unless, of course, you think opposing something you don't think to be in the country's interest is radical."

"Of course not. That'd be a little rigid. But expounding views supporting the Communist government in Hanoi doesn't seem to be in the country's interest, to say nothing of our SEATO allies in Saigon."

Beth bristled. "Vietnam is a complicated issue. Lots of people have different views on the war. Everyone's entitled to an opinion."

He drained his scotch. "And what happens if that opinion gives aid and comfort to the enemy? What about the impact on our troops?"

The conversation got louder with each point and counterpoint. Mike interrupted Sean midway through a diatribe about antiwar demonstrations. "Sean, come here for a moment; help me with these steaks. Come on, move."

Sean quickly followed Mike to the balcony.

"Hey, asshole, cut the talk about the war," Slattery said. "Beth was engaged to a doggie lieutenant. He got it in the Ashau Valley last spring. That gives her the right not to love our little war."

"Shit. Feel like such an ass," Sean replied. *Why didn't she say something? If I'd known she lost someone …*

Val called the group to dinner. It looked like a great meal—steak, red wine, the works—but Sean felt like a jerk. When he saw Beth's blue eyes well up as Val asked Mike to say grace, he felt worse.

Sean did his best to alter the mood and amused the trio with tales about his Brooklyn neighborhood and colorful friends. He had Beth in a fit of laughter with the story about the guys slipping dozens of pigeons into the Avalon movie theater at exactly the right moment during Alfred Hitchcock's memorable scene in *The Birds.*

The scotch and wine had the two debaters a little tipsy. Val motioned to Mike to prepare some strong coffee and suggested Sean and Beth move to the small balcony.

The cool autumn air had a sobering effect. They made small talk about law school, and then Sean spoke in a low, contrite voice. "Sorry about the way I mouthed off about the war. I didn't know about your loss. That must have been rough."

Beth turned quickly, and Sean expected a verbal blast. Instead she forced a sad smile. "It was. It's still rough. I think of him every day. Every time I watch the news or pick up a paper and see the casualty reports, I think of how he held me and teased me. How he loved to laugh. How he loved the Army. How committed he was. And now he doesn't exist anymore." She looked out on the black Virginia night. "What about you? Is there a girl back home?"

Sean half nodded. "Yes. Not really. I mean, we just met a month ago, only a couple of times. Don't think I'll pursue it."

"Pursue it, Sean. If you think you care for her and she cares for you, make it happen. Grab all the happiness you can." Beth ran her hand through her long hair, blue eyes teary. "Just remember she's going to war too. She's going to live in fear and doubt every day you're gone. She's going to cry at night. She's going to try to lose herself in work, but something deep down will gnaw at her gut." She broke into tears. "Christ, I hate this war. Be careful, Sean. Be careful and come home to her."

Sean reached for Beth as she wept. Was grabbing happiness worth the price of someone keeping vigil for him, wondering if he'd make it home? Was it fair of him to ask Sandy to risk going through what Beth was going through?

★   ★   ★

Beth drove on to I-95 toward DC and gunned her Mustang. Had she given Sean the right advice—grab all the happiness you can? She thought about Val and Mike, the cute apartment, the lovely meal, how innocent they seemed. Was Val really prepared for what lay ahead? Mike was an academy graduate, a gung-ho Marine. Risking his life was all part of the game. And Val was now on the team. Sean seemed less military and fairly rough around the edges but equally committed. He was smart and a tough debater, probably would make a good prosecutor. A little myopic about the war, to say the least. Typical Marine. She hoped he'd make it home.

The highway was dark, almost deserted, until she crossed the beltway that ringed DC. The Capitol lights began to come alive in the distance as she exited in Arlington and pulled into the driveway of her barrack-like three-story apartment. The one-room studio crammed with law books, journals, and legal-sized yellow notepads was a grim reminder of her life as a third-year law student and of an internship that had become a twenty-hour-a-week commitment.

What a mess—just like her life. Six more months and that was it for school. With some luck, her internship would turn into a full-time job. What then? Would she bother with the bar-review course or just focus on the job? Despite her scholarship, she still had loans to repay. The job was the priority.

She glanced at a picture that hung over her cluttered table. It was a grainy black-and-white photo of a smiling Army lieutenant leaning against a sandbagged bunker wall. Would she ever be happy without him? She hated the thought but realized, deep down, she wanted someone in her life—someone to lean on, to share her passion, her joys, and her frustration in trying to do something for those in need. Someone to love her. Just not now, and probably not anytime soon.

Chapter 6

Detective Jimmy Napoli joined his old friend, carefully placing a handkerchief before he sat on the brick front stoop. Clad in a charcoal-gray suit, blue silk tie, and highly polished wingtips, he looked more like an IBM executive than an NYPD detective. He was in sharp contrast to his lifelong buddy Frank Cercone. The heavyset Korean War vet wore khaki pants, brown loafers, and a green sweater with a yellow globe-and-anchor symbol over his left breast.

"Still got that Marine buzz cut, Frank? When you gonna let it grow out?" Napoli laughed.

Frank brushed his head. "You know what they say—once a Marine! So what brings ya to the neighborhood, Jimmy?"

Napoli shook his head. "Had to bust a kid up on West Ninth. Running a stolen-car ring. Shit! Known the family for years—went to high school with his dad. You can't imagine the scene. His parents went off the wall. His dad cursed a blue streak at me." Napoli pounded his fist on his leg. "Damn, hate busting neighborhood kids. Makes me feel like some kind of traitor!"

"It's your job, Jimmy!"

"Yeah, maybe. On days like today I wish my job was pounding a beat in the Bronx. When is Sean coming? Bet Ann's all excited."

"Should be pulling in anytime now," Frank said. "Yeah, his mom's all excited, having him home for the holidays."

"You did a great job taking care of your sister-in-law and Sean since Tom was killed on Iwo," Napoli said in an admiring tone. "He's one hell of a young man. Got a lot of guts, just like his dad."

"Yeah, just hope he's luckier than his dad. He's grown up fast—got himself a new girlfriend," Frank said. "Most of his crowd are good kids too."

"Maybe!" Napoli frowned. "That Ryan friend of his gives me real agita. I warned Sean about him. Fairly certain Mr. Frankie "the Brain" Ryan is the guy who flooded Brooklyn with thousands of phony World's Fair tickets couple a years ago. Think he's also behind a major cigarette-smuggling racket. He's also involved with some wise guys in a limo company. Love to find out where he got that money."

"The Brain is a wild one all right." Frank laughed.

"A wild one." Napoli laughed. "If he keeps it up, he's gonna make Willie Sutton look like Mr. Peepers. Hey, look who's pulling in the driveway."

Napoli grinned as Frank rushed to greet Sean. *Good old Frank. Been Sean's godfather—part dad, part uncle, part friend—and now he was a fellow Marine.*

Frank embraced his godson in a bear hug, lifting him slightly off the ground. "Hey, Marine, may just be a junior noncom from the old Corps, but I can still handle a second louie." The barrel-chested veteran released Sean from his viselike grip, stepped back, and choked out a different greeting. "You look terrific, Sean. Image of your dad. Great to have you home, Marine."

Sean approached the stoop. "Hey, Jimmy, good to see ya."

"You're looking good, Marine." Napoli rose, scooped up his hanky, and extended his hand. "Take care of your uncle here, and say hello to your mom. I gotta run. See you next week at the party. Looking forward to meeting that new girl of yours."

Sean recoiled. "Girl? What girl?"

"The chick up Avenue T, what's her name, Sandy," Frank said. "The one you been writing. Sal goes to school with her at Brooklyn. Says you write all the time. Sounds like a relationship to me. Whata ya think, Jimmy?"

Napoli threw his hands up. "Who knows? A horny lieutenant, a good looking woman, a letter here, another letter there, and bing bang bing, you got a relationship."

"This entire damned neighborhood is filled with old washwomen," Sean cried. "Can't mind their business. Christ, only met the girl once or twice. We never dated. She's just a friend."

"Hey, don't get upset," Napoli said, moving to his car. "It's okay. She's just a friend. No problem. Next week bring your friend to the D'Angelos' Christmas party. You know, the one you're not having a relationship with."

Frank motioned to the woman smiling in the kitchen window of the gray stucco house. "Come on, lover boy, let's say hello to your mother. And watch your mouth. This ain't the damn Marine Corps."

Napoli smiled as he pulled out onto Avenue T. Still upset about the arrest earlier that day, he thought about Sean. *Great kid from a great family. A Marine officer. Tom would have been real proud.* Sean was one kid he'd never have to worry about getting busted.

★ ★ ★

The smell of onions sizzling in Italian sausages and green peppers drew Frank and Sean to the small dining area off the galley kitchen. Sean gave his mother a hug and grabbed two sandwiches. Frank poured beers into frosted mugs. Ann Cercone beamed with contentment as the two devoured her handiwork.

Sean wiped red sauce from his chin and gestured to his sandwich. "This is great, Ma, really great." He paused and grinned. "So, have you taught my girlfriend how to make this sauce? You know, the good-looking woman you been telling Frank about. The nice girl everybody thinks I'm having a relationship with."

Ann stiffened. "She seemed like a fine young lady when I met her. It was rather obvious she had more than a passing interest in contacting you."

"Okay, Ma. Sandy's a nice girl, and I'll probably see her again. Let's just not make it a big deal."

"Well, I'm glad you feel that way. About seeing her, I mean," Ann said with a smile. "I met Sal Lente on the avenue yesterday. He invited Sandy to Christmas dinner at the D'Angelos'."

"What's going on? I'm gonna get Sal for this one."

Frank roared, "Loosen up. Sal's just trying to do the right thing. We're all gonna have a ball like we do every Christmas. This year we added a little more spice. In addition to your Irish mother, we got your nice Jewish girl, who, of course, is just a friend."

"You may see her before then. I invited Sandy over." His mother gave Sean a wide-eyed look. "For this afternoon."

The front doorbell rang. Frank glanced out the alcove window. "Well now, Lieutenant, we got company."

Ann ushered Sandy from the foyer through the narrow kitchen. Sean and his uncle both rose. Her long braid hung over a light tennis jacket. She awkwardly extended her hand to Sean. "Hi! Good to see you again. You're looking great." She blushed and squeezed into a chair that barely fit between the alcove wall and the oversized butcher-block kitchen table.

"You too, Sandy," Sean said, thinking she was far better looking than he remembered. "This is my uncle Frank."

Frank smiled and sat down in front of his half-eaten sausage-and-pepper sandwich. "Ann, you gonna let this young lady watch us eat? How about a beer and a hero, Sandy?"

"No thanks, really, Mrs. Cercone."

"Nonsense. With all that volunteer activity and all those children you teach, you need all the strength you can get," Ann said, placing a sandwich before Sandy.

"What's this volunteering all about?" Sean asked.

Sandy unzipped her nylon jacket and smiled. "Since I couldn't play tennis because of my ankle, I decided to volunteer at a settlement house on Washington Street near Bedford Avenue. They really need help with preteen girls. I'm there two nights a week, half a day on Saturday."

"Bedford-Stuyvesant's the bad lands," Frank said, brushing his napkin across his mouth. "No place for a young white girl, especially at night."

Sean frowned. "Actually, it's not a place for anyone at night."

"It's a terrible neighborhood," Sandy said, raising her sharp jaw. "Crime, dope, filthy streets, pimps, drunks, and lots of children. Those children are in desperate need of help, precisely because of that environment. It's a cycle of poverty and ignorance with young girls paying the price." She raised her shoulders and locked her lips. "Yesterday, one of the women I'm helping broke down. She found out her thirteen-year-old is pregnant. She's going to be a grandmother at thirty. Something has to be done."

Sean shook his head. *She has a lot of guts going into one of the worst neighborhoods in the city alone at night.* "How long will you be volunteering?"

"Until I graduate next May. Then I'll be applying for a permanent position."

"A permanent position at a settlement house in Bed-Stuy! Sandy, that's quite a commitment," Sean said in a pleading tone.

"It's a big commitment, Sean." She smiled. "Funny, they say the same about guys joining the Marines. Think that makes us compatible?"

He grinned. "Guess it does."

★   ★   ★

The chilly December breeze pushed at their backs, and the couple walked hurriedly under the naked oaks that lined Avenue T. Small hedges fronted most of the modest single-family homes that sat a few feet from the sidewalk. After a few blocks, the houses became larger, sitting farther back on wider lots with impressive lawns. They slowed as they approached Sandy's house.

"Your friend Sal is quite a guy," Sandy said. "And Frankie, he's certainly different. They talk as if you're brothers."

"We've been together since kindergarten. Went to different high schools but always hung out together in the neighborhood. Then Sal joined the Navy, I went to St. John's, Frankie did his own thing. Didn't matter; we stayed close. They're both great guys, smart as hell and real straight shooters, but very different."

"How so?"

"Tough to explain," Sean said. "Different approaches to life, I guess. Sal likes to ponder, look at things from different angles. He's pretty sensitive and deep, almost like a philosopher. Always thinking about good, bad, right, and wrong. Really cares about people's feelings. A hard worker too. Night job at the *Brooklyn Eagle*—while taking a full load of poli-sci classes at Brooklyn College."

They reached Sandy's house. Sean propped himself up on the side of her stoop and zipped up his blue parka. "Frankie is a whole other story. We've been friends since first grade. Was with him in third grade when his mom died. Been living with his dad, a truck driver, ever since. He's gotten kind of wild over the years. Gets involved in all kinds of capers." Sean flashed a smile. "Never gets caught. Always one step ahead of teachers, cops, wise guys, anybody he takes on. Thinks quick, figures out an issue, decides what has to get done, and does it. He usually knows what he wants and doesn't care what anyone thinks."

"What do they think about your decision to join the Marines?" Sandy asked.

"Sal's all for it. Guess because he did his time in the Navy, maybe because he has a strong sense of duty. Sees the world much as I do. Frankie thinks I'm nuts, told me so a number of times. Said he respects my decision, but the only time he'd join up is if the Commies invade Coney Island."

They both laughed.

"We argue about the war and foreign policy all the time," Sean said. "Sal pitches the danger of isolationism. I usually approach it from the aspect of global responsibility, the spread of Communism." He smiled. "Frankie doesn't buy any of it. I'll give him his due—he reads a lot. Thinks Vietnam is a sideshow, and we're getting sucked in." He motioned over his shoulder. "Talking about foreign relations, I take it your dad isn't too wild about you seeing me."

"Afraid not." Sandy blushed. "Thank God, Mother worked on him. He's backed off a little, probably because he's never seen me spend so much time in my room writing letters."

"I guess being an Italian Irishman isn't a big plus either," Sean said, throwing his arms up in mock frustration.

"Right again." Sandy laughed. "Mother says you're nice, but isn't comfortable with—how did she put it, 'moving outside our circle.' Thinks it's fine to have a gentile friend just so long as it's not a boyfriend."

"What do you think, Sandy?"

"I can handle the gentile part. Actually, we're not that observant," Sandy replied with a sheepish frown. "It's the Marine Corps and Vietnam I've a hard time with. I know we've written about this, but is there any way they might not send you to Vietnam?"

Sean looked at her for a long moment. "Always a possibility, but odds are pretty good I'll be going over in late spring." He failed to mention that he had raised those odds considerably just a week before by requesting assignment to the Western Pacific as his duty preference upon graduation.

Chapter 7

GRAVESEND, BROOKLYN
CHRISTMAS AT THE D'ANGELOS'

Sandy stepped into Sean's Fairlane, dark brown hair flowing over her camel-hair coat. "Hi."

"You look great, Sandy. Ready to see the other side of Gravesend?"

"Sure am! But never thought much about our neighborhood being called Gravesend. Sounds like a desperate place to live."

"Maybe so, for some folks. I like the history of the place," Sean said, starting the car. "Gravesend dates back to the Dutch crossing the river from New Amsterdam. One of four towns that existed when the Dutch ceded Brooklyn to the British. Think that was in the early 1700s. Did you know the town was founded by a woman, Lady Moody, a refugee fleeing religious persecution?"

"Remember learning something about her in junior high. But they never gave any details."

"She was the first woman elected to run a town in North America. How's that for some detail?" Sean said. "Gravesend had a colorful history. Many of the residents were Tories during the revolution, and the town was home to a fair number of crooks who ran brothels when Coney Island first got going last century." He stopped at a light and glanced at Sandy. "It was sparsely settled until the late twenties and early thirties. Then a whole bunch of Italians, some Jews, and a few Irish got themselves out of the tenements in lower Manhattan to settle in Gravesend. The place became another Brooklyn neighborhood laced with tree-lined streets, attached houses, and great people."

"How about the Tories and the crooks?" Sandy laughed.

"Not a lot of Tories—lots of Democrats though. And we're home to at least one major don and a host of wise guys. Nice people. I'll tell you about 'em sometime. First let's find a parking space."

Sandy wrinkled her brow. "So who are the D'Angelos? Are they wise guys?"

"Anything but!" Sean laughed as he maneuvered into a tight space. "Joe Senior is straight as they come. Started as a subway track repairman in the depression. Became motorman on the BMT, and now he's a chief dispatcher. Joe and Mary saved every nickel. Left one of those six-story railroad flats in lower Manhattan. Bought a two-family house over here with Mary's mother, Rosa. Wait till you meet them. You'll love 'em. They're family. Can't remember ever spending Christmas Eve anyplace else."

Sandy dark eyes widened. "I'm a little anxious. Been to a lot of Hanukkah parties, but this is my first real Christmas party. And what's this about a backyard ceremony?"

"It's quite a story. Mrs. D had a tough time trying having a baby. She miscarried four times. Doctors said it was never meant to be." Sean gave one of his sideways smiles. "Mrs. D didn't buy it. Like all good Italian women, when faced with the impossible, she prayed to Saint Jude. After ten years of praying, Joey was born on Christmas Eve in '43. Every Christmas Eve since, Joe and Mary invite friends to join them in prayers of thanks to Saint Jude. That's what it's all about." He switched off the ignition. "Come on, we don't want to be late for the ceremony."

A cold wind swept through the alleyway that separated the house from the two-car garage and blanketed the group gathered in the D'Angelos' backyard. They huddled close, shivering in front of a statue of St. Jude encased in a clear plastic box on a small cement altar topped with votive candles. Joey D and his dad stood arm-in-arm with Mary as she gave her litany of thanks: "To all the angels and saints, amen. To our blessed mother and baby Jesus, amen. And most of all, to St. Jude, who gave us our son, amen."

Sean clutched Sandy tightly, arm over her shoulder, their faces almost touching.

"It's beautiful," Sandy whispered.

Turning his head slightly, lips tightly closed, Sean nodded, a tear working its way down his dark cheek.

Once the group had uttered their last responsorial "amen" to Mary's final invocation, Joe Senior issued the command. "Manga, manga! Let's eat. Come on, everybody in the house."

Sandy and Sean joined the single-file line piling down the narrow cement stairs to the D'Angelos' basement. The aroma of baked fish, garlic, and spices greeted them as they entered the large one-room basement, which seemed to serve no other purpose than to accommodate dinner gatherings. It wasn't a fancy place—muted white-tiled floor, pale yellow walls, and a low ceiling. Half of one wall was shelved with dozens of jars containing sauces, spices, noodles, and an assortment of other eatables. An L-shaped counter protruded into the room, dividing the cooking and eating areas.

Joe Senior motioned from the far end of the room, where an aged woman dressed in black sat pensively at the head of the table. "Hey, Sean, bring your friend down here."

Sandy's dark eyes widened. She gave Sean a Bambi-like helpless look.

"It's okay, Sandy," Sean said. "Joe just wants you to meet his mother-in-law, Rosa, Joey's grandmother. She's the senior one in the family. She'll be offended if she's not shown respect, especially from a young woman. Just kiss her and say *Buon Natale*."

Sean maneuvered Sandy to the head of the table. "Grandma Rosa, I'd like you to meet Sandy Gold."

Sandy smiled, extending her hand. When the frail-looking old woman clasped it, Sandy gracefully kissed her cheek. "Buon Natale."

"Merry Christmas to you too, my dear," Rosa replied in a deep voice with excellent elocution and little hint of an accent. "I may be an old lady who came over on the boat from Palermo, but I learned my English before I came."

Earlier that day, Sean had spoken with Sandy about Mary Rosa Acendi emigrating from Sicily to lower Manhattan in 1917 at the age of twenty-three. She'd been a schoolteacher in Palermo. She had made her move to the New World in quest of the father of her unborn child, a well-to-do wine importer named Cosmo Vincent La Porte. Cosmo had made the mistake of not doing the honorable thing and ignoring Mary Rosa. Soon after, they had fished the dapper wine merchant out of the East River with a longshoreman's grappling hook imbedded in his skull.

"I was widowed young, taught school in the city for twenty-two years," Rosa said, "then moved over here to Gravesend with my daughter Mary Ann and her husband, Joe. Been here over twenty years."

Sandy beamed. "I hope to be a teacher myself!"

The old woman gave a catlike smile. "Sit down, Sandy. Tell me how such a beautiful creature got mixed up with the likes of this one." She motioned to Sean, who grinned. "Bad enough I had a grandson who jumped out of planes, now this one joins the Marines. He makes his poor mother suffer so. He makes me suffer too."

Frankie poured red wine into a tall water glass. "Grandma Rosa, stop breaking Sean's chops. It's Christmas."

Rosa shot back, "Shut up, Brain, before I come over there and kick you in your chops."

Amid roars of laughter, Frankie retorted, "But Rosa, it's a holy day. You gotta have more respect."

"You're right, Frankie, it's a holy day. I should be praying." She straightened up, drew in her wrinkled cheeks, and raised her head before continuing in a melodic voice, "I'm gonna to pray to the baby Jesus, and then to his blessed mother. Then I'm gonna pray to St. Anthony, and St. Rocco, and St. Jude. And when I'm finished praying, then I'm gonna come over there and kick you in your goluneos! But first I'm gonna eat."

Rosa looked at Sandy, shaking her head. "You gotta be tough with this bunch!" She frowned, pointing to Sean. "Because I knew Mr. Big Shot Marine wasn't gonna get you here when we started dinner before Mass, I saved you some antipasti, some fish, and a little pasta."

Sandy was wide-eyed. "Well, I'll try a little bit of everything," she said, blushing.

"That's good, my dear, because we have everything in little bits," Rosa said, preparing a plate for Sandy. "These silver fish are whitebait. Just dab on a little lemon and eat them whole. This is fried calamari. It's squid. Dip it in that red sauce, but be careful of those red pepper flakes." Rosa snapped at Sean, "Make yourself useful, Mr. Marine. Fix up a plate for Sandy with that pecorino cheese, some red peppers, and some black olives. Then get her some of that eggplant caponata. I pickled it myself last September."

"Yes, Mama Rosa," Sean laughed. "We'll have to catch up with all of you who started eating this meal yesterday."

"See what a wise guy he is, Sandy," Rosa handed her a plate. "Start on this while I get you my special pasta dish. A recipe from Palermo—pasta with sardines and fennel."

Sean noticed Sandy living up to her commitment to try everything. He winced when Joe Senior presented a large platter of sausages sizzling in peppers and onions. Sandy, to Sean's amazement and Rosa's delight, took a generous portion. *Pretty good for a girl who's only attended Hanukkah parties!*

★ ★ ★

They left the party well after 4:00 a.m. Both unsteady from the strong red wine, they stumbled up the stairs and down the narrow alley.

Sean put his arm around Sandy's waist. "So, what do you think?"

"It was unbelievable. They made me feel so at home. What warm people. Grandma Rosa is adorable, and what candor. She thinks we're more than we are—friends, I mean." Sandy giggled. "Rosa actually cautioned me about getting pregnant."

"Don't feel alone. I got the same lecture from Joe's mom. Think they know something we don't?" He reached for his car door. "Didn't have the heart to tell them we haven't even kissed."

Leaning her back against the car door, Sandy grabbed the collar of Sean's jacket, drawing his face close to hers. "That's something we should change right now."

Sandy's arms slipped around Sean's neck. They stood motionless against the car, cold breath streaming about their faces.

Minutes later, the couple was again locked in an embrace on Sandy's stoop. Both were startled as Mrs. Gold appeared in the partially open door. She glared at her daughter. "Good morning, young lady." Without looking at Sean, she continued in the same stern tone. "Good night, Sean."

Sean unlocked his embrace and stood stone-faced on the stoop like a schoolboy caught in the act. *I really screwed up this time.*

"Mother, how rude!" Sandy protested.

"Don't how rude me! It's almost five. If your father catches you—"

"What the hell is going on down there? I'll be a son of bitch! It's five o'clock! Juliana, is that my daughter?"

★ ★ ★

Later that day, an anxious Sean phoned Sandy. Her mother answered. "Good afternoon, Sean. No, I'm afraid she's not available. Her father's very upset about you two staying out all night. Thinks you're a bad influence. I'm not certain I disagree."

Sean winced and let out a deep sigh. "I'm really sorry. I apologize. It's my fault. Maybe I could speak with Mr. Gold."

"Appreciate the apology, Sean, but don't think it would be a good idea to talk with Sam. Best leave that to Sandy."

"Look, I'm sorry. It was a big party, lots of friends. We do it every Christmas. We just lost track of the time."

"I understand Christmas is a special time, Sean. We enjoy Hanukkah ourselves but manage to make it home at a decent hour."

Sean went silent.

"I'm not blaming you. Sandy's a big girl and should have known how her father would react. And once he's made up his mind, that's usually it." Juliana paused. "He told her she can't see you again."

Chapter 8

Friday afternoon, the Hawkins room bar and all of the two dozen tables in the lounge area overflowed with second lieutenants. Echo company had completed a tough training week in near-freezing weather. Today had seen an especially rough field exercise made worse by a four-mile run in sleeting rain back from the training area. Several lieutenants hadn't bothered to shed their soggy utility uniforms and had gone straight to the bar. Sean and BW were among them.

"Hey, man, you did well today," BW said, shoving a beer in Sean's hand. "They're gonna make you a captain. Hell, you'll skip right over first lieutenant. Second time this week—first you get the top score on that tactics exam, and now you ace-out in your billet as the company commander in that tank-assault exercise."

"Thanks, BW, but everybody did their job. Made me look good," Sean replied, glancing across the room. "Hey, look! This is a first. It's Slattery coming to drink with us, not going home to his blonde bride. Must be trouble in paradise."

Slattery moved to the bar and mounted a wood-frame stool, barely acknowledging his roommates. He ordered bourbon and a beer. Seconds after being served, he downed the whiskey, slamming the thick shot glass embossed with the globe and anchor on the bar. He gulped half his beer.

"Shit, Mike, you're doing some serious drinking at five thirty in the afternoon. What's going on—what's wrong?" Sean said, watching Slattery clench his jaw.

Slattery looked at Sean, his face contorted and flushed. "Two of them, both on the same day—my roommate at academy and my closest friend. We were in each other's weddings. Jim was my best man. Rocco and I were teammates for four years. Both fuckin' KIA, can you believe it! They couldn't have been in-country more than two weeks."

He spoke rapidly, almost in panic. "Val got a call from Jim's wife. Then she called Ann to let her know. Ann's mother answered the phone and said a Marine was just at the house to inform them that Rocco was killed. Two of 'em, both gone, both fuckin' dead!"

Sean winced. "Jesus, Mike, I'm sorry. Was Jim the guy we met right before Christmas leave? Lived up in Philly not too far from Val?"

"Yeah, that's him. Val and I visited Jim and his wife over the holidays." Slattery gulped his beer, motioning for the bartender to do it again. "I can't fuckin' believe it. He was slated for the Third Division. With travel and all, he must have just gotten to his battalion."

BW nodded, his face expressionless. "The Third is up at Dong Ha, right below the DMZ. No VC up there, just main-force NVA, badass area." He moved closer to Slattery and continued in a low voice. "Listen, Mike, shit happens. Guys get hit; there's nothing you can do about it. Afraid we're gonna see a lot of that in the next few months. I know it sucks, but you gotta get used to it."

Sean watched Slattery clenching his teeth, staring at the floor as BW continued. "Mike, best thing you can do is to send a note to their wives and folks. Wait a couple of days. You never want to forget these guys, no way. You just put them in a different part of your mind. You don't forget them ever. But you gotta move on."

A tall, thick-necked lieutenant sat at the bar next to Slattery. "Rather easy for y'all to say, you being a grungy mustang." Easing his lanky frame off the stool, the interloper moved toward BW, speaking in a smooth southern drawl. "Then again, it should be no surprise for your kind not to be sensitive to a gentleman's loss. Do y'all really think you can—"

"You're out of line, Lieutenant," Sean snapped, "and I don't remember anyone asking you to join the conversation."

The big lieutenant took a wobbly step toward Sean. "Y'all are correct about that, sir!" A full head taller, looking down at Sean, he coldly remarked, "Cercone, you're absolutely correct! As a gentleman from the South, I make it a point never to converse with wops or niggers."

"Is that right?" Sean took a quick step and whipped his forearm up and forward as he had done so many times as a linebacker, smashing it directly across the smirking face of the gentleman from the South.

★   ★   ★

"Lieutenant Cercone reporting as ordered, sir." Sean stood at attention three feet before the desk of his company commander, Major "Ax" Dalton, a Princeton graduate and a Korean War veteran. He stared over the balding head of the thin officer sitting behind the gray steel desk.

Without raising his gaze from the material he was reading, Major Dalton barked, "Sit!"

Sean moved to a metal folding chair slightly to his right. Except for the chair and the desk, the room had no furniture. He sat with his back pressed against the chair, hands flat against his thighs, staring straight ahead. He couldn't help but focus on the ribbon-laden chest of his company commander.

For what seemed like an eternity, Dalton continued to ponder the material. Sean assessed his company commander's ribbons: a Silver Star, a Bronze Star, two Navy commendation medals, a Purple Heart, Vietnam campaign ribbons, and several ribbons Sean couldn't identify.

Still not looking directly at Sean, Dalton said, "Know why you're here, Lieutenant?"

"Yes, sir. I guess it's about the incident in the Hawkins Room."

"Good guess!" Dalton replied sarcastically. Closing the folder, he clasped his hands on the desk and stared straight into Sean's eyes. "You're also present to tell me why we shouldn't convene a special court. Why we shouldn't charge you with striking a fellow officer, conduct unbecoming of an officer, and maybe some other charges."

Sean's green eyes widened, clearly shocked by the reference to a special court-martial. He remained silent and continued to stare into the major's chest.

"Come now, Mr. Cercone, it says right here you had a whole year of law school; surely you can mount a defense of your actions." Dalton looked up from Sean's record book and the serious incident report filed by the officer of the day. "Let me take a shot while you collect your thoughts. Let's see, you probably don't like being referred to as a wop. I can understand that, especially since I spent some time in New Jersey and have a reverence for an Italian American Marine from Jersey named Basilone. Happen to know of him, Lieutenant?"

"Yes, sir," Sean replied. "Sergeant John Basilone was awarded the Congressional Medal of Honor for action against the Japs on Guadalcanal." He went on to describe the details of the action and the fact that Basilone had volunteered to return to the Pacific and had been killed on Iwo Jima in 1945.

"Well, I'm impressed—someone who knows a little about our history," Dalton said, retaining his laser-like stare. "Continuing with my speculation, I guess you would object to having your roommate, Lieutenant Farnsworth, referred to as a nigger. Is that accurate, Mr. Cercone?"

Sean pushed his chest forward. "Yes, sir."

Dalton didn't react to Sean. "Think racism is a problem in the Marine Corps, Mr. Cercone?"

Sean hesitated. "Racism is a major problem in our society, sir. I suspect the Marine Corps, drawing from that society, could find itself with more than a few racists." He looked directly into Dalton's pale gray eyes. "Like the lieutenant I busted up last night. We can't allow that kind of talk in the Marine Corps, sir. We just can't."

The major stared at Sean, saying nothing for a long moment. "Absolutely correct, Lieutenant." He paused again. "And we need officers who understand that. Officers who will ensure racist comments don't go unheeded. I assume you are that kind of officer."

Sean exhaled. He began to relax. "Yes, sir."

"That's too bad," Dalton said, his facial expression blank, eyes still riveted on Sean. "I'm not sure we can keep you as an officer. You can't control yourself! You lost control last night. You let your anger get the best of you." Glancing down at the record book on his desk, Dalton continued, "Your instructors have you slated as an 0-3—infantry platoon commander with an immediate assignment to West Pac upon graduation. That graduation is eight weeks away. Do you think with your obvious control problem I should let you graduate? More importantly, put you in charge of a rifle platoon of Marines?"

Sean was stunned. *Jesus! Selection as an infantry officer, overseas orders, not being able to graduate, the whole thing going down the tubes.* He pleaded, "Sir, I made a mistake. It'll never happen again. I swear it will never happen again."

"I am not sure of that. But I might be inclined to believe you and let you graduate if you show contrition and perform penance for your sins." Dalton pushed the button on his intercom. "Gunny, send in the exec and Captain Franco."

Major Mike Shay, executive officer of Charlie Company, and Captain Bob Franco, Sean's platoon commander, entered the CO's office.

"At ease, gents." Dalton nodded to the two officers. "Captain Franco, I've decided to defer my decision on this incident until graduation eve. Between now and that time, Lieutenant Cercone is restricted to the base—no leave, no off-base privileges. He may go main-side to the PX or to the chapel. He may not go to any club on base, and he may not visit Quantico town. He's banned from the Hawkins Room. Is that understood, Bob? Understood, Cercone?" Dalton looked over to Major Shea, raising his finger. "Mike, lest we forget our southern gentleman, when he gets out of sick bay, inform him he is under the same restrictions." He looked at Sean. "Now get the hell out of my office, Cercone."

As he left, Sean heard Dalton address his executive officer. "Mike, at your earliest convenience, but sometime today, meet with each platoon. Pass on this word. First, if anyone causes even a minor disturbance in the Hawkins Room, the entire company will be restricted to quarters. Second, if I hear any member of this company utter a racial or ethnic slur, I'll personally write the unsat fitness report and do everything to see that man is cashiered out of my Marine Corps. Okay, gents, that's it. Let's get to work."

Chapter 9

Sal Lente sat at a table eating a tuna sandwich while scanning the *New York Times*. Unfolding the paper in disgust, he moaned to Sandy, "Listen to this crap:

> 'Silence at Vassar on the war is assailed ... Alumnae express concern over the lack of protest. Thirty-nine Vassar alumnae and former faculty members have written the college expressing concern that Vassar students had not participated in student protests against the war.'

Next thing, they'll be giving course credit for demonstrations!"

Sandy frowned. "Vassar's not my problem. Seems my Marine got himself in a brawl. Now he's confined to quarters—no leave. Won't see him for eight weeks!" *How could he let this happen, especially after my dad caved on me not seeing him?* "And talking about those demonstrations, I think we're having one today."

Rain kept most students in the large cafeteria and off the main quad that was to be the site of an antiwar demonstration. Dozens of professionally made posters with crudely drawn pleas to end the bombing of North Vietnam were stacked against the wall. Disappointed student protesters huddled in a semicircle around Jay Delfano, the protest leader, who waved his arms as if he were leading a band. His straggly blond hair hung over the collar of an Army utility jacket with a yellow peace symbol etched on the back.

Delfano cried, "Screw the quad. Get all your people in the lounge. We worked too hard to have this rained out. The hell with the administration. We'll have our protest in here. If people don't like it, they can leave. Matter of fact, I'll announce that right now."

He jumped up on a table and shouted for the attention of the three hundred or so students, most of whom were eating lunch. Despite his less-than-imposing five-foot-seven frame, his act worked, and the room fell silent.

"We're taking over this place for an antiwar rally. Anyone who's against Johnson and his bombing is invited to stay. Anyone who isn't can leave." He pointed in the direction of Sandy's table. "This table first."

The room remained silent. One of Delfano's henchmen, a tall, skinny protester, moved in the direction of the table, "Okay, you with us, or—"

"Wait a minute! Who do you think you are?" Sandy jumped to her feet, pointing to Delfano, who was still on the table top. "You have absolutely no right to order anyone out of this building for any reason. You can take your protest and …"

"Shove it up your ass!" Sal cried and leapt to his feet.

The lanky protester stopped a few feet from the table.

An image of Sean in his Marine uniform flashed in Sandy's mind. She stood, hands on hips, and faced Delfano. "I'm not moving!"

"Guess we'll have to move you," Delfano shot back, motioning to his cadre behind his table.

"Forget about moving her, wiseass. How 'bout moving me first? I'm not moving either." The booming voice came from a squarely built, broad-shouldered guy with a dark day-old beard. He wore a windbreaker embossed with the letters NYFD.

His table mate, a tall, lean redhead with the same New York Fire Department jacket, stood. "I ain't moving either, pal."

"Neither are we!" shouted three coeds at the far end of the lounge. Others began standing with the same defiant cries. "Neither are we. Neither are we."

Delfano's face reddened. Confronted with most of the room standing and chanting, he was beaten at his own game. Embarrassed and made to look like a fool, he jumped off the table and shouted in the direction of Sandy. "Fascists! Fascist pigs!" He hurried toward the closest door, followed by a dozen of his zealots. Sandy heard his ranting. "I'm gonna get that bitch. I'm gonna get her. I'm going to make her pay."

★   ★   ★

Delfano and three of his friends sat at a table drinking egg-cream sodas in the rear of a Brighton Beach luncheonette. "See you guys. Gotta get home," Delfano said, slipping on a tan leather jacket. "Thanks for your support the other day. We showed that bitch. She's no match for people who know what's going on in the world."

He approached a long counter cluttered with stacks of newspapers and plastic jars filled with pretzels. A frail older man with a head that seemed too large for his body pushed the keys of an antique-looking cash register. "Vell, Jay, congratulations on getting into NYU Law. Your dad must be proud."

"Thanks, Abe. Yeah, dad's very happy. He went to NYU."

"You don't look so happy, Jay. Didn't you and your friends have a successful demonstration last Monday?"

"Not exactly, Abe. It was disrupted by the weather and a loudmouth bitch that turned the crowd against us." Delfano shrugged, tossing a dollar and some change on the counter. "But we got some payback the next day. Couple of us corralled Miss Loudmouth in the hallway. Had a little discussion about the war, about the corrupt Vietnamese government and America's imperialist policies. After we tongue-lashed her for a few minutes, she got real upset, took off in tears."

Abe Paser shook his large head, wiping his hand on his gray apron blotted with stains. "Several of you tongue-lashed this girl. Doesn't sound like a fair debate—more like a verbal gang rape. Vas she that supportive of the war?"

"Yeah, she was all for the war." Delfano smirked. "Kept whining about men putting their lives on the line, and the standard right-wing crap about Communist expansion in Asia. We heard all that before, right, Abe?"

Abe stared back at the young man. "Vell, I've heard it before. Don't like war, Jay. As you know, my boy, like most old Jews in this neighborhood, I suffered through a war. Certainly think it right to protest about this war, but we have to respect the opinion of others." He pushed the register drawer closed with more force than usual. "That woman had a point, Jay. There are young men risking their lives. And people who support them."

Delfano moved toward the door and turned abruptly. "Sure, Abe, lots of young men. Most of them drafted right out of high school. A few even volunteer. They're the real schmucks. None of them have a clue about foreign policy, world politics, or global responsibility. No, Abe, like the song says—the times they're a changin'. And it's up to us to change the world, create a new order. Make it all better."

Abe shook his head. "A new vorld order. I seemed to have heard that line before, Jay."

"Yeah, right, Abe." Delfano stormed out the door.

A damp wind blew off Sheepshead Bay, and Jay wasn't pleased with his decision to walk to his Manhattan Beach home. But it gave him time to think about Sandy and his failed protest demonstration. Maybe the protest thing wasn't worth the trouble. He'd gotten into law school. He'd get deferment for sure. No sweat for a couple of years. It was getting risky funding this thing. Who needs this hassle? Approaching the low fern hedges that rimmed his long driveway, he heard a deep voice.

"Excuse me. Can you tell me where …"

The voice came from a black limo parked close to his driveway. A hand clutching a small photo extended out the rear window.

"Where's this place?"

Moving toward the car window, he tried to view the postcard-sized picture and get a glimpse of who was asking for help. A hand sprung out, grabbing Delfano's collar and heaving his upper torso through the open window. The car started moving, and another set of hands clasped over his head and mouth, pulling the remainder of his twisting body into the car. Stuffed on the rear floor, his face pressed against the gray carpet, he was frightened speechless. He could feel the car picking up speed as one of the men who held him spoke.

"Listen, scumbag, and listen good. If you ever go near, or hassle, or ever fuckin' touch Miss Gold, you're gonna have a big problem." The hands pressed harder, mashing Jay's face against the floor, making it difficult to breathe.

The voice became a low growl. "Let me show ya what the problem gonna be."

Jay felt a hand between his legs and screamed as he felt a crushing grip around his testicles.

"Ya know that gavel your daddy uses in court? We gonna get one of them and mash these balls of yours flat—flat as a fuckin' pancake. Ya understand, Mister College Guy?"

The hand squeezed harder and caused Jay to cry uncontrollably as he tried raising his head from the car floor.

"Lou, pull over so we can get rid of this prick. Jesus! He pissed his pants."

The car stopped abruptly and the left rear door flung open. The one holding Jay's head to the floor eased out of the car. He reached back and grabbed the slobbering Delfano, pulling him out of the car and tossing him to the gutter.

The frightened peace activist crawled to the grassy separation between the curb and the sidewalk. He grasped his loins and felt the humiliating wetness. His mouth was parched; he'd never experienced such fright. The fear ebbed. He wasn't going to be tortured or killed. He began to feel rage at being violated. Stumbling down the tree-lined street, he now hated Sandy Gold more than anything in the world.

★　★　★

The Wrong Number Lounge was empty except for one or two regulars. Frankie and Sal hunched over a small table in the rear of the bar and were joined by a heavyset, silver-haired grandfatherly looking man. "Hey, Geno." Frankie smiled. "That thing going down?"

Geno nodded. "Yeah, I got Lou on it—should be tonight."

The phone behind the bar rang. Pauli "Black" picked up the receiver and grunted. The balding, rail-thin bartender, always dressed totally in black, placed his hand over the phone. "Geno, you here? Some guy says he was told to call ya. Wants to report about a job."

"Yeah, Pauli, it's for me. Excuse me, guys. Think this is our call."

Geno moved behind the bar and grabbed the phone. "That's good, that's good. Nobody saw nuttin'. You sure?" Motioning across the bar, he gave thumbs up to Frankie and Sal. "You used Connecticut plates. Good, ya get rid of them? Good. Whaddaya mean, you gotta clean the car? What the fuck you do? Did you cut him up? I just told ya to scare him." Geno pulled the receiver from his ear, gritted his teeth, and growled, "You asshole!" He stopped his ranting and burst into laughter. "What, you're kidding. He pissed all over the back floor?" Geno laughed. "Hey, that ain't so bad. Lucky you didn't scare the shit out of him—you really woulda had a fuckin' mess. Okay, Lou, you did good. See ya at the wedding next month. I owe ya one."

Frankie and Sal praised Geno for the well-executed job. After making a brief phone call, Frankie motioned it was time to leave. He whispered to Geno, "Let's keep this one to ourselves." *Don't think we want to tell Sean. Shit, someday he may be a DA, and he'd have to arrest our asses.*

"No problem, Frankie." Geno grunted. "Diz one of them unsolved crimes that fuckin' nobody gonna find out about."

As they left the bar, Sal asked, "What's Delfano gonna do? Think he'll report this to the cops?"

"Nah." Frankie grinned. "Just called a friend at the Sixty-Second Precinct. Said there were no assaults reported in Manhattan Beach tonight. Then again, don't think Delfano is ever gonna forget what happened. Better keep an eye on him."

Chapter 10

The graduation ceremony for basic class 3-67 was a brief, somber affair held in an auditorium at the main side area of the Quantico Marine base. Sean and several hundred Marine lieutenants heard Colonel Peter Kerrigan, commanding officer of the Basic School, deliver a speech about what lay ahead for the young officers and those who waited for their return. He spoke of the sacrifices and uncertainty facing the graduates, many of whom were slated to be in Vietnam in the next six weeks. It was anything but an uplifting speech and was over in twenty minutes. After a brief session naming the class honor men, the ceremony ended. The lieutenants spilled out into the parking lot, gathering in small groups, shaking hands, and saying good-bye to classmates. Everyone understood this would be the last time they would be together as a group, and for many it would be the last time they saw one another.

Sean sought out his company commander, Major Ax Dalton, wanting to thank him for the handwritten note on Dalton's stationery delivered to his room the previous afternoon: "Show up at graduation tomorrow. You're a good Marine. Just keep that temper in check. Take care of your Marines. Semper Fi."

Sean also wanted to congratulate Dalton on his recent promotion to lieutenant colonel. He searched the crowd, but Dalton had left. Deciding he would forward a note when he got home, Sean sought to meet up with BW to say good-bye to the mustang who had taught him as much about the Corps as any of his instructors.

After meeting with his roommate, Sean drove to the Slatterys' Woodbridge apartment to attend a bon-voyage brunch. He was surprised to see Beth Wilenski at the end of the teak bar helping Mike distribute Bloody Marys to classmates and their wives. Her long black hair was worn up in a twist. A light brown silk blouse blended nicely with dark slacks, and a slight heel on her gold sandals added to Beth's sophisticated bearing, a clear contrast to the other women, who seemed dressed for a sorority social.

Sean ambled across the room, waving to Slattery, who flashed a depressing grin. *Mike's down. Got word of another academy classmate KIA, not in a party mood.*

"Hi, Beth. Good to see ya." *God, she's a good-looking woman.*

"Hello, Marine!" She greeted him with a warm smile. "Mike tells me you've been a bad boy, restricted to base. How's it feel to be going home? Is that girl still waiting?"

"Hell, sure hope so. With luck I should see her this afternoon."

Beth laughed. "Don't envy her having to deal with a Marine who's been cloistered for eight weeks." She took a long sip of her drink. "My suggestion is to have one good Bloody Mary, kiss the hostess, wave good-bye to your friends, and get your butt in your car." She handed Sean a drink, drew his head close, kissed his cheek, and whispered, "Be careful, Sean. May God be with you."

Sean clicked his glass with Beth's. "Thanks. Better check out with Val. I'll see you when I see you. Watch out for that Kennedy guy!"

After an emotional good-bye with Val, Sean turned to Slattery, extending his hand. "Well, Mike, we're both going to the First Mar. Div. Hope I'll see you over there."

Slattery gripped Sean hand. "You bet. I'm sure we'll be meeting up. Good luck, Marine."

★   ★   ★

The late-morning traffic on I-95 was light. Sean crossed the Verrazano Bridge into Brooklyn just over four hours after leaving Virginia. How fast life had changed. In less than a year, he'd gone from a freshman law student to a Marine officer, from playing touch football to learning how to lead men in combat. During the past months at Quantico, he had begun to grasp the enormity of his commitment and the price he'd be paying to follow his father and serve his country, a price made far greater by his feelings for a new person in his life.

Sean pushed Sandy's front doorbell and braced himself, not knowing how he'd react to her appearance. The door opened, and he was taken aback. "Good afternoon, sir—Mr. Gold. I was wondering if Sandy—"

"She ain't home. She's out with her mother," Sam replied with a blank stare that faded into a grin. "You want to come in and wait, maybe have a cup of coffee."

Sean's body stiffened. Sandy had told him her father had relented about them not seeing each other, but he still expected some flak from Mr. Gold. He was apprehensive following the burly man down a richly decorated hallway into a large eat-in kitchen.

"Sit down." Sam motioned to a round glass-topped table. "How ya like it?"

"Black, please, no sugar," Sean said, easing into a high-backed wrought-iron chair. After an awkward silence, he spoke while Mr. Gold poured the coffee. "Wanted to apologize about keeping Sandy out so late last December." He hesitated. "Also wanted to say I'm sorry for being such a wiseass the first time we met."

Sam finished pouring and put a cup in front of Sean. "Yeah, well, I wasn't such a nice guy either. You know, those remarks and all. Far as Sandy staying out late, she's a big girl. Just don't do it again—or I'll break your legs." He locked his jaw and gave Sean a menacing look and then laughed.

Sean grinned. "Understood!"

"So, ya really into this Marine thing? Sandy tells us you're going over. They give ya some leave?"

"Thirty days counting today." He dropped his head. "Guess I feel a little different now that I'm under orders. You were right."

Sam raised his hands in a puzzled gesture. "Me, right? Right about what?"

"What you said first time we met." Sean looked up at Mr. Gold. "About me not knowing shit about war. You're right. It's all about killing and getting killed. I guess that's hit home in the last couple of months at Quantico."

"Ya scared?"

"Sure, I'm scared. Mostly about screwing up, getting men killed. Maybe not coming home in one piece. Kind of scared for my mom too."

Sean shook his head, brow foiled. "I'm not—I don't know … Maybe I'm not doing the right thing with Sandy. I mean …"

In almost a whisper, Sam said, "It's gonna be okay. We'll take care of Sandy. Just be careful and come home."

Hearing a noise in the foyer, Sam turned and smiled. "Hey, looks like the ladies are home."

Having spotted Sean's green Fairlane, Sandy ran into the kitchen, almost colliding with her father. She stood facing Sean for a moment and then threw her arms around him.

Sam motioned to his wife. "Come on, Juliana, let's get the groceries. Give the kids a little privacy."

★   ★   ★

"So where's the handsome Marine?" Sam said, entering the kitchen.

"He wanted to run over and say hello to his mom. She took a half-day off just to prepare for his dinner tonight. He'll be back soon." Sandy pushed her long brown hair off her shoulder. "Dad, can I ask you something?"

"Sure, princess."

"Dad, I really appreciate you accepting Sean. He said you two had a nice talk. But I've never seen you change your mind so abruptly. Mom said you were adamant about not discussing Sean. What happened?"

Sam took a breath and exhaled with a smile. "You remember my friend Mickey Cohen? You know him—a little guy, Brighton Beach handball champ. I've known him for what, about fifteen years. Tough guy, but a real gentleman. Found out he was in the Korean War, a sergeant with the Marines, no less. So I asked him about Sean and you, what he thought about a guy dropping out of law school to become a Marine officer, volunteering to go over."

My God, that's all I need—advice from Mickey Cohen, Sandy thought. "What did he have to say, Dad?"

"Mickey said he didn't have any kids. If he did, and his son did what Sean is doing, he'd hate it. Said he'd also be the proudest man alive." Sam gazed into Sandy's beautiful dark eyes. "And if he had a daughter who got hooked on a guy like that, he wouldn't get much sleep. But he'd know his little girl was now a real woman who made a good choice for a man to love. Mickey said Sean was gonna see some rough times. You'd be going through hell waiting for him. Said you're gonna need a lot of support from us."

Sandy grasped her father's hand, and her eyes moistened.

"Then Mickey asked me if I believed in God. I laughed. Told him I'd seen too much to believe in any God. Said he felt the same way. He said that was too bad, because the Sean and Sandy thing was now in God's hands. He said we can't do anything except try to understand you, support you both, and hope the God we don't believe in will look over Sean. That's what Mickey Cohen said."

Sandy's eyes welled with tears, and she wrapped her arms around her father.

Chapter 11

HOME LEAVE
GRAVESEND, BROOKLYN
MID-MARCH

Buoyed by the reception and acceptance of her father, Sandy was determined to spend every waking moment with Sean during the next thirty days. He offered to go to class with her, but she declined, deciding instead to cut most of her classes. She told Sean of the frequent antiwar demonstrations but never mentioned her incident with Delfano at the student lounge.

An unseasonably mild spring enabled them to take morning walks along Ocean Parkway. Leaves were just beginning to appear on the giant oaks that lined the thoroughfare down to Brighton Beach. They strolled along the wide boardwalk that separated the white sand beach from an aquarium, a giant Ferris wheel, and blocks of amusement rides that formed the backdrop of Coney Island. The couple spent most afternoons back at Sean's house, alone, in blissful passion.

Today the weather looked threatening. They decided to forego the beach and drove north on Ocean Parkway, passing through several upscale neighborhoods before reaching Prospect Park, a lush oasis occupying hundreds of acres in the middle of the city's most populated borough. Sandy thought the low green hills, winding paths, and beautiful lake would offer some tranquil privacy from the other two million people who called Brooklyn home. "If I'm going to cut class again today, this is great place to play hooky." She laughed. "Let's go find a bench by the lake."

They sat in silence, watching tadpoles leap through the reeds at the lake's edge. She moved closer to Sean, grasping one of his arms, head on his shoulder. "Sean, I'm scared." Her voice cracked. "I'm so frightened about you going to Vietnam." *What happens if—my God, I don't know what I would do.* She pressed her head into his chest, fighting back tears.

Sean put his arm around her. "I'm a little scared too, Sandy. Feel guilty as well. I never considered anyone else. My mom's beside herself. Just feel, way down inside, I've got to go. My dad would have expected me to go. It's the right thing for me on a lot of levels. But now I'm putting you through all this." He hesitated. "Maybe we should never have—"

She bolted upright from his grasp. "Never have what? Fallen in love, shared our bodies? It's happened, Sean. I'm glad it did. Whether it's for a month or a lifetime, I wouldn't want it any other way."

$$\star \quad \star \quad \star$$

During the month, everyone wanted them over for dinner. Most evenings didn't end before midnight in Sandy's backyard, living room, or front stoop. On the third weekend of Sean's leave, the family was invited to a wedding at their club in Deal, New Jersey. They planned on leaving Friday night and coming home Sunday. Much to the consternation of her mother, Sandy begged off with an excuse about an engagement party for a close friend on the tennis team.

Dressed in jeans and a tailored button-down shirt, Sandy made her bed and looked forward to sharing it with Sean that weekend. Her mother entered the room. "Hi, Mom. Dad already go? Thought I'd catch him for breakfast today."

Juliana smiled and glanced around the room with its light tan walls and sleek sofa festooned with dolls. Her smile faded after looking at a framed tennis championship banner hanging above a cedar dresser topped with pictures of Sandy in various stages of her youth. "He's left. Too bad you didn't mention it. I'm sure he would have loved to have breakfast."

Turning to her mother and tightening the sheets on her four poster bed, Sandy frowned. "Mom, what's the matter? Something wrong?"

"No, nothing. Just wanted to talk. We haven't talked in a while, especially since Sean's been home." Juliana sat on the narrow sofa, clasped her hand, and spoke rapidly as if she wanted to get past something.

"What will you do after the party Friday night? Will you and Sean be coming over here? Will he stay? Have you and Sean been—intimate?"

Sandy stood erect and spoke in a deliberate tone. "Yes, mother, we have. And we'll be staying here, together."

Her mother's face flushed. "Are you using protection?"

Sandy nodded and inched cautiously around the bed, eyes fixed on her mother's anxious face. "I love him, Ma. I love everything about him. I want to be with him. In ten days he's leaving. I may never …"

Juliana stood, extending her arms. Sandy rushed across the room to the comfort of her mother's grasp as she had done so many times in this room. "I may never see him again. Ma, I'm so scared. I can't bear to lose him."

★ ★ ★

The Wrong Number Lounge had been the neighborhood bar for as long as anyone could remember. Drinking had never been a big deal for Sean and his friends, but hanging out in Wrong Number was special. The bar was a mecca for an array of local legends, most of whom had made their mark as athletes, ladies men, gamblers, or wise guys connected to the lower rungs of the local organized crime family.

Frankie Brain had hung out in the Wrong Number since his late teens and could qualify as a legend in all categories with the exception of wise guy. Francis Xavier Ryan was too smart and too independent. His knack for meticulously planning successful capers, however, garnered him the confidence—and most importantly, the respect—of virtually all the connected guys in the bar. He had put these relationships to good use over the years.

Given his prince-like status, it was no surprise that Sean, one of Frankie's closest friends, was held in high esteem by the locals. They decided Lieutenant Cercone's going-away party would be held at the Wrong Number Lounge.

The affair took place on a Friday night, the day before Sean's departure. The lounge was packed to capacity. A six-foot-long banner hung on the wall opposite the bar. One end of the banner had an American flag, the other end a large Marine Corps globe and anchor. The middle section was used to pen words of farewell to Sean.

Sean and Sandy slithered through the crowded, narrow lounge, exchanging comments with the well-wishers. It was an eclectic group—

regulars from the bar, mostly older men; several of Sean's frat brothers from St. John's clad in T-shirts and madras shorts; even a couple of out-of-place law school classmates in blue blazers. Sean's Gremlin teammates milled about, carousing with a half-dozen local ladies who sported presummer tans and low-cut halters. Several of the older crowd were present, including Joe and Mary D'Angelo along with Grandma Rosa. Platters of food, all of it homemade and contributed by friends, were served. Pauli Black, Geno, and Sal worked frantically pouring wine and beer courtesy of the Sons of Italy Club located across the street from the lounge.

Sandy sat with Rosa and the D'Angelos, and Sean approached a table with his mother, his uncle Frank, and Jimmy Napoli. The dapper NYPD detective was a lifelong friend of the Cercone family. A dedicated, hard-charging professional, he'd recently been promoted to chief of detectives for Brooklyn South.

"Hey, Jimmy!" Sean cried. "Haven't seen you in a while. Congratulations on your promotion. Thanks for coming."

"Sean, I'm honored to be here. I'm even gonna get rid of this tie in your honor." He laughed and removed his stripped silk tie, folding it carefully into his jacket pocket. His tone changed and his smile faded. "As I was saying to your mother and uncle, I wasn't pleased about you leaving law school. But I can't argue with you becoming a Marine officer, especially nowadays." Sliding out of his chair, Jimmy extended his hand. The would-be handshake turned into a hug, and he spoke in a low voice. "We're all proud of you, Sean—very proud. Take care of yourself. Your uncle and I'll watch out for your mom."

Frankie Brain stepped to the table. "Hey, anybody up for a drink? How 'bout some wine, Mrs. Cercone?"

"Thanks, red wine would be fine. By the way, Frankie, do you know detective Napoli?"

"Sure, I know him," Frankie said, turning to face the detective standing next to Sean. "We've met several times. Catch any bad guys lately, Nap?"

Sean tensed. He remembered the last time he'd seen Napoli in the park. *This is trouble. Any conversation between Jimmy and Frankie could be bad news, if not incriminating for Frankie.* He tried in vain to change the subject.

Napoli wrinkled his brow and cast a hard stare at Frankie. "Yeah, Frankie, just got a bad guy. That punk friend of yours, what's his name—

Sonny somebody. Got him smuggling cigarettes up from the Carolinas. Eight hundred cartons! He may be doing some time. Maybe not, if he tells us who was behind that caper. Wouldn't know anything about the subject, would you, Mr. Ryan?"

"Why, Chief Napoli, how could ya have such thoughts? I don't partake in that awful smoking vice." Frankie moved closer to Napoli, lips set in a pained expression. "But I'm sure, with that analytical mind of yours, should be rather simple to deduce the problem. Let's see … eight hundred cartons, that's eight thousand packs or one hundred sixty thousand cigarettes. No doubt about it. Looks like poor Sonny is a fuckin' chain-smoker and should be charged as such."

Those within ear shot burst into laughter. The new chief of detectives of Brooklyn South tightened his jaw, hissing in a low voice, "Fuck you, Ryan. One of these days you're gonna to slip, and I'm personally gonna—"

"Whoa, guys. Got one war to go to; let's not start one before I leave," Sean said, stepping between Frankie and Jimmy. When he had settled things down, Sean turned to his mother and uncle. "Sandy and I have to go. We've got a few things to do. See you all in the morning."

Ann Cercone raised her chin, a faint smile appearing on her otherwise stoic face. Her brother-in-law Frank grinned. "By all means, Lieutenant. Please take your leave with your lady."

Chapter 12

Sean and Sandy walked hand in hand down the lengthy corridor a few steps ahead of his mother and his uncle Frank. The rest of the group followed at a discreet distance. The tubular corridor with gray brushed cement walls made the walk from the bustling terminal to the planeside lounge almost surreal, as if they were moving to another world. In a sense, Sean was.

At the departure area, Sean turned to face the group. Standing in his tropical tan uniform, a bit snug after thirty days' leave, he took off his cover and walked toward his friends. He shook hands with Sal and then with Joey. Both uttered the same comment. "Good luck, Sean."

He extended his hand to Frankie. The lanky six-footer pulled Sean into a hug and whispered, "Do what you have to do, Sean, and be careful." He ushered Sean toward Frank Cercone.

The former Marine grasped his godson in his traditional bear hug. With their eyes inches apart, he growled in a low voice, "Don't forget what I said, listen to your noncoms, and take care of your men." His voice lowered, "May God bring you home to us, Sean."

Barely out of his uncle's hug, Sean was embraced by his mother. She wrapped her arms around his neck and cried as she had done many times in the past few days. "Mary, mother of Jesus, please have your son bring my son home."

Sean almost lost his composure as he felt his mother's trembling, wet cheek against his face. He held her tightly. "I'll come home, Mom,

I promise. I'll make it back." Still embracing his mother, feeling guilty about a promise over which he had little control, Sean looked over to the other woman in his life. Sandy stood a few feet away, a light blue blouse accentuating her deep tan, her dark eyes wide and sad. Her shapely lips quivered.

Sean motioned to his uncle, who unlocked the trembling mother from her son.

Sean and Sandy embraced. She placed her arms around his neck and delivered a passionate kiss. Parting her lips from his, she murmured, "I love you, Sean. Please come back to me."

Sean whispered, "I'll love you forever and—" A loud, melodic voice announced the immediate boarding of American 960 to San Francisco.

Joey unlocked Sandy from Sean's embrace. Frankie handed him his Valpak with "Lt. Sean Cercone, USMC" stenciled across its side. Sean turned away and quickly joined the line of boarders filing onto the plane. Just before reaching the door, he stepped out of the line to take a last look.

Sal tried to help Frankie with Ann, grasping her arm. Neither could do anything about the tears and the look of anguish frozen on her pale face. Joey reached to hold Sandy, who managed a weak smile, raising her hand in a slow wave.

Sean stared. *Leaving everyone. Everyone that counts. Hope I'm doing the right thing.* He nodded, flashed a smile, and stepped back in line to begin his terrible journey.

Book II

Chapter 13

Quang Nam Province
South Vietnam
Early May 1967

Sean bounced uncomfortably on the wooden slats of a truck the Marines called a "six-by." The discomfort of the ride was offset by air rushing into the open truck bed, making the intense heat somewhat bearable. The convoy of two jeeps, half a dozen trucks, and two amphibious tractors crawled on a narrow dirt road winding through the flat Vietnamese countryside. Two hours had passed since the slow-moving convoy left the relative security of the port city of Da Nang with its sprawling airfield and network of blacktop roads connecting dozens of Marine units. Rice fields dominated the landscape in every direction, punctuated every mile or so by clusters of shoddy thatched huts. The putrid smell of excrement hung in the dusty air, its stench intensifying as the convoy passed each tiny hamlet.

Sean fought a sense of anxiety. He had never felt so intensely about someone. Bad times lay ahead, and he'd be tested over the next thirteen months. He hoped he'd measure up, get through it in one piece, and get back to the girl whom, after only a week's separation, he missed desperately.

The convoy reached its destination at Hill 55 without incident. It wasn't much of a hill—just a slight rise completely devoid of vegetation. A string of bunkers behind rolls of concertina wire formed a perimeter halfway up the hill. On the far side of the road was a battery of well-camouflaged howitzers. Within the perimeter were more sandbag bunkers and a few tin-roofed plywood huts, walls covered with wire-mesh screens. Shallow slit trenches flanked each of the huts. All the bunkers and huts were covered in a light yellow-brown dust. A cluster of slender poles, each jutting twenty feet in the air, formed an antenna farm that even a rookie second lieutenant knew was the sign of a headquarters unit.

Hill 55 was the field headquarters of the Fifth Marine Regiment. The regiment had more than five thousand Marines spread over twenty square miles, including several infantry battalions, an artillery battalion, and attached companies of trucks, tanks, amphibious tractors, and other supporting units.

Sean suspected this visit to the regiment would be a quick stop on his way to one of the infantry battalions. He was right. He entered one of the screened huts that had a red sign with the designation S-1 painted on it in yellow. A shirtless man wearing a crushed utility cover with a major's oak leaf greeted him with a pensive look. "Lieutenant Cercone reporting in, sir."

The very detached major grunted. "Cercone, right. Welcome aboard, Lieutenant. You're going down to Fifth Battalion. Supply chopper is leaving in twenty minutes. Be on it."

Late that afternoon, Sean sprinted down the ramp of a CH-46 helicopter. Running hunched over from the backwash of the twin rotor blades, he slid past several Marines moving into the chopper to off-load boxes of rations, five-gallon water cans, and tins of ammo. The only other passenger, a lance corporal with a field radio strapped to his back, trotted behind Sean.

The landing zone consisted of a small clearing bounded on one side by waist-high brush with a stand of thick trees arching around the remainder of the area. Running toward the cluster of trees, Sean spotted two bunkers fifty meters into the tree line. One bunker had a tarp extending from its roof large enough to shelter a field desk and a map board.

A lone Marine sitting under the shelter on a small canvas chair motioned for Sean. "Welcome to Five/Five, Lieutenant Cercone. Regiment told us you were coming in. Glad to have you aboard. I'm Jim Ward, battalion XO. See you stowed your gear at regiment. Good. We're gonna be in the bush for a while. You brought us a radioman as well." The major pointed to the lance corporal, who was maintaining a respectful distance from the two officers. "Son, go over to the comm bunker and report to the gunny, Spitz. He's the comm chief. Tell him I want you in Alpha Company. Then come back here tomorrow morning first thing."

"Glad to be aboard, sir," Sean said, extending his hand.

Ward nodded and gave Sean a strong handshake. "Let me fill you in, Lieutenant, then we'll have you say hello to the CO. Too late to get out to Alpha. You'll stay here tonight."

Grasping a small black notebook, Sean listened as the major motioned to a plastic-covered map covered with black and red circles.

"Been in this area for the last ten days. Had several contacts with main-force VC units and at least one NVA company. NVA contact was significant. They generally stay in the hills surrounding the valley, leaving most of the fighting to VC units. Their presence means something is up. We want to stop whatever it is."

The lean, square-jawed major turned away from the map, sat down on the corner of the field desk, and stared as if he was studying Sean. "Alpha Company engaged the NVA unit and did well, got thirty confirms. Alpha paid a price. They lost a platoon commander and his radio operator. You and the lance corporal will be taking their place."

★ ★ ★

Early the next morning, Sean and Lance Corporal Tim Odom, a thin, pale eighteen-year-old from Tyler, Texas, were escorted to Alpha Company, where they met Captain Robert Lee, the company commander. Captain Lee, a graduate of the Virginia Military Institute, was tall, lean, and completely bald, a career Marine officer with ten years of service. He addressed Sean and Odom in a businesslike manner. "You two are just in time. First platoon needs an HQ element. You've got a good buck sergeant who's been acting as platoon commander. Make sure you use his experience. First thing to do is make sure you know how to call for fire. Check in with our Arty FO, Lieutenant Mason. He's over in the next hole. He'll check you out on our procedures." Nodding to Odom, the captain narrowed his pale eyes. "I want a sit rep every four hours. Make sure the lieutenant and you work it out."

Lee bent his slender frame, put his hands on his sides, and gave Sean a tired look. "We'll be moving out at 1300, about three clicks west. Make sure you keep contact with second platoon. They'll be the point. The gunny will give you the scoop on your platoon. Sorry I can't spend more time. Gotta get over to second platoon. Join up with you tonight and we'll get acquainted. Any questions, Cercone?"

Before Sean could say anything, the long-limbed captain turned and left. Sean shot Lance Corporal Odom a blank stare. "Let's go see the FO and then find our platoon."

Sean and Odom jogged quietly down a trail of matted grass, cutting through a green and brown thicket of tall weeds. Rustling movement sounded to their front. Both men froze.

"Welcome to first platoon. Better get a little low. Took some sniper fire yesterday." Peering above a shallow hole, a Marine pushed himself onto the trail. He stood hunched with a crooked smile on his bearded face. Thin, well-developed arms protruded from the flak jacket, which he wore over a filthy green undershirt. His pants were faded and splattered with mud. "Name's Clawson. They call me Spider. You must be our new lieutenant."

Sean extended his hand. "Lieutenant Cercone. Good to meet ya. This is Lance Corporal Odom. Can you can take us to the platoon sergeant?"

"That'd be Sergeant Murphy," Spider replied. "About thirty meters down the trail. Can't take ya, sir; gotta watch this trail. Sorry 'bout that."

Sean gave an understanding nod and took off down the trail, Odom following, both hunched over trying to keep their heads below the shrub line. Shallow holes, most with gray rubber ponchos draped on sticks to protect against the elements, lined both sides of the trail. The holes were filled with sleeping Marines. Sean spied a short radio antenna protruding from one of the holes and figured that to be the home of Sergeant Murphy.

"Tom Murphy, sir. Welcome aboard."

Except for his reasonably clean-shaven face and well-trimmed thick black mustache, Sergeant Murphy appeared much like Spider. He wore his flimsily protective flack vest over a green undershirt. His boots were mud-caked and his utility trousers faded and torn. Innocent, light-blue eyes gave him a youthful appearance.

Sean sat on an ammo crate on the side of Murphy's hole, which had a string of sandbags around its edge. Odom sat against the far wall and winced in relief when he slipped the twenty-pound radio from his back. Sean took off his helmet and put on his soft cover utility cap, a sign both men were moving in. "Good to meet you, Sergeant. The CO says you're doing a great job with the platoon."

Murphy gave a half-smile. "Do my best. Got a couple of good squad leaders. Men are good too. Couple of shirt birds, but even they get it together when we're in the bush. We do okay, I guess." He let the last phrase hang as if prompting Sean for a comment.

Sean knew Murphy had been in this situation before. He'd been briefed back at the company. For the third time in six months, Murphy was turning the platoon over to a new lieutenant, an inexperienced rookie brown bar. Both men eyed each other for a long moment. Odom tended to his radio, looking as if he wanted to be somewhere else.

Sean grinned. "I'm certainly gonna be the new guy for a while. Be relying on you to get me up to speed. When I think it's necessary, I'll call the shots. If you think I'm stepping on my dick, let me know." Murphy smiled. Sean went on, "We got orders to move out at 1300. How long will it take to get 'em ready to go?"

"We can move in thirty minutes, a lot less if necessary," Murphy said. "Most of the platoon is catching some sleep; had a tough couple a days. You want me to roust them up so you can meet them before we shove off?"

Sean took off his cover, moved his hand through his close-cropped hair, and made his first decision as platoon commander. "Nah, let 'em sleep, unless you've got something you want 'em to do. I will want to meet with the squad leaders when you brief them on the move. I'll meet with each squad separately when we get to where we're going. Make sense?"

"Good call, sir." Murphy kept his smile. "It'll give me some time to give you a map read of the area. Give you some scoop on the platoon."

The positive initial rapport between the young platoon sergeant and the new lieutenant continued over the next few weeks. Sean and Murphy spent time each evening, sometimes up to an hour, reviewing the day's activity.

"Ya gotta lean hard on them sometime, sir. Especially when they think it's slack time. Or the opposite, when they're dog tired. That's when they don't pay attention, when they let details slip, maybe forget to check an ammo pouch, store the claymores right, don't get out of wet socks. Then we get in some shit and it's too late."

Sean nodded. "Got it. Make sure they pay attention, don't let anything slide. Not that I should talk. Didn't pay attention to that jock itch; now I've got crud all over. Who leans on lieutenants when they fuck up, Murph?"

Murphy brushed his thin mustache and smiled. "That's an additional duty for the platoon sergeant—politely, of course."

Sean's opennes—along with his willingness to listen and learn impressed Sergeant Murphy. He was eager to share his experience with his new lieutenant. Sean understood how lucky he was to have Murphy as his platoon sergeant. He recalled his uncle's parting advice at JFK: "Listen to your noncoms."

Little contact occurred during Sean's first two weeks with his platoon except for two brief firefights that were handled by the squad leaders. He did call in artillery twice and supervise two emergency evacuations. He learned more each day, but in the eyes of his Marines, he was still a newbie, yet to be tested. All that changed during Sean's third week with the platoon.

Chapter 14

The Fifth Battalion had again been ordered to sweep the northwestern part of the Que Son Valley. The mission was to engage the 354th NVA regiment that was reported to have entered the valley. Alpha was the lead company. Its task was to sweep through a series of hamlets making up the village of Phu Duc that sat astride a hill mass know to be an infiltration route. Sean's platoon was the point. Its mission was to move down the main road that snaked through the series of hamlets and engage any NVA. In the grand scheme, Sean and his platoon of thirty-two Marines were bait for luring the NVA into a fight.

The platoon entered the outskirts of a good-sized hamlet of more than two dozen huts clustered on about three acres of dry land. Rice paddies surrounded the hamlet, which was designated as PD(1), with two similar hamlets, PD(2) and PD(3), about a quarter-mile down the road. The three hamlets composed the village of Phu Duc. There was no way into the village complex except a single road ten feet wide and a foot higher than the surrounding paddies. Muddy water partially flooded the paddies, and the mounds of dirt dikes crossed the fields parallel and perpendicular to the narrow road. The midmorning heat intensified and propelled the pungent, sewer-like smell of the paddies through the nostrils of the advancing Marines.

Sean crouched, dropped his radio handset from his ear, and spoke loudly to Sergeant Murphy a few meters away. "The six wants us to move through this vill quickly. Says the main resistance will be in PD(2) and PD(3). I'm not so sure. Make sure we're at five-meter intervals. Get an M-60 with the point fire team. When we're halfway in, about two hundred meters from the vill, get the platoon off the road."

Murphy responded, "The whole thing sucks. Think we're just bait, LT. If we take fire from that vill, just blow it away."

"Too many civilians." Sean frowned. "We'll see what we see. Just make sure you get off the road halfway in. Get the extra radio up with first squad. I'll take Odom and get behind second squad. Let's move."

The sweat-drenched Marines formed a staggered column and inched down the road. Halfway to the vill, each fire team halted on Murphy's order and slid into the foul-smelling paddies.

Kneeling on the paddy edge, Sean pulled out a pair of binoculars, adjusted the focus, and scanned PD(1). There were few villagers in the hamlet, most working behind the vill and to the south side of the road. No villagers were in the paddies to the right front, north of the road. Sean scanned his right front and detected something unusual. A portion of one of the dikes parallel to the road was higher and looked thicker than the normal dike. Peering slowly, he detected a similar configuration a few meters away.

"Odom, get first squad and give me the handset," Sean ordered. He barked into the handset, "This is one actual. Over."

Corporal Statsi, first squad leader, responded, "Over, sir!"

Sean blurted, "Fire mission for your M-60. Your right front, the paddy dike, about two hundred meters out. Hit the two mounds that are higher than the dike. Now!"

The machine gun sounded off with a metallic roar, spitting red tracers across the dikes. The initial rounds were high. The gunner adjusted, and the rounds impacted on one mound and then the other. Sean's hands and face were sweat-covered, but he kept his binoculars on the target. He smiled. *Movement behind the mounds.*

A loud explosion erupted at the front of the column, an entire section of the road blown skyward.

Sergeant Murphy's voice came over the radio. "They had a 105 round rigged for command denotation about fifty meters to our front. Nobody hurt." A static hiss interrupted the transmission. "You spooked them with that recon fire, and they pulled the switch. Good call, LT. That round woulda taken out one of our squads."

Sean responded, "Don't think that's all they had planned. Get everybody on the north side of the road. Get first and second squads on line. Be prepared to assault the vill with the road on your left." He paused. "I'll bring up third squad in trace. I'll call for fire on that dike with the mounds. When the arty comes in, move both squads out. Hold up at the dike in front of the vill."

Sean ordered Odom to switch the artillery frequency. He grasped the handset and pulled out a plastic-covered map from his pack. He studied the map, hands trembling as he followed the procedures for calling an artillery-fire mission. Sean realized he hadn't depressed the transmit button on the radio handset. Cursing to himself, he repeated the procedure.

Five miles to the southeast, an artillery battery came alive. A 105-millimeter shell tore through the air on a course calibrated to the eight-digit map coordinates transmitted by Sean.

"Shot," Odom cried, monitoring the arty frequency. Sean peered in the direction the round should have impacted and saw the explosion about 150 yards beyond the dike and 50 yards north of the vill.

"Left fifty, down one-fifty," Sean cried.

The second round hit fifty yards beyond the target. Sean adjusted. "Down fifty. Fire for effect."

Seconds later, the area around the long, narrow dike erupted with watery mounds of earth and steel. A close two hundred meters away, the two squads of Marines sloshed across the open paddy, weapons blazing as the artillery covered their right flank. The screeching of the incoming shells and the roar of explosions had everyone in the hamlet scrambling into holes and slit trenches, including four Viet Cong poised to defend the dike.

The charging Marines threw themselves against the mud dike, peering over the low wall as four figures dashed away. Fire from the entire first squad hit three men, tumbling them forward like rag dolls as rounds tore through their bodies. The fourth one ducked into an underground shelter twenty meters forward of the dike now occupied by second squad.

"Get that little fucker," screamed Roach Man, the first squad leader.

Two Marines darted forward. The first man emptied his weapon into the bunker entrance. His partner, a wiry left-hander, whipped a grenade into the shallow entrance as if delivering a sidearm baseball pitch. Taking a step back, he pulled the pin from another grenade and whipped it into the bunker.

Sean and the third squad arrived as Sergeant Murphy had first and second squads in position to cover the village. Crouching next to Sean, a winded Murphy blurted, "We got four of 'em. Look like VC. We'll know when we check the bodies. You want us into the vill, LT, or wait for the rest of the company?"

"No, hold here," Sean said. "I want first and second squads to move to the far end of the vill. Set them up so we can move into the vill or direct fire down into the vill. I'll move the third to cover your rear. Before you set up, get a fire team to check that dike we hit with arty."

Sean radioed a sit rep to his company commander. "We're on the north side of PD(1). Triggered an ambush. Assaulted the vill just north of the road. Got four confirms and four individual weapons. Arty got four more, one crew-served destroyed. We got three RPGs." He paused to catch his breath. "Holding at the extreme north side of the vill."

Captain Lee's voice came over the net. "Report friendly casualty count."

Sean replied curtly, "Zero friendly, zero Ks, zero WIAs."

After a moment, Captain Lee replied, "Outstanding job, Lieutenant! I'll be in your pos in ten minutes. Stay put."

On arriving in PD(1), Lee shouted, "Good job, Lieutenant—really outstanding. Nice job, Sergeant Murphy." Lee pointed back at the cratered roadway. "Sneaky bastards, that 105 round woulda caused a few casualties. We woulda called in a medevac. They woulda taken out the bird with RPGs. Maybe take you under fire from the vill. If you assaulted the vill, that machine gun in that mound woulda cut your assault to pieces." Lee smiled. "You did good, Lieutenant." His smile fading, he looked to Murphy. "But they all ain't this easy, are they, Murph?"

Lee yelled to his radioman several yards away, "Get me second platoon." He turned to Sean, barking instructions. "Get two of your guns on PD(2). Get as far out as possible to provide direct fire support into that vill. Lift fire when you see green smoke. That'll signal second platoon is assaulting from their line of departure."

Sean deployed his men with two M-60 machine guns pouring narrow volleys of fire into the cluster of huts five hundred meters away. He watched the assaulting platoon close on the objective.

"Green smoke!" Sean cried. "Cease fire, cease fire."

As the thirty men from the second platoon stormed into the hamlet, Murphy yelled, "Shit, mortar fire! Ya hear it?"

Sean didn't hear anything but did see explosions rippling through the second hamlet.

"They let 'em walk in and had the place bracketed." Murphy spoke in monotone. "Those guys in second platoon are in the hurt locker."

The mortar fire continued until Marine artillery fire erupted on the lower slopes of the hill mass two thousand meters south of the village. "Looks like the skipper got some counter-battery fire going," Sean said with an air of relief.

The artillery silenced the mortar fire, and the attack continued. Captain Lee and his third platoon moved into PD(2), passing through the bloodied second platoon, and on to PD(3), where they met light resistance. The objective was secured, and Alpha Company occupied all three hamlets of Phu Duc by midafternoon.

★   ★   ★

Captain Lee called a meeting of his platoon commanders in PD(2). Sean left Murphy in charge of the platoon and arrived in the second group of hamlets just as a medevac chopper was landing. He found himself next to an exhausted corpsman straining to help a black Marine whose lower right arm was wrapped in a bloody bandage. The three watched in silence as Marines struggled to get two canvas body bags up the chopper's ramp. One of the bags had a trail of blood and entrails seeping out of its end.

The wounded Marine's fierce, bloodshot eyes opened wide. "Coulda been me in one of them bags. Fuckin' round landed twenty meters away. Took that dude's head off. Sorry for him, a good dude. Ain't sorry for me. I'm getting the fuck outta this place. Semper fi, man, and all that shit. They can keep my hand. I'm going home."

The corpsman turned to Sean. "Four WIAs, two gonna lose limbs, two KIA. Fuckin' mortars."

Staring in silence as the corpsman ushered the wounded Marine toward the chopper, Sean was joined by Lieutenant Jeb Wilkerson, commander of the second platoon. A veteran who had been in-country for almost eight months, Wilkerson's utilities were mud-caked and smeared with the blood of the men he helped evacuate. He stared in the direction of the departing chopper, expressionless.

"Sorry, Jeb." It was all Sean could think to say.

The distraught lieutenant, face flushed with anger, turned back to Sean. "Shit happens, Cercone. Sometimes it happens bad. You'll see soon enough. Shit happens." Looking away, Wilkerson murmured, "And there isn't a fuckin' thing you can do about it. Not a fuckin' thing."

Sean moved toward the CP. *Coulda been my guys on that chopper.* What Lieutenant Wilkerson said struck him. Someday, it might be his men, and he might be with them. Time would tell. He had 331 days left in Vietnam.

Chapter 15

Rosa's seventy-fifth birthday party was in full swing. More than thirty people crammed into the D'Angelo backyard on the mild summer night. Frankie showed up to pay his respects to Joey's grandma and have some laughs with the outspoken neighborhood matriarch.

Frankie grinned at the backyard scene. *Can't beat the D'Angelos when it comes to food.* Joey's mother Mary and several women busied themselves shuttling platters of baked ziti from the basement kitchen to an apron-covered table in the backyard. Joe Senior scurried about making sure everyone had a drink. Rosa sat on a chair in the corner of the yard, holding court for a dozen neighbors who applauded her feisty remarks. Amid the laughter, she stood abruptly and walked to the far corner of the yard.

"Hey, Frankie, bring the boys over here. Got something I wanna talk about."

"Over here, guys." Frankie beckoned to Sal, Joey, and three of the younger guys. They gathered in a semicircle in front of the tiny woman in her straight black dress.

"So when's the last time any of you paid a visit to Sean's mother?" Rosa asked, holding up her frail hand to signal she wanted no interruption. "And what about his girl, Sandy? How's she doing?"

Sal Lente offered a sheepish reply. "I went to school with Sandy. We're pretty good friends. Just saw her on the avenue last week."

"Oh, you saw her last week, how nice. What about this week? What about next week? You got any plans?" Rosa's raspy voice rose. "Any of you got plans to see Sean's poor mother, maybe bring her a piece of cake?"

Pausing, she could see the uncomfortable looks. The young men stared at the ground like schoolboys who had missed an assignment. She lowered her voice, folding her thin arms across her chest. "Look, we got a situation here. Sean's away, God knows where, in that damned Vietnam. I think he did a crazy thing." She raised her gray head, trying to push back her bent shoulders. "But you know what? He's doing it because he thinks it's right. He's doing it for his country. He's doing it for us."

Joey spoke up. "Grandma, we all love Sean. We love the country; most of us served. We respect Sean and what he gave up. We'd do anything for him."

Rosa raised her wrinkled face in the direction of her grandson. "Good! You would do anything for him. Good! First thing to do is shut up. Let me tell you what you gotta do. The best way to support Sean is take care of the two women he loves. Don't make them go through this thing alone." The old woman's voice gained strength. "Visit Sandy twice a week. Same for Ann Cercone. I mean *twice a week*. I don't wanna hear about football practice or going to the shore or 'I gotta go to the city.' No bull crap excuses. Two of you, twice a week. And don't go empty handed—bring something to eat."

Frankie was moved by the frail grandmother's plea. It was an embarrassment. He cleared his throat with a cough. "Grandma Rosa, gotta say a couple of things. First, with respect, thank you for reminding us what we shoulda been doing. We're ashamed you had to do this on your birthday." He snapped his head toward his friends, narrowing his eyes like an angry don. "Second, this is Gravesend, Brooklyn. We're tight in this neighborhood. We're family. If one of us is at war, we're all at war. We're that way 'cause our parents made us that way and 'cause women like Grandma Rosa ain't gonna let us forget what we gotta do."

Frankie tugged on his ponytail and placed his arm around Rosa's narrow waist. "Grandma Rosa, we'll do whatever you tell us to do, whenever you want us to do it."

The old lady from Palermo leaned her frail head against Frankie's chest and whispered, "God bless you, Frankie, you and all the boys."

★   ★   ★

A cool breeze stirred the leaves on the oaks hovering above Sandy's backyard patio—a perfect evening with summer not yet descending on the city. Even in the treeless Bedford-Stuyvesant where Sandy spent most of her days, the sweltering heat and humidity normal for June had yet to arrive.

Sandy sat on a lounge chair reading a letter from Sean. She thought of him constantly. His letter seemed upbeat, but she had her doubts. A cry came from beyond the thick hedges on the barely visible street.

"Hey, we got ya some lemon ice!" Sal Lente shouted as he pushed open the wrought-iron gate leading into the backyard. "Our friend here," Sal jibed at Joey, "now that he's a big protector of the people, gets free lemon ice at Santo's."

"Hi, guys. Good to see you," Sandy said. "Come on in. Just got a letter from your buddy. Hadn't heard from him for a few days and was starting to worry. This one is funny. He's telling me about some of his men."

Joey handed Sandy the lemon ice cup with great flair. She smiled, adjusting her low-cut blouse. "It is so great for you guys to stop by again. And I love lemon ice. Let me read you some of what Sean has to say. It sounds as if his men all have strange names."

Sal and Joey pulled up chairs as Sandy began reading:

I've got a great platoon of Marines with a rock-solid platoon sergeant, a young guy named Tom Murphy. Murph is out of South Boston from a neighborhood that sounds like ours. He attended Boston College for a year before he joined the Corps. Said he couldn't stay in college when so many of his high school friends were in. He said his class of '65 already had five dead and over a dozen guys wounded. That's unbelievable for one high school class. Then again, if these Southey guys are all hard chargers like Murph, I can understand. He's actually two months into a six-month extension of his tour. That's almost fifteen months in-country. He has more combat time than anyone in the battalion. Murph is teaching me a lot about the bush and how to keep the platoon going.

I have a good radio operator, an eighteen-year-old named Odom. He's from Tyler, Texas. Looks more like a choir boy than a Marine. Matter of fact, his dad is a preacher. No big surprise he's called Preacher.

We've two experienced squad leaders and a rookie who just took over his squad. He's a sergeant with a couple of years of stateside duty but no combat time. He's got a loud, booming voice. His squad named him Boomer.

Everybody gets a name. Our senior squad leader, who just made buck sergeant, is Ray Statsi. He's known as Roach Man. I've no idea why. I guess it's because the fire team leaders in his squad are called Spider and Black Beetle.

My third squad leader is Hollywood. His name is Erick Olsen, a well-built Swedish kid from some town in Minnesota. Olsen looks like a twin to that good-looking actor, Tab Hunter. I think Hunter actually played a Marine in one of those John Wayne movies. He has that same square jaw, perfect smile, blue eyes, and white-blond hair. Despite his pretty-boy looks, he's a good leader and one tough Marine with two Purple Hearts and a Bronze Star. They wanted to transfer him up to battalion to complete the last three months of his tour, but he opted to stay with us as a squad leader.

"Sounds like a great bunch," Sandy laughed. "And here's some really good news."

PS: Almost forgot! I just got word Mike Slattery will be joining the Fifth Marines. He was up at division for two months and finally got a platoon. Hopefully I'll get to meet up with him.

"Isn't that great!" Sandy giggled. "Sean might get to see one of his best friends from the Basic School. He's one of the married guys. I think his wife's name is Val. Bet they'll have a ball together."

Joey raised his eyebrows and smirked at Sal. "Yeah, Sandy, bet ya he's gonna have a good time with his buddy." He kissed Sandy's cheek. "We'll see ya in a couple a days. Say hello to Sean for us."

Sandy hadn't missed Joey's expression. She remained on the patio and reread the letter. *He never mentions anything about the war or the fighting in his letters. How much of what's happing is he keeping from me? Do I really want to know?*

Chapter 16

Alpha Company was exhausted and beat up after grueling days of constant movement in sweltering heat. The temperature was so extreme, battalion decided to rotate in each platoon every few days. Sean's platoon was given a day and a night back at a relatively secure base camp. The platoon, now thirty-one men, reached the camp after dawn and had their first hot food in ten days. A small, quick-flowing stream ran through the base camp surrounded by dense, double-canopy foliage. A few feet of the narrow stream, dug out in the middle to a depth of a foot, provided a way for two men at a time to wash off the slime that caked their bodies.

Sean was the last to bathe. He then began one of his daily rituals. Using the end of a plastic spoon to extract oily C-ration peanut butter from a small round tin, he carefully spread the brown, gooey substance on three dry crackers, placing them on the piece of cardboard torn from a C-ration box. After pouring water from this canteen into a used juice can, its metal top pried back to form a crude handle, he ignited a blue wafer heat tab under the can. In a few moments, the water boiled. Sean tore open a packet of instant coffee mix and dumped the brown crystals into the boiling water as if it were a magic potion.

He sat back on the sandbag wall of his shallow, half-completed bunker, munching on his peanut-butter crackers and sipping the hot, bitter coffee. He put down his cup and opened a letter he had received that morning.

Dear Sean,

Glad to hear you are doing well. I hadn't gotten any letters for over a week, and yesterday I received two. I hope you are getting mine regularly.

The guys were over the other night. It was Sal and Joey. I read them the letter about your men. That Hollywood guy sounds interesting. I've a few friends who might like to meet a Tab Hunter look-alike.

After some great weather, summer has arrived. We're being hit with a heat wave, and Brooklyn is boiling. It was 96 yesterday with humidity above 80. It's especially tough at the settlement house, since we have no air con and we can't get half the windows open. Thank God we have some fans.

I'm planning to take four of my thirteen-year-old girls to the beach. They all need bathing suits, so I took them down to A&S today and spent half my paycheck on four Janzens. Of course they all wanted a bikini, but I told them it was out of the question. Looks like I won't be wearing my bikini, the one you liked so well. Don't want to set a bad example.

Sean's mind flashed to the first time he had seen Sandy in her bikini.

"Yo, Lieutenant, got some word. Afraid it ain't good," Gunny Sergeant Ray Katamana said as he leapt into Sean's hole. The squat, heavyset Gunny had a dark, round face with all the features of a Pacific islander. His soft-spoken voice seemed out of place given his physical stature. "Gotta move them out again, sir. Skipper wants you on the move by 1400."

"Bullshit! We're supposed to be in for a day and a night. Where the hell's Captain Lee? No fuckin' way. I wanna speak to Lee about this crap."

"Wouldn't do any good, sir. Orders came from battalion," the gunny said. "Skipper was already on the horn to the ops officer—said he wasn't going to send you out again. Got in a shitload of trouble. The old man said he would relieve his ass if he didn't obey orders."

Sean took a breath and stared over the rim of the bunker at his men, most of them dozing under whatever shade they could find. He exhaled and nodded to the gunny. "Okay, tell the skipper thanks for trying. What do they want us to do?"

★　★　★

Sean led his platoon in a wide sweep of an area battalion wanted checked out due to reports of fresh enemy activity. Crouching through waist-high brush and small clusters of hedgerows, Sean had two squads moving abreast, covering about one hundred meters of frontage. He positioned himself with the trailing third squad.

The foliage thinned out as the platoon approached an open area appearing to be a thirty-meter-wide firebreak. Small-arms fire from the far side of the break hit the first squad on the platoon's left flank. Signaling the trailing squad to halt, Sean sprinted forward, diving to the ground beside Sergeant Murphy, who was positioned between the two lead squads.

Murphy gave a quick assessment. "Looks like about half a dozen of 'em about a hundred and fifty meters left of that tree line. No automatic weapon fire. They aren't stupid enough to engage with only small arms. Must have a crew-serve weapon out there somewhere."

"Yeah, you're right. Want us to make a frontal assault. Then they'll open up," Sean said. "Hold first squad in place. Get some fire discipline going. Get third squad to flank them wide on the right. Once they cross this open spot, tell 'em to drive to the right of that tree line. Once they're over, get second squad across to join the assault." Sean shouted, "Odom, get me on the arty net."

Hollywood Olsen's third squad of eleven men prepared to rush across the thirty meters of open area toward heavily scrubbed ground well north of the firefight. Once into the bush, they would flank the NVA.

Sean and Murphy moved to the far end of the second squad to better control both squads. They arrived in time to see the first fire team of four men from Olsen's squad dash across the open space.

"Jesus," Murphy cried as a stream of green tracers flashed two feet in front of them and a foot off the ground.

Sean watched in horror as the closest assaulting Marines doubled over, crashing to the ground. Another man a few meters to his right faltered and slipped but made it to the far side of the break. Sean couldn't see what had happened to the other two assaulting Marines, but a man lay face down without a helmet about fifty meters away.

The closest fallen Marine lay in full view, only a few meters from Sean and Murphy. Both pressed to the ground, green tracer rounds flashing in short bursts inches above their heads. The wounded Marine, a new guy who had joined the platoon a few days before, screamed and clutched his lower midsection, pieces of his innards seeping out. Looking in the direction of Sean and Murphy, he screamed something that couldn't be heard over the firing.

Sean yelled for the man to hold on. *Christ! Can't remember his name.* "Can we get him?" Sean cried.

"Gotta get that gun first!" Murphy screamed as they crawled backward away from the machine gun fire.

"Wait, let's put out some smoke," Sean said. "Maybe we can mask that gun and bring him in."

"Worth a try!" Murphy pulled the pin on a gray canister. It hissed and began emitting dark green smoke. He lobbed it to the middle of the open space ten meters left of the wounded Marine. Someone from the third squad tossed another canister gushing white smoke.

The open area was engulfed in billowing green and white smoke, but the hidden machine gunner kept up a steady stream of fire. The smoke did hide the Marine who had made it safely to the far side of the break. Crawling out to the edge of the smoke-filled area, he began firing his M-79 grenade launcher. He reloaded the thick, four-inch projectiles into his launcher half a dozen times while deadly bursts of machine gun fire probed the smoke-filled area. He adjusted his rounds twenty-five meters up with each shot.

After the sixth pop of the launcher, the grenadier got lucky. The stream of green tracers arched skyward, falling off to the ground several hundred meters out.

"He got him!" Murphy screamed.

Sean cried back, "Get those men in. Regroup third squad. Call in the medevac. I'm gonna take second squad across."

He led the second squad in a desperate rush across the clearing. Sergeant Statsi, without any direct orders, led his first squad in the same manner. The experienced squad leader did as Sean had hoped. The two squads closed in on the heavily scrubbed tree line. They found blood trails but no sign of any enemy. Sweeping back in the direction of the concealed machine gun, first squad found the gunner slumped over his automatic weapon, its barrel still smoking. His assistant gunner was down with his head half gone. They had been taken out by a direct hit from an M-79 round.

Sprinting back to the rear position of third squad, Sean found Doc Jackson. "What's the status on the emergency medevac?"

"Just changed the status, Lieutenant. We got no emergency. We got two KIAs." The twenty-year-old corpsman glared down at a Marine wrapped in a rubber poncho. The putrid smell of human waste emanating from his stomach wounds hung in the air. "He bled out a few minutes after we got him in. Machine gun ripped him right below his flack vest, woulda never made it."

Looking away from the dead Marine, Sean saw two men struggling to carry a poncho. He rushed forward to help, and the man in front spoke in a low voice. "Hollywood got it, sir. Shit, the man was short. Only six weeks to go, fuckin' six weeks."

The Marines stumbled, and the poncho thumped to the ground, revealing a body. Erick Olsen had no face. His thick neck was there, and his white-blond hair was matted and still prominent, but his face was a mash of bones, teeth, torn flesh, and blood. Sean felt queasy and then very sick. He spun away from the litter, went down on one knee, and gagged as vomit crept through his throat.

One of the Marines who had carried Olsen put his hand under Sean's arm, supporting him as he spewed green bile. The other offered his canteen. The warm and chalky water helped wash away the taste of vomit. Sean's eyes watered, and he cast an embarrassed look at the two Marines.

"Don't worry 'bout it, sir. We've all done it," said a lanky black Marine called Slink. Taking back his canteen, Slink poured water on a dirty green towel he pulled from his pack. He placed the towel over the back of Sean's neck. "Hollywood liked you, sir. Said you were a good officer. Said we should take care of you."

His eyes still watery, Sean replied, "Thanks. Corporal Olsen was a good Marine."

"The best," Slink said, pouring more water on the towel. "One good-looking dude too." Pausing for a moment, he continued to rub Sean's neck. "When you write his folks, Lieutenant, just don't say anything about his face. Just tell 'em he got hit and died. That's the truth, ain't it? You don't have to tell 'em 'bout his face."

Sean nodded. Tears crept down Slink's dirt-stained black cheeks.

Corporal Odom, trailing Sean from the time of the assault, extended the radio handset. "Company wants a sit rep. They want it now, sir."

Grabbing the handset, Sean spoke. "Thumper, this is Bearcat actual. Sit rep. Over." Straining to keep from vomiting, he heard the familiar, businesslike voice of Captain Lee.

"This is Thumper actual. Nice of you to finally report in. Over."

Gritting his teeth, Sean responded, "We were engaged. Two hundred meters north of checkpoint blue. Reinforced NVA squad. Area now clear. Two NVA KIA. One crew-serve weapon captured. Two Marines down, both KIA."

Lee responded in his usual matter-of-fact tone. "Not such a good trade, Bearcat. Over."

Sean depressed the talk button. Voice trembling, he screamed, "Not such a good trade? No shit!" *You asshole!* "Bearcat out."

Chapter 17

RUSSO FUNERAL HOME
GRAVESEND, BROOKLYN
MID-AUGUST 1967

Frankie and Sal Lente joined a quiet crowd of mourners in the spacious foyer of the old funeral home. The gray, stucco-walled building resembled a Tuscan mansion—long narrow windows trimmed in black wrought iron giving way to oversized dark cedar doors. The interior walls papered in gold-leafed biblical scenes contrasted with a pinkish brown Italian marble floor. The funeral home sat on a half-acre corner plot, making it the dominant, but very out of place, structure in the neighborhood of attached two-family homes. The Russo brothers had hosted wakes in their mansion for over thirty years, enabling the people of Gravesend to provide a fitting send-off for mothers, fathers, and elder family members. Today it was different. Today they were waking one of their young sons, nineteen-year-old Private First Class Thomas V. Penalli.

Frankie whispered, "This is gonna be a bad one, Sal. Sealed coffin! Ann Penalli ain't gonna get to see her son."

"Yeah," Sal replied in a low voice. "Spoke to his dad, Tom. Said Ann had a breakdown when the coffin finally arrived. Took a week from the time they got the telegram. And you know what? Today is their twenty-first wedding anniversary."

They inched through the crowd to the rear of a massive room made larger by the removal of a sliding wall. Toward the front, flower bouquets, some standing six feet high, surrounded a gun-metal-gray coffin, giving the room a garden-like smell. A silver-framed eight-by-ten photo of Tommy Penalli in his All-Star baseball uniform sat awkwardly atop a slender table just to the right of the coffin.

"Yeah, this is a bad one," Frankie murmured. "Great kid, and what a ballplayer. Coach Franco said Seaton Hall over in Jersey offered him a full ride. Mets and Braves were both interested. They were talking double A. Of course, the problem was his draft status."

"Oh shit, there's Coach Franco going up now." Frankie motioned to a heavyset man with thinning dark hair wearing a red baseball jacket with white leather sleeves. The back of the jacket said Brooklyn All-Stars. He was on the far side of the room, midway in the line of mourners, all of them waiting to perform the ritual of kneeling and praying in front of Tommy's casket before offering their respects to his parents.

"Yeah, I see him. Looks like he's carrying some kinda bag," Sal said. "He's right behind Sean's mom and Rosa. Damn, everybody in the neighborhood is here—Jimmy Rizzo, the grocer; the Fryers from the deli; Pappy from the bar; and even Freddie Cohen and wife from the diner."

Frankie motioned over the dozens of rows of mourners to the twenty or so purple-jacketed young men sitting silently behind their teammate's grieving family. "Looks like the entire Lafayette baseball team is here. Can't imagine anybody not coming," said Frankie. "But what about the reserves? Thought Coach Franco got the kid into the six-month National Guard program."

"He did." Sal sighed. "The kid goes in the Guard. After basic he goes to advanced infantry training. Then he calls home, tells his folks he respects the Army, feels it's his duty to serve a tour in 'Nam. He transfers out of the Guard on the condition they send him airborne, which of course they do in a heartbeat. Off he goes to Fort Bragg." Sal shook his head. "Saw him when he was home on leave two months ago. He looked good. Spit-shined boots, jump wings, and an airborne patch on his sleeve, really a proud kid. Now this."

"You never know what makes guys do what," Frankie said. "Didn't have to go. He wasn't a dumb kid. Maybe he thought he had to do the right thing. Maybe the kid—" He stopped in midsentence, raising his jaw and motioning to the front. "My God, catch this."

Coach Franco carefully placed a worn baseball glove on top of the closed coffin. After kneeling before the casket for few a moments, he rose and faced Tom and a heavily sedated Ann Penalli. The grieving brick mason extended his arms to his son's coach. The two embraced. The low murmur, normal for a room full of mourners, gave way to soft cries and weeping.

"Frankie, this is a bad scene. Let's get out of here and get a drink."

Placing his hand over his mouth, Frankie whispered, "Yeah, this sucks." *I'm not going up there—not tonight anyway.* "Let's hit the Wrong Number."

★   ★   ★

Frankie and Sal were among the first of many mourners seeking solace in the neighborhood watering hole that dreadful evening. Frankie nursed a double scotch while flipping through the pages of the *Daily News*. "Look at this crap! You see this, Pauli?" He turned the paper to the bartender, who refilled his glass.

"Looks like one of them peace demonstrations." Pauli Black shrugged. "So what else is new?"

Frankie's face contorted. "Take a close look at the center picture. See that cocksucker waving a North Vietnamese flag?"

Sal came from the end of the bar and leaned over. "You're right, Brain. That's an NVA flag. Guy is really pushing the limits of legitimate protest."

"Legitimate protest? I'll give him a fuckin' legitimate protest right up his ass. These bastards! We got kids like Tommy coming home in coffins, guys like Sean fighting over there, and they're fuckin' waving an NVA flag!"

Frankie slid off his stool, slamming the newspaper down in disgust. "These pricks aren't antiwar. They're for the fuckin' North Vietnamese! That's giving aid and comfort to the enemy. That's fuckin' treason."

"Take it easy, Frankie," Sal said. "Think that's bad? Next month they're gonna have a big antiwar demonstration in the city, right down Fifth Avenue. The mayor personally signed the parade permit. Said he'll be marching too."

"There's nothing you can do about them protestors," Pauli said. "Fuck 'em. Have another drink. This one is on me, for the kid."

Frankie clenched his fists on the bar and looked up at the tobacco-stained ceiling. He pondered a moment and then cried, "Bullshit! There's something we can do about that parade. We can kick the shit out of the marchers."

"You out of your mind?" Sal cried, his blue eyes open wide in disbelief. "There'll be hundreds of cops. What do we do? Just walk up and pop a couple a protesters, then get our asses thrown in the can?"

"Tell you what, Scribe, we're gonna do better than that. We're gonna kick the shit out of a couple of hundred of 'em." Frankie glared at Sal. "My house, tomorrow night, we start to plan this thing."

Chapter 18

QUE SON VALLEY
EARLY SEPTEMBER

Sean and Murphy shared a hole partially shaded by tall grass and a fallen log. Both Sean's platoon and the second platoon were in a stand-down mode in the company rear collated with the Fifth Battalion headquarters. Rumor had it the third platoon would be joining them that afternoon.

"First time in weeks we've had the entire company together. What do you think is up, Murph?"

"Means we're moving out of the area, probably lining up to make a battalion-size operation. God knows where," Murphy said, trying to get comfortable in the shallow hole. "As soon as the third gets in, I'm sure we'll get the word. Just enjoy this little lull. It ain't gonna last."

Nodding, Sean reached inside his flak jacket and pulled out a letter from Sal. Most of his letters were brief, but they came often, almost weekly. This letter was different, over five pages beginning with a summary of the recent elections in South Vietnam.

"Hey, Murph, did you know that 80 percent of the South Vietnamese went to the polls last week?"

"No shit, an election with 80 percent participation! Musta missed it in those two vills we worked last week. Didn't see any elections polls. Guess there was a Que Son Valley absentee ballot for villagers. A.k.a., a fuckin' death certificate."

Sean laughed. "Hey, how about this—they want Johnson to consider a bombing halt."

"Yeah, well, I don't know who the fuck *they* are or what *they* think a bombing halt is gonna do," Murphy said, waving his arms, "except of course allow the NVA to resupply. Just what the fuck we need. Yeah, they. *They* ain't here, and *they're* full of shit."

Sean started to say something about the political and diplomatic ramifications of a bombing halt but thought the better of it. He went back to Sal's letter, which described the details of Tommy's wake and funeral.

His gut tightened at Sal's description of Coach Franco placing the glove on Tommy's coffin. *Remember coaching him in the park, skinny little kid with a good arm. And Coach Franco—who could forget him? Tommy's mother suffered a breakdown. Wonder if Mom heard?*

Murph watched Sean, staring in silence. "Anything wrong back home, Lieutenant?"

"Yeah, one of the young kids in the neighborhood got it. With the Air Cav down south. Tommy Penalli—what a nice kid. Coached him when he was about twelve. Shit, couldn't be more than eighteen now. My buddy said the whole neighborhood is taking it bad. Can't imagine what my mom is thinking."

"Sorry, sir, you're not gonna have much time to think about it. Here comes the gunny. I'm sure the skipper wants us up at his CP."

★   ★   ★

After a brief meeting at the company CP, Captain Lee led his three platoon commanders and his HQ group a few hundred feet down a narrow path to the battalion command bunker. The group assembled in a hot, musty sandbagged bunker barely large enough to hold them and the half-dozen officers who composed the Fifth Battalion command group.

Lieutenant Colonel Paul Hansen, tall and thin with speckled gray hair, ignored his sweat-drenched condition and began the briefing. "We got a bad situation on the other side of the AO." He gestured to a map that took over half of one of the bunker walls and depicted an area of operation running from the battalion's current position in the northwestern end of the Que Son Valley over to the South China Sea. "We've been tasked to provide a relief force to help out. We're going to chop Alpha Company to operational control of Second Battalion,

Fifth Marines. Our S-3, Major Duff, will brief the situation and the mission."

Hanson stepped aside, and a small, heavyset major squeezed by him, pointing to a spot on the map. "The NVA slipped the better part of two regiments into this area fifteen clicks from the provincial capital of Tam Ky. Estimated strength: two thousand NVA regulars, brand-new radio gear, new gas masks, clean uniforms, and well-maintained weapons. Both Two/Five and Three/Five been in contact for the past four days. Looks like the NVA wanted to capture or at least level Tam Ky, cut Route 1 midway between Da Nang and Chu Lai."

The major went on in a brisk fashion as if he were an evening news commentator. "They probably wanted to disrupt the elections last week. That didn't happen, but it cost us. We took over a hundred twenty killed, more than three hundred wounded. Second battalion took the most hits. Two of their companies pretty chewed up. They even lost their chaplain. NVA losses estimated at seven hundred, maybe eight hundred, but they're hanging around, holding up in bunker complexes in these hills. Alpha, your mission is to augment Two/Five and become one of their rifle companies. We'll begin to lift you out at 1700 today."

Sean and the others from Alpha Company remained silent. *Jesus, Slattery's letter said he was a platoon commander in Delta Company Two/ Five.*

★ ★ ★

Less than two hours after the briefing, Sean and his platoon, twenty-nine men plus a three-man mortar crew, gathered in squad groups in a shallow trench line that formed one side of a hastily prepared landing zone. Sean briefed his three squad leaders, all of whom seemed tense but anxious to lead their men. Passing along the trench, he couldn't help but notice the ways his Marines used the waiting time. Helmets off, leaning on their packs, some wrote letters, others read, and more than a few cleaned weapons. One squad was sharpening knives and bayonets. Several Marines stared. A few smiled as Sean worked his way down the line. No words were spoken.

Slipping down into the trench next to Murphy, Sean smiled confidently. "They're ready to go, Murph. Looks like the squad leaders did a good job."

"Yeah, Statsi is a good man. So is Slink. This is Boomer's first time leading his squad into some shit, but I think he'll do okay."

Sean used the remaining hour of daylight to finish reading Sal's letter. Replacing his helmet with his soft cover utility cap, he wrapped himself in his rubber poncho and propped himself on one side of the narrow trench.

Saw Sandy the other day. She's working full time at that settlement house but spends a lot of time at Joey's, hanging out with Rosa.

Tommy's death has really set off Frankie. And the antiwar demonstrations have him going wild. Last Monday, I spent half the night listening to his plan to poison a couple of hundred peace demonstrators at a parade in the city next month. Actually, it's not poison. He plans on passing out hot chocolate drinks spiked with Ex-Lax. Can you imagine that? Picture the scene—several hundred of those scumbag demonstrators shitting their pants all down Fifth Avenue!

Four of us plus Frankie are on the job. It's secret, so I can't give names. Frankie says when we pull it off, it will hit the papers. He says there's going to be a lot of heat, so nothing is discussed with anybody. You know how nuts Frankie is about details. It's like he's planning the Normandy invasion.

He's already arranging for alibis down in Philadelphia, which I have yet to figure out since we're going to be in New York. He got a van, stolen plates, and special dissolving paint for a quick change on the van. He's gotten four twenty-gallon drink dispensers, the kind the guys wear on their backs at the ball park. I think he stole them. It doesn't matter, 'cause we plan to dump them in a swamp over in Jersey after we do the job. He's even buying the Ex-Lax in drugstores way down in South Jersey, never more than two packs per store. With Frankie planning this thing, I think we just might pull it off. I'll tell you all about it when it's done. Hope I won't be writing from some jail. Wish us luck.

Take care,
Sal

Sean burst into laughter. Murphy asked, "What the fuck's so funny, Lieutenant? We're getting into some serious shit tomorrow."

Sean shot back, still laughing, "We're not the only ones that are gonna be in some serious shit!"

Chapter 19

The evening lift was delayed, and the helicopters arrived the next morning, eight in all, including two CH-53s capable of lifting the heavy 81 mortars and the entire weapons platoon. Over a hundred Alpha Company Marines were lifted some fifteen miles, landing next to the Fifth Regiment headquarters at 0700. While Captain Lee and his platoon commanders received a briefing, three choppers flew back to the valley to pick up the remaining three dozen Alpha Company Marines.

By midmorning, the company was augmented with a fire-support artillery team and several Second Battalion Marines who wanted to get back to their unit. Alpha Company, with attachments, now included more than 160 Marines. Captain Lee moved them over the flat terrain in three parallel columns a hundred meters apart. Sean stepped out of line to look over his platoon. Had it not been for their helmets and weapons, the young men could have been farm boys moving through a field to do a day's work. They moved through thick, waist-high grass, trying to maintain five-meter intervals, in three long lines, snaking across the open ground toward a small hill mass, the location of Second Battalion—or what was left of it. Beyond the small hill lay two larger hills that dominated the surrounding terrain. Sean and his Marines ducked on instinct as artillery rounds whistled overhead like unseen screaming birds. Someone cried, "Get some, get some!" as white puffs of smoke appeared on one of the large hills.

The pace of the company quickened. When the lead elements closed to within a thousand meters of the small hill mass, platoon commanders began moving their squads out of their columns into a tactical formation. While rearranging his squads, Sean glanced to his rear at the fire-support team provided by the regiment. A Marine removed his helmet, attaching headphones that snaked from a large, jeep-mounted radio. Sean grinned and shouted, "Hey, you candy-ass mustang, do they actually let you arty guys in the field?"

Lieutenant B. W. Farnsworth, leader of the fire-support team, stared for a moment, pointing at Sean, who was walking in his direction. "Well, if it isn't the mob boss from Brooklyn. Shit, I better get on this radio and call the NVA. Let 'em know they're in for some serious trouble."

Sean and BW crouched down next to the team's radio jeep. "Hey, man, what's the scoop on Slattery?" Sean asked.

BW wiped his sweat-drenched head. "Not good news. He was with second platoon, Delta Company. They got hit bad." Pulling a map from his pack, he motioned. "See this draw? It's between the small hill mass and the larger hill, just ahead about five clicks. That's where Delta got hit. They were able to disengage but left half a platoon. We put a lot of arty in. I was monitoring the net. I'm sure it was Slattery calling it in. We lost comm with them day before yesterday." BW raised his dark eyes and stared. "It don't look good, Sean."

★ ★ ★

Over the next hour, Captain Lee positioned his platoons around the severely depleted Second Battalion headquarters. The battalion was at less than 50 percent strength. BW moved his fire-support team into position and started planning close air-support missions. Sean's platoon drew the assignment of recovering the missing from Delta Company. The eight MIAs were thought to be four hundred meters into the draw that BW had shown him on the map.

"I don't like it, Murph. Even with arty and air, if we go down that draw, we're going to get hit same as Delta."

"Roger that," a sergeant from Delta Company said in a gruff voice. "There's a smaller ridge you can't see on that map. That's where we took the most fire from. Couldn't see 'em. Musta been in concealed bunkers."

The sergeant, along with two other Delta Company Marines, had requested to join the body recovery effort. At first, Sean didn't want the Delta Company Marines along. Their haunted faces and blank stares, forged by days of combat, belied their determination. They were exhausted. But they knew the ground. At the last moment, he agreed. It proved to be a good decision.

A heated discussion ensued on the battalion tactical radio net with the ops officer and Captain Lee, both rejecting Sean's request to change his axis of advance. Wanting to attack the unspotted secondary ridgeline first and then enter the draw from the far north, Sean acknowledged the scheme of maneuver might take hours.

A new voice crackled on the radio net. "This is six actual. Be advised this is Bearcat's call. You may proceed, Bearcat. Inform when you have enemy pos in sight. Make sure you call for prep fire before you assault. Affirm, Bearcat. Over."

Sean replied. He'd heard that voice before but had little time to think about it. He signaled Murphy to direct the platoon around the edge of the draw. Rough, heavily scrubbed terrain slowed progress. Two hours passed with no sign of the suspected enemy position. An intense clatter of small-arms fire erupted. *Christ, point squad is in contact, sounds like a hundred meters up.* Sean screamed to his 60 mortar crew, "Get that tube ready!" He grabbed his handset. "Murphy, give me some fire direction."

The engagement lasted a long, bloody twenty minutes. Boomer's squad on the point took the brunt of the initial contact. Under the cover of the mortar fire, Murphy and Sean maneuvered the other two squads into the fray. "Get those M-60s up," Sean screamed. "Rake that small ridgeline. Odom, get some arty going on coordinates …"

Aggressive movement by the squads coupled with the fire support enabled them to dislodge the NVA from their hidden positions. Two bunkers, both with automatic weapons, faced the draw and couldn't be brought to bear on the attacking Marines. But the fourteen NVA, all of whom died in their spider holes and secondary bunkers, didn't go without a fight.

Sean had five men hit, including one of the volunteers from Delta Company. Two were dead. Boomer was seriously wounded, shot in the arm and groin. He and the KIAs were evacuated shortly after the position was secured. Two other wounded were treated in the field and stayed with the platoon.

Sean caught up with Murphy as the sergeant destroyed the last bunker with C-4 explosives. Sean's face was caked with dirt and sweat, his hands sticky with blood from helping one of the wounded with a sucking chest wound.

Murphy grinned. "Christ, we ever walked into that draw, they'd have cut us to ribbons."

"The men did a great job. So did you, Murph. Thanks."

"You made the right call on the approach, LT. Bringing that mortar section was smart too. By the way, you look like shit. Sir."

"Not exactly looking like a picture poster Marine yourself, Sergeant." Sean grinned. "Let's move down the draw in ten minutes. I'll take third squad and the guys from Delta. Give us two hundred meters and bring the rest of the platoon. Just watch our backs."

The oppressive midafternoon heat and the brutal fight took their toll. The adrenaline rush that accompanied intense combat gone, the Marines inched through the draw at a slow, zombielike pace.

"God, ya smell that? Can ya smell it?" the point man cried. "Over this way. Shit, look at 'em. Goddamn, I don't want to touch 'em."

"Fuck you. We'll take care of our dead," the Delta Company sergeant mumbled, pulling canvas body bags from his pack.

Sean ran forward and stood motionless. His head pounded. The smell from the decomposing bodies attacked his senses as if he were being hit by an unseen gas. His eyes watered. His throat closed. He went down on one knee and shouted, "Two men to a body—make sure they have tags. Check the boots for tags. Get them in a bag. Body parts too—everything in the bag. Watch out for booby traps."

Sean rose and walked toward the decomposing corpses of the eight Marines. Some were still bloated, all yellowish black. He promptly vomited, as did several others. He stared at one of the bodies, horribly shredded and gashed from multiple gunshot wounds. The left hand clutched a handset, the radio portion stitched with bullet holes. He knelt down and gingerly placed his hand inside the man's flack vest, removing his dog tag. The body, blackened beyond recognition, was Mike Slattery. He stared at the remains and lifted the body, dropping it in a frozen panic as maggots crawled out of a large hole in the base of Slattery's back.

"I'll take care of him, sir," one of the Delta Company Marines said. "He was my platoon commander. His name was—"

"Lieutenant Mike Slattery, Naval Academy '66, married to Val Pruett, son of Captain and Mrs. Mike Slattery. He was my roommate, one of my closest friends in the Corps."

"Sorry, sir. He was a good officer. Just joined us six weeks ago."

Sanding up, almost losing his balance, Sean kicked at the maggots, hands trembling, face flushed in anger. "Get him in a bag. Get those fuckin' maggots off him!" *Christ, what will I tell Val?*

★ ★ ★

The bodies were airlifted out, saving the platoon the task of carrying the corpses two kilometers back to their lines. Sean led his platoon back to the Two/Five headquarters area as the late-afternoon sun cast a beautiful orange-purple hue over the end of a horrible day.

Entering the battalion lines, Sean's voice was flat, almost mechanical, as if he were on autopilot. "Get 'em settled, Murph. Clean weapons first, then get 'em some rats. Some water to clean up. I'll give the ops people the brief."

He made his way to the command bunker entrance, removed the magazine from his M-16, and locked his weapon. Before entering, he poured water from a five-gallon can into his canteen cup. Gulping half the cup, he poured the remainder over his hands, trying to clean off the blood and grime. He removed his helmet, refilled the metal cup, poured water over his head, and wiped his face with a dirty green hand towel. He put on his soft utility cover and entered the makeshift bunker, headquarters of the Second Battalion.

Three Marines, all wearing flack vests over green undershirts, huddled over a map board. Two radio operators behind field desks facing the bunker wall transcribed messages on small notepads.

A smallish, thin man sitting on a cot in a darkened corner rose and addressed Sean. "Good job, Lieutenant. Damn good job. Hell of a job, Cercone." Lieutenant Colonel "Ax" Dalton, commanding officer of Second Battalion, Fifth Marines, extended his hand.

After a moment of hesitation, Sean grasped Dalton's handshake. "Good to see you again, Colonel." He spoke in a whisper and stared at the floor.

"Good job, Cercone," Major Joe Files, the battalion operations officer, said, looking up from his map board. He laughed. "Look like one of your grunts. Smell like one too."

Sean glared at the operations officer, reached down, and fumbled through his trouser pocket, producing eight dog tags. Smashing them down on a field desk, he shouted, "Would the major like to smell these grunts!"

Lieutenant Colonel Dalton grasped Sean by the arm and barked, "Gents, let's clear the CP. I'll debrief the lieutenant. Get some chow. Go—now!"

The staff rapidly exited the bunker.

"Cercone, sit down over here." Dalton eased his grip, motioning Sean to a small canvas field chair. Reaching into a duffle bag next to his cot, Dalton produced a bottle of Jim Beam. He poured a generous shot into a canteen cup, extending it to Sean. Gripping the cup with both hands, Sean gulped the whiskey, wincing as it burned his already parched throat. Dalton motioned him to take another swig. As the warmth started to take hold, Sean felt light-headed.

Dalton took back the cup. "Begin with your assault on that position. Take me through what happened until you evacuated the KIAs."

Sean covered the attack on the NVA position, crediting the Delta Company sergeant for the plan and Murphy for the success of the assault. Dalton nodded in understanding silence. Sean's speech became rapid. "Once we secured the area, we moved out and found the MIAs. It was awful—the smell and the remains. They were all black and stiff as boards. They didn't look human. Everybody was vomiting." Sean looked up at Dalton. "Lieutenant Slattery and I were close at TBS."

"I remember. He was your roommate."

Sean shook his head. "Musta had forty rounds in him, one leg nearly torn off. Fuckin' maggots crawling out of him—maggots!" His voice cracked, and he burst into tears. He dropped his head, cursing as he wept.

"That's okay, Lieutenant. Let it out. It's okay." Dalton handed him a towel. "Sean, maybe you need some downtime. A bad loss like this can—"

"I can hack it. I'm ready to go, sir." Sean wiped his face.

"We're attacking in a few hours, Sean. Sure you can lead your platoon?"

"I'm sure, sir."

Chapter 20

Sean worked his way toward Alpha Company, positioned almost a full kilometer forward from the battalion CP. They'd be attacking at dawn. He had to focus on the platoon and get over Mike. He recalled BW's words to Slattery back at the Hawkins Room: "You have to put them away in a different part of your mind. You never want to forget them. But you gotta move on."

"How'd the briefing go, Lieutenant?" Sergeant Murphy said, huddled with Slink, trying to read a map in the fading light.

"Fine, just fine, Murph. How many effectives we got?"

"Twenty-five, counting Sergeant Statsi. We're trying to get him to the rear to take care of his arm. Refused to get on the last bird. Said he can make it for another day or so."

Sean's eyes narrowed. "Bullshit. Order him to get his fuckin' ass to the battalion CP. Then make sure everybody is set to move out. Did we get an ammo resupply—any M-60 stuff?"

"Not yet. Ain't seen the gunny," Murphy said.

"Well, find the fuckin' gunny. Tell him I want a resupply, and I want it now." He bolted off toward the far side of the perimeter. *Mike's gone. Can't let it get to me. Gotta focus on the platoon. Gotta blank Mike out.*

★   ★   ★

Late that evening, a surprise order was issued. Both rifle companies slated to attack the hill mass were directed to reposition under the cover of darkness to a rear location five hundred meters from the line of departure.

"What's going on, LT?" Murphy said as Sean passed the order.

Sean gave a sideways smile. "Dalton knows these guys. Probably figures the NVA will move in real close to what they think to be our lines. They'll want to engage us close in when we attack. Try to reduce our fire support out of fear of hitting our own guys."

Twenty minutes before dawn, a massive, earsplitting artillery barrage fell on what had been the Marines frontline. A mix of high-explosive rounds and proximity-fused shells timed to erupt twenty meters from the ground rained steel-splintered death on those below.

As soon as light pierced the predawn darkness, sharp commands rose above the sounds of the barrage. Hundreds of shadowy figures rose up from the muddy earth as if resurrection day had come. They moved forward, slowly at first, hunched over like old men. More shouts, and the adrenaline pumping in their bodies caused their pace to quicken as squad leaders and platoon commanders tried to control the movement of the attacking Marines. As they approached their former position, the barrage shifted across the field in a slowly creeping wall of thunderous eruptions.

Sean's platoon, now on Alpha Company's right flank, sprinted in three and four-man teams across the ground cratered by artillery fire. Corporal Washington, leading the point squad, yelled, "LT, there're wounded gooks in these trenches! Send up Doc and a team."

"Bullshit, keep going!" Sean cried, leaping to the right front of the lagging second squad. "Kill anything that's moving. Just keep going. Can't hang around these trenches out in the open. Come on, move!"

The deafening artillery fire ceased. Sean waved his arm in a signal to sprint toward the base of the hill. With the exception of a single casualty, the platoon made it to a position on the lower part of the hill, where Captain Lee planned to regroup before the final assault.

"Murph, Slink, hold 'em up! Keep 'em on line, but hold them up!" Sean screamed.

Nodding, Slink pointed skyward to an A-6 streaking parallel to their lines over the forward slope of the hill. Two jets followed seconds later, both releasing silver-gray canisters of napalm. Thunderous eruptions engulfed the middle level of the hill. Eighty-meter-long, twenty-meter-wide swaths of molten flame incinerated and suffocated all in their wake. One strike came dangerously close to Sean's position as it engulfed a trench line and a concealed bunker. Brush fires bellowing gray smoke clouded the hill. Artillery began again to whistle overhead and tore into the hill.

Stunned by the closeness of the napalm strike, Sean pulled his canteen from his belt holder. Hands trembling, he drew it to his month. His mind flashed back to a close-air-support demonstration training exercise. *Never that close back at the Basic School—never told us about the screaming and that smell.*

After a short pause to regroup and get mortars positioned, the Marines shifted a few yards up the hillside to a protected fold, waiting to begin the final assault. An artillery round fell short, erupting in a slight draw only meters in front of Sean. His body shook from the concussion. He pressed against the ground, cursing the impact and the wetness running down his legs. He hoped most of the NVA bunkers had been destroyed by the overwhelming firepower. The putrid smell of burning flesh indicated many had been. Flashes of green tracers and the metallic sound of automatic-weapon fire to his far right revealed some had not.

Sean tried to ignore the fear that griped him. He rolled over and cried to Odom to shift to Sergeant Murphy's position on the left flank. Hunching as low as possible, he ran behind the line of Marines lying flat in muddy earth at the base of the hill. A few yards down the line, he tapped two Marines on the legs. "Flame team! On me, follow me. Let's go." On reaching the platoon's flank, he positioned the two Marines behind him. The trio went to the ground, awaiting the signal to attack.

A red star cluster burst several hundred feet in the air. Sean leapt to a crouch. "Let's go! Follow me!" He ran hunched over in the direction of a barely visible mound spitting green tracers.

Gotta get that bunker. Hope it's not covered by something bigger up the hill. Gotta chance it. Hope this kid can use that flamethrower.

Chapter 21

CHINA BEACH, DA NANG
CONVALESCENT CENTER
EARLY OCTOBER

"Lucky you didn't lose the leg, LT. That 12.5 millimeter coulda taken your leg off. Musta got hit by a ricochet," Doc Jackson said. The husky, square-faced Navy corpsman removed his sunglasses as he and Corporal Slink Washington stood in the entrance of the raised hut.

Sean lay in a mosquito-netted cot next to the door. Three unoccupied cots filled the remainder of the screen-walled hut. He moved the netting aside. "Got that right, Doc! Felt like someone put a hot poker on my leg, but it beat hell out of a direct hit!"

He was surprised to see two of his men in the convalescent rest area on China Beach just outside the port city of Da Nang. Several dozen huts and squad-sized tents made up the rest area in a treed section of beach three hundred meters from the shoreline, a place the slightly wounded were sent to mend before rejoining their units. A strong breeze off the South China Sea kept the place cool, and the massive airbase to the rear made the area very secure, if noisy at times.

"What are you guys doing here? Look at those clean utilities—really squared away." Sean frowned. "Thought they'd be sending the company back to our battalion."

"Yes, sir." Slink smiled. "We're going back. But on the way, Colonel Dalton got the company three days in-country R&R. He's good people, that colonel. We're a half-mile down the beach. Sergeant Murphy heard you were here. Sent us to deliver your mail." He tossed a pack of letters to Sean. "Supposed to leave day after tomorrow—back to battalion, wherever that is."

"That's great. I'm due out of here tomorrow," Sean said. "I'll just come down and join you. How's everybody? What happened to that new kid with the torch? Really did a job on that bunker. What's his name—Loral or Laurel or something? He was right in front of me when we zapped that bunker."

Doc shrugged his wide shoulders and shook his head. "He didn't make it. That gun that almost got you—it got him. Cut him in half. Best you can say is he went quick."

Sean grimaced. "Anybody else hit since I got evacuated?"

"Things died down after you left," Slink said. "One of the guys in first squad caught some metal. He'll be okay—be back in a couple of weeks. Saw Statsi yesterday. They did a nice job on his arm. He ought to be back in a couple of days. Got three new replacements too. That puts us at about two dozen effectives. Ain't that bad for all the shit we been in."

"Yeah, guess so," Sean said. "Any word on the skipper or the gunny? Right before I got hit, the company CP took an RPG. And what about Boomer? How's he doing?"

Doc Jackson turned away and talked to the mesh wall. "Boomer didn't make it. Bled out on the bird. Thought I had him tied down good; don't know what happened."

Slink put his arm around the corpsman's shoulder. "Did your best, Doc. You saved a lot of guys, just can't save 'em all. The gunny is gonna make it, LT. All the way back home to Hawaii. Don't know about the captain. He was hit bad. Last we heard, they got him out to the hospital ship. Ain't heard nothing since."

The sound of Boomer's voice rang in Sean's mind and gave way to the image of the ever-calm Captain Lee. "Good Marines." He exhaled. "Be sure to save me a couple of beers. See you guys tomorrow. Thanks for the mail."

Christ—the skipper, the gunny, and one of my squad leaders. Who's next?

★   ★   ★

Leafing through the pack of letters, Sean saw two from his mother. He hadn't written her in almost three weeks. He'd vowed to try to get her at least one letter a week but found it difficult to say anything about what he was doing or how things were really going. After quickly glancing at the beautifully penned letters detailing her constant anxiety and fears, Sean wrote to his mother.

3 October 1968
Dear Mom,
Sorry I haven't written in a while. We've been in the field for the past couple of weeks chasing the bad guys. It's difficult to keep paper clean and to find a place to write, especially with all the rain. Actually, the rain cools things down.

The Vietnamese are good people. It's sad to see them caught up in a war, especially the kids. We do all we can for them whenever we can, but it's never really enough. We move around a lot, so we don't ever get real friendly with the locals. Matter of fact, some of them are the bad guys, but that's another story.

We're now in a rest area on a beach in Da Nang. We're having a good time getting cleaned up, having some good food, and just relaxing. I'm using this slack time to get caught up on my letter writing. Tomorrow I'll be taking my men for a swim in the South China Sea. After that, we are going to have burgers and beer. Not as good as your burgers, of course, but we'll make do.

Hope all is going well. Thanks for having Sandy over. I'm sure her and Rosa are good company. Please tell Rosa to say hello to Mary and Joe. Sal tells me he visited a couple of times. Said he can't get enough of your sausage and peppers. Be sure to call on Sal or Frankie if you need anything done on the house. They would be offended if you needed anything and didn't call them. Say hello to Uncle Frank. Let him know I'll write soon.

If you think of it, send more of those hand wipes. They're a great cleanup tool. A big help when we have to chow down in the field. Please keep them coming. Don't worry about me; things are going well. I'll be home before you know it.
All my love,
Sean

After addressing the letter to his mother, Sean sifted through the packet of mail, noticing familiar return addresses. He didn't recognize one of the addresses, but it had a familiar name on the rear of the envelope: Beth Wilenski.

Dear Sean,
Hope things are going well for you. I was up in Philadelphia visiting Val last week and got your address from her. She said you and John might be meeting up soon. She hadn't gotten any letters in almost two weeks and was a little uptight. If you see Mike, tell him to write.

The reason for my writing is to let you know I'll be spending some time in your hometown. Senator Kennedy's family is making a commitment to the Bed-Stuy section of Brooklyn. They want to open a facility to provide social services to the neighborhood—that I understand is in a bad way. I remember you telling me your girl (you never told me her name) was doing social work in that area of Brooklyn. I would love to connect with her and get her take on Bed-Stuy. On the personal side, I know what she's going through, having you over there. Maybe I could be helpful. Please drop me her name and address. I'll look her up next time I'm up that way.
Take care and be careful.
Beth

Christ, Sean thought. At the time of Beth's meeting, Val hadn't learned of her husband's death. By now, she surely had gotten the terrible news. Sean hated the thought, but it was now time to send his condolences. He just didn't know what to write. He decided instead to walk down to the shoreline and compose his thoughts.

Sitting on the hard-packed sand a few feet from the water's edge, Sean inhaled the briny smell of the sea. This beach was magnificent. He glanced up and down the expansive shoreline. To the north, a jagged hill rose from the shore and curved out to sea, forming a protective flank for the long strand of beach. The locals called the hill Monkey Mountain. Two miles to the south, a massive rock formation, dubbed Marble Mountain, shot vertically from the surf line like a small Manhattan office tower. Between the two flanking mountains lay China Beach, a ribbon of pure white sand separating the gentle surf from dense groves of trees shading wooden shacks and limestone villas built by the French during better times.

He peered over the calm water of the South China Sea. It was a lot like Coney Island without the rock jetties. He could almost hear Sandy's voice.

"Hey, Lieutenant Cercone, can you see all the way to Brighton Beach?"

Sean grinned at the sight of a Navy chaplain he'd met when he first arrived. "I sure am trying, Padre. Maybe you could talk to your boss. Didn't he do some tricks on the water?"

"Hold on, just because you were an altar boy doesn't give you the right to blaspheme. Last time I checked, he was your boss as well," Chaplain Raymond Flynn shot back. The thin-framed Irishman with short red hair, freckled face, and slightly protruding teeth had just emerged from his midday swim.

During the past few days, he and Sean had talked frequently and had become fast friends. Sean had spoken about his feelings about Slattery's death and the things he had to face as an infantry platoon commander.

Standing to greet the chaplain, Sean grinned. "No blaspheme intended, Padre. But you Jesuits from Fordham probably didn't get the word. The holy father decreed all us Brooklyn guys from St. John's to be papal wise guys. As such, we get blanket dispensation on all church related jokes."

"I'll take that into account when I determine your penance. How's the leg doing?"

"Pretty good. Should be moving out tomorrow. Just learned my company is down the beach at an R&R center. Hopefully I can hook up with them and get back to work."

Flynn countered in his clipped Bronx accent, "Think you're ready to go back, Sean?"

"Yes, sir. The leg is good, or will be by the time we move out."

Wrapping a green towel around his neck, the former theology professor stepped closer. "Not talking about the leg, Sean. You seemed pretty upset the other night about not being able to feel anything, not being able to get close to anyone, not being able to display any emotion. And, as you put it, not giving a shit about anything."

"Probably the drink talking, Padre. But those are pretty good traits if you run a rifle platoon, except the not-giving-a-shit part." Sean flashed his sideways smile but it disappeared as he looked away. "I do care about my men. Want to get as many back as possible. If we have to kill a bunch of North Vietnamese along the way, so be it. The platoon is all I give a shit about."

"What is it you don't like? Do you—"

"With all respect, Padre, you don't get it. I want to get all my men back, but we both know that's not gonna happen. Some will get killed, others hit bad, lose an arm or a leg if they're lucky. So I don't like the odds in this game. I don't like what the killing does to you. Feel a little of me going wacko every time we waste some of them. I understand why we're here. I hate the damn Commies and what they're trying to do. It's just that the killing can get to you. Maybe worse, after a while, it doesn't get to you."

Flynn's lips tightened, and he lowered his milky blue eyes. "As I said the other night, Sean, your reaction is normal. War is brutal. Its takes a terrible toll, especially on frontline guys. God is asking a lot of you and your Marines. I wish I could tell you why, except to say he suffered just as much for us."

"Yeah, but he didn't waste anybody along the way."

"Killing is maybe the worst part." Flynn nodded. "But I'm sure you remember your theology and St. Thomas's teaching on the concept of just war. In an awful way, having the right to kill may be the heaviest cross of all."

Sean grimaced. "Just war concept, the right to kill—yeah, we covered it all at St. John's. But now I see the problem with the theory. St. Thomas Aquinas never had to run a rifle platoon."

Flynn gave an understanding nod. "Good luck, Sean. May God give you the light to know your duty and the strength to do it."

Sean flashed a twisted smile. "Thanks, Padre. That prayer suits me well. I've got some letters to write. Hope to see ya again."

Chapter 22

"Hey, Sal, how ya doing? Let's have a drink over here in the back." Frankie motioned to an empty table in the rear of the bar. "Pauli, give us a couple of beers, will ya! So, Sal, you get the tickets for the Giants game in Philly next Sunday?"

"Yeah, Frankie, got four tickets. The game starts at twelve thirty," Sal said, raising his cupped hand. "Mind telling me what we're doin' with them, since we're gonna do our thing at that antiwar rally in Manhattan the same day?"

"All part of the plan—gonna be our alibi when the shit starts flowing." Frankie laughed as Pauli Black approached the table with two beers. He lowered his head and whispered, "Don't want you telling the others just yet, but we're going to be spending Saturday night in a motel just outside Philly. We're taking two cars. We'll leave real early Sunday in one of the cars." He nodded to the smiling bartender. "Thanks, Pauli."

Sal threw his arms in the air. "Frankie, what alibi? We got this thing down pat. Shit, we rehearsed the thing three times last Saturday morning. Four of us filled five hundred eight-ounce cups in less than ten minutes. We're in, and then we're out. No way are we gonna get caught. You really think we need an alibi?"

"You never know. You just never know," Frankie said, raising his dark eyebrows. "Somebody might recognize one of us. Maybe somebody in the neighborhood does too much talking, maybe somebody rats on us. Who knows what could happen." He tapped his finger on the table. "There's gonna be a lot of heat after this goes down. I want an air tight alibi, just in case."

"Well, I'm really up for this," Sal said, clenching his fists. "I've had enough of this antiwar crap. We had an incident just the other day. Some left-wing assholes tried to stop a couple of Navy recruiters from setting up a table in Boylan Hall. Then there was a demonstration by the local SDS pukes, and the cops hauled their asses away. Can you believe the student government called a strike because the administration let the cops on campus!"

"Yeah, well, it just ain't Brooklyn College. Look at this." Frankie unfolded the *Daily News* to a picture of the folk singer Joan Baez being escorted into a police van. "This hippie bitch was leading a protest to close the draft board in Oakland. She gets arrested, posts bail, and in three or four hours she's out on the street. The problem is these fuckin' liberal judges. They just don't want to enforce the law. Mark my words, these protests will take off once these pricks find out there'll be no real punishment for occupying buildings, assaulting cops, or resisting arrest."

"I can't wait for next Sunday. I'll tell you straight out, Brain. This has gotta be your greatest stunt ever!"

Frankie frowned, flicked his ponytail, and thought for a moment. "It's not just a stunt, Sal. It's a counterprotest. Kind of a form of civil disobedience directed at those motherfuckers who don't mind breaking the law when it suits their cause." He laced his figures and shook his hands. "Call it a form of self-expression in reaction to those pricks wrapping themselves in the First Amendment while giving aid and comfort to the fuckin' NVA. Or maybe we should call it a counterinsurgency caper. It's definitely not just a stunt."

"That's actually eloquent, Brain." Sal grinned. "Just keep those thoughts, case we get caught. It would be a perfect—"

"We ain't getting caught." Frankie slammed his fist on the table. "Sure, it's risky. Just remember we're doing our little counterinsurgency caper for the kid Tommy, and for Sean, and for all the guys over there. Definitely think they're worth the risk."

★　★　★

Sandy rushed through her kitchen, barely acknowledging her parents finishing their late-morning breakfast. "Just got two letters from Sean. I'll be out back. Catch breakfast later."

Ignoring the cool October breeze, she sat on a lounge chair and tore open the two envelopes, selecting the letter with the oldest date. Sean wrote that he was well and out of the field for a few days at a place called China Beach. He described meeting a Navy chaplain from New York with whom he had good time. He went on at length about a beach party with his platoon. Sandy was feeling giddy until she turned to the last page of the letter.

Before we got our little rest on the beach, we were in a pretty big fight—several battalions engaged, including John Slattery's. John didn't make it. I know that for sure, because I recovered his body. It was the worst experience of my life. I just wrote Val yesterday, another horrible experience. You may remember me talking about John's wife, Val. She is living with her folks in Philadelphia. John's loss really hit me. I also lost Boomer, one of my squad leaders, and we may lose our company commander, Captain Lee. He was in pretty bad shape when they got him out. Both he and Boomer are married and have kids.

I'd be lying if I didn't say I'm down. I'm trying to stay positive, especially in front of the men. Actually, I'm feeling kind of numb to it all. They say that's the best way to handle it. I don't know. I feel responsible for every man in the platoon. It's hard to just blank out losing a man. We draw strength for each other. When a guy is lost, we all feel part of ourselves going with them. I can't describe it except to say it's terrible.

Sorry to be so heavy, but I didn't want to con you about what's going on. God willing, I'll get through this. Just thinking of you and knowing you are waiting for me can get me through anything. I love you.

Sean

PS: Give my regards to your folks. Tell my mother and Rosa to keep lighting those candles. Don't mention anything about Slattery or the others.

Sandy shivered. She folded the letter and anxiously tore open the second.

We're back with our battalion. We were lifted out yesterday with several new replacements. In addition to two lieutenants and a dozen new troopers, we have a new company commander, a new gunnery sergeant, and a staff sergeant. Our new CO, Captain Frank Mallick, is a California guy who played some football at San Jose State. I spent a lot of time with him yesterday; seems like a good leader. The gunny is rock solid, a Korean War veteran. The new staff sergeant, Finbar Lynch, who actually has an Irish brogue, was assigned to my platoon. The plan is to have him as my platoon sergeant for a few weeks, then take over as my replacement. I'll be moving up to be the company XO, replacing Jeb Wilkinson, who is due to rotate home next month. I hate to leave the platoon, but they usually rotate you out between four and six months. At least I will be staying with the company.

As luck would have it, Sergeant Murphy served with Finbar Lynch back in '66. He says he is a great NCO. Rumor has it that Lynch was sent to America by his folks because he got involved with the IRA at the age of seventeen! Evidently, he found a home in the Corps and picked up staff sergeant in five years—no easy feat for a guy who is only twenty-three. Murphy says Lynch got a Silver Star during his first tour along with a meritorious promotion.

Talking about awards, both Murphy and I were put in for Bronze Stars for our work in the last operation. It's certainly an honor, but both of us were just doing our jobs. I feel guilty for being singled out. Murph now has two Bronze Stars to go along with a Navy Com and a couple of Crosses of Gallantry. He says we wear them for all our men, especially the guys who didn't make it.

Sorry to have been so down in my last letter. I feel a lot better now. Having you in my life makes all the difference. What happens, happens—but there's nothing I can't face knowing when I get through it I'll be with you.

Please don't worry about me, and try to get out once in a while. That Halloween party your tennis team pal is having in Manhattan Beach sounds like fun. Make sure you go—just don't look at any other guys.

Give my best to your mom and dad.

I love you,

Sean

Sandy stared at the green hedges that formed the rear wall of her patio. *Oh my God. Val Slattery—what must she be going through? What if something were to happen to Sean?*

Suppressing the terrible notion, she craved his return. To have him hold her again, to feel the strength of his body, to have him inside her. The thoughts brought a depressing realization. Sean's tour wasn't scheduled to end until May of next year, seven long months away.

Chapter 23

Staff Sergeant Lynch took charge and made his presence felt. Sean watched the hard-driving Irishman strike up an immediate rapport with his young Marines, always laughing and joking while he instructed them on how to function and survive in the unforgiving world of a rifle platoon. Sean knew Lynch stayed up half the night, spending twenty to thirty minutes in different foxholes, getting to know each man. During the two contacts the platoon encountered in his first week, Lynch moved to the center of the action, directing fire with decisive but calm commands, all the while cursing loudly at the NVA.

The presence of Staff Sergeant Finbar Lynch didn't go unnoticed by the new company commander, Captain Mallick. He sought out Sean on the matter. "Cercone, what's your take on Staff Sergeant Lynch? The gunny had some good things to say about him."

"He's a pro, sir," Sean replied with no hesitation. "He's a natural leader with an uncanny knack for understanding men. Damn good at running a platoon."

"Well, there it is. We'll give him your platoon and move you up to be my XO. Let's do it this afternoon. Wilkerson has been with this rifle company for almost his entire tour. He's got a little over three weeks left in-country. I want him to spend that time in the rear."

"Aye aye, sir." Sean smiled. "That's a good call for everybody concerned."

Sean sought out his new staff sergeant. He found Lynch in a forward position huddling under a poncho, trying to stay dry in the monsoon rain that had plagued the area for the past several days. Wrapped in his own soaked poncho, Sean slid down next to the Irishman.

"Top of the morning, LT. Sorry I can't offer any coffee. All me heat tabs are soaked." Finbar shuffled to give Sean some room in the muddy hole.

"No sweat, Finbar. Got us some better refreshment." Sean produced six miniature bottles of scotch, a constant supply of which was mailed to him by Joey's cousin, an American Airlines stewardess.

"Praise be to God! And if you're not the best platoon commander of the best platoon in the Corps."

"I had the best platoon, Finbar. Now it's your platoon. I'm being moved up to XO. This is kind of our change-of-command ceremony. Take care of them, Finbar. They're a great bunch of Marines." Sean unscrewed one of the tiny bottles and downed its contents.

"That I will, Lieutenant. God help me, I will. And I'll take some help from the devil as well." Lynch laughed, raising the miniature bottle and letting the scotch drip slowly into his mouth

A week had passed since Sean assumed his duties as executive officer of Alpha Company. The monsoon rain curtailed operations, making life miserable for the grunts. On the plus side, with the exception of an occasional mortar attack, there was little contact with the enemy. Sean missed the men in his platoon. He was reminded of their presence each time he heard the determined voice of Corporal Odom calling in situation reports on the company tactical net.

Late that morning, the rain slackened, and a resupply helicopter was called in. Sean left his bunker to supervise the off-loading. A lone Marine sprinted in from one of the forward positions. It was Corporal Odom.

"Hey, Preacher, what ya up to?" Sean said.

"Hi, LT. Looking for some batteries. We're getting pretty low."

"You're in luck. Resupply chopper is just about to arrive. Why don't you help us off-load and grab all the batteries you can carry."

The CH-46 circled the hillside once before dropping onto the mud-soaked piece of flat ground topped with strips of steel matting that was the landing zone. Odom and three other Marines rapidly off-loaded the supplies. In less than two minutes, Sean gave the thumbs-up to the crew chief. The twin-blade CH-46 rose slowly, passing within yards. Its roaring engines masked all sounds.

The mortar blast slammed Sean to the ground. A sharp, burning sensation ripped through his thigh and arm. He screamed in pain, spitting mud from his mouth. Two Marines came to his aid, tearing off his trouser leg. A still-hot steel splinter protruded from his thigh. Smaller fragments peppered his upper left arm, causing rivulets of blood to gush forth.

"Gonna hurt a little, Skipper." One of the Marines gingerly removed the jagged piece of steel. Sean moaned and lost consciousness. A shot of morphine kept him in a twilight state during his evacuation to Charlie Med.

Later, he vaguely recalled lying on the floor of the chopper, smelling aviation fuel despite the cool air rushing about, and staring at the interior roof with its web of exposed wires and thin strands of steel running the length of the aluminum hull. His torso shook in sync with the vibration of the helicopter as it strained to remain airborne. His body was jostled to one side as a corpsman tied a belt around the leg of a Marine the lower half of whom was a blood-soaked mass of torn flesh and protruding bones. He remembered raising his head to catch a glimpse of the wounded Marine and looking into the anguished face of Corporal Tim Odom.

When he regained consciousness, Sean found himself staring into the bearded face of a field doctor with a green surgical mask pulled down below his chin. "You'll be fine, Lieutenant. That was a deep, nasty gash in your leg, but no permanent damage. We got all of that metal out of your arm and stitched it up. You're gonna be sore for a while, but you'll be good as new in a week or so."

Taking a deep breath, Sean drifted off, images flittering in his mind as if someone were flashing cards. The images stopped abruptly, and Corporal Odom appeared.

★   ★   ★

"Well, looks like we can't keep you out of this place." Chaplain Flynn laughed. "Checked the roster last night and saw your name on the list of new arrivals. Guess some guys will do anything to get back to China Beach."

"Hi, Padre. Good to see you again," Sean said, rising to draw back the mosquito netting from his bunk. Failing to reach the netting, he grimaced in pain and fell back on his cot. "Ouch! They said I'd be hurting for a while; guess they meant it."

"A little pain is good for your soul, Sean," Flynn said with a half-smile.

"Really?" Sean replied, gritting his teeth. "Tell me, is it a grave sin to curse at a chaplain?"

"Oh, God is all forgiving, but the Navy might have a problem."

Sean nodded. "That's good. Then you can go fuck yourself with that good-for-your-soul bullshit. And when you rat me out to the Navy, just report I suggested you self-fornicate. You know, to address that state of celibacy that no doubt accounts for your sick sense of humor."

Flynn burst into laughter. "Sean, you certainly have a way with words."

Sean sighed. "I was evacuated with another Marine. His name is Odom, Corporal Tim Odom, a nice kid from a small town in Texas. He was my radio man. I wonder if you can find out his status."

"Saw them take him out of the OR," Flynn said, his smile fading, his voice somber. "He'll be going back to Texas, but I'm afraid he'll be leaving one of his legs here."

Sean fell back on his cot, gazing at the ceiling. He recalled the day he and Odom had dashed off the chopper to join the battalion and all they had been through in the past several months. He and Odom had moved as one through every engagement, experiencing the special bond known only to platoon commanders and their radiomen.

"He's a good kid, Padre, a damn good Marine."

"You're all good Marines, Sean. I pray to God every day that he embraces those he takes. And that he provides special love and strength for those like Odom, who'll be carrying this war for a lifetime."

Chapter 24

For eight weeks, Frankie Brain pored over the details of his counterinsurgency caper. Saturday evening, Frankie, Sal, and two others pulled into a motel in a northern section of Philadelphia just off the New Jersey Turnpike. He blasted the car's distinctive horn to ensure everyone in the motel office would remember the red Bonneville.

Making small talk with the clerk, he paid for the rooms in cash, requesting a receipt. "Sorry, didn't get your name," Frankie said, stuffing the receipt in his wallet.

"Morris. My name is Stu Morris. I kind of work here weekends, make some money on the side."

"That's good, Mr. Morris. You on duty until tomorrow?"

"Till noon," the balding clerk said with a frown. "A guy's gotta do something to make a little dough."

"Hey, that's great," Frankie said. "We need a wake-up call at eight thirty. Want to grab a quick breakfast, then get out to the stadium to watch the Giants warm up before they kick the Eagles' ass. Tell you what, here's a fiver to make sure you don't forget to call at eight thirty."

★   ★   ★

At six thirty Sunday morning, it took a little more than an hour for the gray van with yellow peace symbols painted on its sides to travel to Exit

16 on the Jersey Turnpike. Ten minutes after leaving the turnpike, the van exited the Manhattan side of the Lincoln tunnel.

"How come we let my brother Porky stay behind and we get to do all the dangerous work?" Kevin Fallon said.

"Shut up, Kevin," Frankie said. "We needed him to answer the wake-up call at eight thirty and to do the thing with the car horn at nine thirty. You did a good job driving up the van last night. Now all you and Phil gotta do is focus on getting the fuckin' cups filled as fast as you can. You got that?"

Sal chimed in, "To say nothing of the fact your brother Porky handled the drink dispenser like a damn flamethrower during our practice run. Better we let him be the wheelman and get the Bonneville back home."

A drizzling rain fell softly on the Manhattan streets, accompanied by a light breeze, making the otherwise mild October morning a little chilly. A few minutes after entering Manhattan, the van, with its four occupants and its cargo of folding tables, cartons of cups, and four five-gallon drink dispensers, came to a halt at a police barrier running across Fifty-Seventh Street between Sixth and Fifth Avenues.

Driving up to the wooden barrier, Frankie poked his head out the driver-side window, addressing two cops who looked very annoyed. "Good morning, officers. We gotta deliver this stuff to where the parade is starting. You know where it's gonna start?" Frankie said, wearing large glasses and a baseball cap with its beak pulled low.

"And what might this stuff be?" a police sergeant snarled as he approached the gray van adorned with peace symbols and a Weiss Construction Company sign.

"We got some hot drinks for those marchers. Got cups and tables too," Frankie said. "Our boss, Mr. Weiss, he's a good friend of the mayor. Wants to show his support for the demonstration."

The sergeant moved closer to the van, gave Frankie a disgusted look, and ordered him to pull over to the curb. After a brief inspection, they drove to the corner of Fifth Avenue and Fifty-Seventh Street. Several minutes later, they unloaded the tables and placed one on each corner of the intersection. Frankie held off on unloading the drink dispensers and the cartons of cups.

A half hour passed, and the crowd of protest marchers with antiwar signs and banners swelled to several hundred. A group of organizers assembled them for the march, with the mayor and some prominent peace activists positioned to lead the demonstration.

"Now!" Frankie said. "Let's move. Be back here in ten minutes or you're gonna walk home."

The four moved out smartly, each carrying boxes of cups and a silver-gray drink dispenser strapped to their backs. Frankie headed for the far side of the street to the table closest to the mayor and his entourage. He cursed under his breath when he saw a Channel Nine news team panning the area with their TV camera.

After hastily setting up rows of white Styrofoam cups on the table, Frankie enlisted the aid of two young ladies to help complete the setup. He began filling each cup with steaming hot chocolate laced with large quantities of Ex-Lax. He called to another bystander, a hippy-looking guy with a peace symbol on his sweatshirt.

"Hey, pal, give us a hand here. Take some of this hot chocolate over to the mayor and his group. They're our elected leaders—putting their asses on the line to support peace. We gotta take care of them."

"Right on, man. Right on!" the young hippy cried. He carefully placed half a dozen cups in the top of one of the empty cartons and ran off toward the mayor to do his duty and support the movement.

With over five hundred cups of Ex-Lax–laden hot chocolate dispensed, they drove south down Fifty-Seventh Street, made a left on Tenth Avenue, and pulled into a car wash at fifteen minutes to nine. When the gray van exited the car wash off-white, Frankie barked at Kevin Fallon, "Get on the Jersey plates while I tip these attendants. Sal, shit-can that Weiss Construction Company sign."

Rather than take one of the tunnels to Jersey, Frankie took the George Washington Bridge. Once on the Jersey Turnpike, he began to relax and turned on the radio. The nine-thirty news reported that a major disruption to a peace demonstration appeared to be taking place, but details were not available. As the van approached Exit 5 on the turnpike, the reporter came back on at ten.

This morning, a major antiwar demonstration in Midtown Manhattan was disrupted when hundreds of participants appeared to lose control of their bowels. Witnesses reported chaos as hundreds of marchers fought to gain entrance to the few restroom facilities open on Sunday morning. Congressman Albert Finemen, a leading antiwar activist and an event organizer, had to be restrained from entering the women's restroom in the Sixth-Avenue subway station. The mayor, who left the parade after marching only a few blocks, was reported to have soiled himself while running for his limo. Early reports indicate the culprits to be several young men who distributed hot chocolate, probably heavily laced with a laxative. The police have put out an all points for a gray van with New York plates and yellow peace symbols painted on its side.

"Frankie, we did it! We did it!" Sal cried as their white van with Jersey plates left the turnpike at Exit 5.

"Yeah, we did. Now let's hope we get away with it," Frankie said. "Right now we go Franklin Field, watch the game, and have a good time. Hey, be sure to keep those ticket stubs."

★   ★   ★

The next day, New York Police Commissioner Tim Murphy convened a special task force to address what the *New York News* described as a "mass movement down Fifth Avenue." Jimmy Napoli represented Brooklyn South at the emergency task force meeting. He sat with a group of senior detectives sipping morning coffee.

"Let's take a look at this shitty situation," Detective Jim O'Donnell of Manhattan South laughed as he turned on a tape recording secured from Channel Nine News.

After watching the tape for a few minutes, Napoli stood up and yelled, "Stop, roll it back. See that guy with the dispenser on his back, the one with the baseball cap and a damn ponytail? I know that son of a bitch. That's Frankie Ryan from Avenue T." He bolted toward the door. *I'm gonna personally pick up Mr. Frankie "the Brain" Ryan.*

Frankie sat at one end of a gray metal table in a basement room of Brooklyn's Sixty-Second Precinct. At the other end of the table, three veteran detectives sat, collars opened, ties undone, and sleeves rolled up. By contrast, Jimmy Nap stood behind Frankie in the windowless room wearing a gray pin-striped suit, a white button-down collar shirt, and a blue silk tie. *This is one neighborhood guy I'm not gonna mind puttin' away.*

"Okay, Ryan, enough of this bullshit about the Giants game in Philly," Napoli barked, throwing the ticket stubs on the floor. "We got ya on tape!" Crouching down, his face next to Frankie's left ear, he shifted to a whisper. "I don't want any more crap. Just tell us who else was in on it. Sign the piece of paper, and maybe, just maybe, I'll talk to the DA. Maybe we can get him to plead this rap down. Maybe classify the incident as a counterprotest that got out of hand."

Never moving a muscle, Frankie responded, "Jimmy, not for nothing, but this guy you got on tape—the guy whose face you can't see but who happens to have a ponytail like mine—I'm not sure that's what you guys would call a positive ID." He wiggled his nose and sniffed the air. "Hey, Jimmy, that Canoe cologne? That shit is strong! Beats the hell out of Old Spice. Do you—"

"Shut up, you asshole!" the flustered chief of detectives screamed.

"Wait a minute—hold it," Frankie said, feigning a look of surprise. "Forgot to tell you guys, we actually stayed in Philly Saturday night at a little motel."

One of the detectives jumped to his feet and pounded the table. "You been telling us for the last hour you drove to the game Sunday morning. You changin' your story?"

"Well, you never asked me where we drove from. Guess I shoulda told ya. Anyway, we stayed over Saturday night. Got up about eight thirty. Left the motel about nine thirty, got some breakfast, and went out early to Franklin Field."

"This motel got a name?" snapped another detective.

"Don't think I can remember the name. Oh, wait a minute, got a receipt." Frankie plucked a slip of paper from his wallet. "Here it is. Yeah, the Whitehall Motel—kind of a dump, but what ya expect for thirty a night. Nice old guy runs the place. Think his name was Morris. Yeah, Mr. Morris checked us in about ten thirty Saturday night. Then I remember him calling us around eight thirty Sunday morning. Like I said, we left the place maybe an hour later."

Pacing behind Frankie, Napoli mulled over the timeline and the prospect that the story might be confirmed. No matter how sure he felt about Frankie's presence at the demonstration, Napoli knew the tape would never hold up in court. He hissed at Frankie, "Okay, Ryan, you can go—for now. We're gonna talk with your Mr. Morris. Better yet, I'm going to have one of my Philadelphia Highway Patrol friends pay him a visit. Hope your story checks, Mr. Ryan. Meanwhile, keep your ass in town."

Chapter 25

GRAVESEND
ALL HALLOWS EVE

Leaving the settlement house early Friday afternoon, Sandy arrived home before five. Most of the thick oaks along Avenue T had lost their leaves, and a good many of them littered the street and curbside as Sandy parked in front of her house. It had been a long week. She looked forward to taking a relaxing bath, writing to Sean, and having a light supper with her mother before going to her old tennis team's Halloween party.

"You look very spry in your tennis whites. That your costume for the party?" Her mother smiled as Sandy joined her at the kitchen table.

"That's it, plus this." Sandy held a white mask over her face.

"How was your lunch last week with that friend of Sean? Tess, what's her name …"

"Her name is Beth, Mother. Beth Wilenski. And she was quite impressive. She's only twenty-four and works on Senator Kennedy's personal staff. She's actually involved in planning community-housing initiatives for a social services center the Kennedy family is establishing in Bedford-Stuyvesant."

"And she knows Sean how?"

"She's best friends with John Slattery's wife, Val. John was Sean's roommate. Sean met Beth at the Slatterys' house down in Virginia when he was at Quantico." Sandy sighed. "Beth is a widow. Her husband was an Army lieutenant—killed in Vietnam last year." Sandy lowered her head. "And now her best friend's husband, John, was just killed a few weeks ago. My God, I can't imagine how she ..." Sandy looked up at her mother.

Juliana grasped her hand. "Let's pray you never have to find out."

★ ★ ★

Jay Delfano arrived at the house in Manhattan Beach to find the party in full swing. Dozens of costumed collegiates milled about an exterior porch that wrapped around three sides of the white and gray Victorian house. Six-foot-high, thick hedges flanked both sides of the property. A dense row of fern trees formed the rear side of a large backyard that held a two-car garage, a gazebo, and a slate pathway that wound through three seating areas, each walled with shrubs to ensure privacy.

Sandy and her former teammates wore white tennis gear and white masks. Several other partygoers, most of them recent graduates from Brooklyn College, sported elaborate costumes, ranging from a half-dozen Frankenstein-like creatures to witches and an assortment of other goblins. A fair number didn't wear any costume except for the obligatory black, full-face cardboard mask presented to each attendee on arrival.

Delfano wore jeans and his green Army jacket with a large yellow peace symbol etched on the back. He put on a black face mask, entered the foyer, and made his way to the bar. He spotted the attractive girl who, despite her fancy white mask, he knew in an instant was Sandy Gold.

Delfano had had a joint before joining the party and consumed several beers while lurking about the crowded room for almost an hour. All the time, he stayed in close proximity to Sandy, whom he hated for the scene at school and for the terror he had endured at the hands of thugs. He got close enough to hear Sandy mention her Marine boy friend, someone named Sean. Returning to the bar, his mind raced and his rage grew. *I'm going to get that bitch alone and scare the hell out of her.*

Delfano left the bar, circled the room, crept behind her, and whispered. "Hey, Sandy, got a message from Sean."

He curled up the collar of his Army jacket and moved toward the veranda, his hand raised in a signal to follow. Sandy followed as he burrowed through the packed room. He shoved two partiers aside, making his way to the porch, down a short flight of steps, and out to the backyard. As Sandy reached the porch steps, he was on the slate path, shrouded in darkness but still visible. Delfano motioned again and entered one of the shrub-enclosed alcoves.

★   ★   ★

He stared in frozen silence. She lay lifeless, eyes wide open, head bent awkwardly over one shoulder. When he had taunted her, she had lunged at him and had torn off his mask. He had grabbed her long hair and swung her around, her head smashing into the white brick wall that ringed the vine-studded alcove. He never had meant to hurt her.

Resisting the impulse to touch her, he rushed out onto a slate path and dashed through the heavily scrubbed yard to the driveway. He slowed down and casually crossed the street. Once in the refuge of the shadowed darkness, he broke into a run. After a few short blocks, he was alone and slowed to a fast walk, sweat dampening the back of his neck despite the cool autumn night. A stately white colonial came into view, and he turned into its long driveway. Home.

Slumped in a wicker chair on the side porch, Delfano caught his breath. *What have I done?* He stared into the blackness of the huge oaks fronting the property and saw his recent life pass before him. Brooklyn College, the hard work that had gotten him on the Dean's list, his leadership in organizing students, his recent acceptance to NYU law school, and his dreams of a political career. All of it could be gone. He had been stupid to confront her again. He hated her and what she had done, but he had only wanted to scare her. Who would believe him after that incident at the demonstration? But nobody had seen him at the party—everyone had been wearing those full-face black masks. How could they prove he had been there?

"Hey, Jay, that you out there?" Judge Benjamin Delfano pushed opened the front door and moved onto the porch. Slightly built with curly gray hair, he took a seat next to his son and lit a cigar. "Your mother told me you were going to some kind of party." Jay didn't answer. The judge puffed to get his cigar going and turned to his son with a puzzled look.

"Decided not to go," Jay blurted. "Didn't want to drive to the city. Thought I'd take it easy. Been out here all night."

Chapter 26

Chief of Detectives for Brooklyn South Jimmy Napoli slammed down the phone and cursed as rookie detective Mike Pierce entered his office.

"Somethin' wrong, boss?" the young detective asked.

"The fuckin' world is wrong," Napoli growled. "Just heard from my esteemed colleague on the Jersey State Police. He finally tracked down Mr. Morris, the clerk at Whitehall Motel. After a supposedly rigorous interview, he reports that Morris is positive he checked in Mr. Ryan last Saturday night and called Mr. Ryan at eight thirty Sunday morning. Mr. Morris is also positive he heard Mr. Ryan's red Bonneville leave the motel lot at approximately nine thirty that morning."

Napoli pounded his desk. "That prick Frankie set this whole thing up. Somehow he wired a perfect alibi." He reached for his white mug, wincing as he downed the stale coffee. He calmly rose, glanced slowly over his shoulder, and threw his mug across the room like a pitcher trying to pick someone off first. He screamed in a fit of rage, startling the young detective. "That son of a bitch wasn't in Philly. He was here on Fifty-Seventh Street. Right here, feeding Ex-Lax to those shithead protesters and our liberal fuckin' mayor. Now I've gotta tell the chief we have no suspect for this heinous assault on the mayor and his peace demonstrators. But before I do, I want to take one more shot at Frankie Ryan."

"Don't think you're gonna have time for that, Jimmy. We got a homicide in Manhattan Beach. Seems the victim is the sister of one of our new ADAs. The mayor and the chief want you on this one."

Saturday-morning traffic was light. Napoli sped along the narrow three-lane Belt Parkway and reached the Sheepshead Bay exit in twenty minutes. He drove around the small harbor inlet along Edmonds Avenue to the upscale neighborhood of Manhattan Beach and parked behind several squad cars. A boyish-looking cop ushered Napoli to the crime scene in the well-scrubbed backyard of a stately home. He was greeted by Max Kline, a balding, old-line detective he had worked with over the years.

The plaid-jacketed Kline began the briefing. "The victim is female, early twenties, identified as Sandra Gold. Looks as if somebody probably smashed Miss Gold's head into this wall. Did it with enough force to break her neck. They took the body downtown an hour ago. We'll know more about the cause of death when we get their report."

Napoli frowned. "Sandra Gold. Name sounds familiar."

Kline reached into his case. "Here's a couple of Polaroids the crime scene guys left us. Pretty good-looking young woman. Know her?"

Napoli shook his head in disgust. "Christ! Yeah, I know her, met her once. Nice kid. She's the girlfriend of another nice kid, Sean Cercone, a Marine over in Vietnam. Known his family for years. Christ! What do I tell them?"

"At this stage, we got nothing to tell anybody, Jimmy." Kline peered over his rimless glasses. "We interviewed some of the partygoers who hung around, but there were dozens more at the party. I got someone trying to develop a contact list. IDs are going to be a real problem with everybody wearing a damn mask."

Kline flipped through his notebook. "The only thing we got is—let's see, a Janie Phillips, dressed as a clown. She reported being shoved by a guy in an Army fatigue jacket, mentioned a big peace symbol on the back of his jacket. Said the guy nearly knocked her down to get out on the porch. Here's the connection. Phillips says she definitely saw one of the tennis team girls following the guy out to the porch, probably Miss Gold, but she is not sure."

"She get a look at the guy's face?"

Kline shook his bald head. "Nope. He was wearing a big black mask like everyone at the party."

"Right." Napoli sighed in disgust. "And his Army fatigue jacket with its big peace symbol narrows him down to just about every third college kid in the city!"

"I'm going to check out a few of the local joints," Kline said "There's a place down on Brighton Beach Avenue where college kids hang out run by a friend of mine, Abe Paser. Old Abe generally knows what's going."

"Check it out," Napoli said. "Nothing much I can do here. Gotta deliver the bad news to my buddy."

★ ★ ★

Frankie sat on the small couch in Ann Cercone's small living room as Sal entered the room. "Just heard about Sandy. How'd this happen? What do we know?"

Frankie shook his head. "Nobody knows nothing. Napoli told us a couple of hours ago. Said they didn't have much, but he's gonna take charge."

"Did anyone try to visit her parents?" Ann murmured, slumping in her armchair directly under the picture of her late husband, Sergeant Tom Cercone. "Mother of God, her poor parents!" She burst into tears. "And what are we going to tell my Sean?" She turned to her brother-in-law, pleading. "Frank, can we get him home? Can he come for the funeral? He would want ..." She covered her face with her hands, sobbing.

Frank grasped his sister-in-law's hand. "Don't think so, Ann. Jewish people bury their dead right away—a day, maybe two. We could never get him home that quickly. Right now, we got to figure out how to let Sean know." Looking at Sal seated across the room, he motioned. "What do ya think, Sal?"

Frankie looked back at Ann and her brother-in-law and knew what they wanted. He turned to Sal, knowing he was the only one who could do it. "Scribe, ya know what you gotta do, right?"

Sal pursed his lips, closed his eyes, and slowly moved his head side to side. "I'll do it. Don't know what I'm gonna say, but I'll do it. I'll write him."

Chapter 27

After a week recouping at China Beach, Sean returned to Alpha Company, now located on Hill 55. The company had been in the bush for two rain-soaked weeks, enduring several sharp encounters with the NVA. Then somebody had decided Alpha needed a break and pulled them out of the field to provide security for the regimental headquarters.

"Good to see you back, Lieutenant Cercone," Staff Sergeant Lynch said as Sean entered the hardback tent, home to the company's junior officers. "Welcome to our humble house. Sure if it doesn't beat hell out of lying in the mud."

"This is true, Finbar." Sean smiled. "How's everybody doing?"

Finbar looked away, fumbling with his utility jacket. Then he turned to Sean. "I'm afraid we took some bad hits last week. 'Tool Man' got it. Sergeant Murphy went out to recover the body and took a burst."

"Jesus, not Murph. He had about thirty days left!" Sean cried.

"We got him out quick. Doc did the best he could, but he was real bad. When we put him on the bird he was still alive. Haven't heard anything since."

Sean threw his duffle bag against the wall. "He's too short. Christ, after seventeen months. It shouldn't have happened."

"Sorry, sir. With some help from the Almighty, he might make it," Finbar said, reaching into a field desk, the only furniture in the hut apart from half a dozen cots. He tossed a packet of letters to Sean. "Your mail caught up with you."

Sitting on an empty cot clutching the packet of letters, Sean made no attempt to open his mail. His thoughts were on the young sergeant from South Boston with whom he had a special bond formed by months of combat—not a friendship, not a brotherhood, but something far more intense. And now Murph was gone.

Lynch reached into the lower drawer of the field desk and produced a pint bottle of J&B. "I was saving this for better times, but maybe this is the right time." He tossed the bottle to Sean.

Clutching the bottle with one hand, Sean opened it, took a long drink, and returned it to the sergeant. Lynch did the same and handed it back to Sean. Within three passes, the bottle was empty.

Sean fell back on the cot, flipping through two weeks of mail. Strange to see only one letter from Sandy. Deciding to hold hers, he sorted the others by post mark. The oldest was a letter from Beth Lewinski.

October 20, 1968
Hello Sean,
Thanks for your letter. I hope you're doing well. We were all devastated by Mike's loss. I'm doing the best I can for Val. I know only too well what she's going through. Of course I'll stay in touch with her, but I'm moving.

I've decided to accept a permanent position with the Kennedy Foundation working at their facility in Bedford-Stuyvesant, Brooklyn. I'm committing to at least a couple of years. A big decision, but working on housing initiatives for the poor is something I want to do, at least for a while. We didn't have much of a house where I grew up, and I know what that feels like. It's tough to be a family without a roof overhead.

The really good news is I had a chance to meet with your girl, Sandy. She's wonderful and quite beautiful. It looks as if we're birds of a feather, with her working at a settlement house only a few blocks away from the foundation. We're of the same mind on a number of social issues. I'm sure I'll be seeing a lot of Sandy. She's worried sick about you. Again, I know about that. I'll do everything I can to cheer her up. It'll be great for the three of us to get together when you come home.
Take care. May God keep you safe.

Sounds like Sandy and Beth hit it off. Not surprised. Two very committed women. That's great for Sandy—like having a big sister. He tore open one of two letters from Sal. The first contained a couple of neatly folded pages from the *New York Daily News*. Sean read the headline: "Mass Movement Foils Protest March."

He began laughing and then screamed, "Yes! Yes! Way to go, guys." He roared with laughter as he read the details in Sal's letter. "Fuck those peaceniks. Beautiful, beautiful."

"Praise to God, what's this all about? Sounds like some good news from home," Lynch said, lying on his cot across the room.

"I'll show ya in a minute." Sean laughed. "Wait till I open this other letter, might have some more stuff. You're never gonna believe what my buddies did. It's unbelievable."

Sean scanned the second letter. His body stiffened. "No! No! Please God, no!" Rolling off the bed, he pounded the floor with his fists. Sobbing hysterically, he buried head between his legs and sat hunched over on the plywood floor.

Lynch jumped from his cot and ran across the room.

"What the hell is this racket about? I could hear you guys down in the company office!" Captain Mallick shouted as he entered the hut.

"Don't know, sir," Lynch cried. "One moment he was laughing like hell. Next minute he was wailing like a wounded banshee. Think it might be something in this letter."

Chapter 28

The battalion staff agreed that Lieutenant Cercone was in no condition to rejoin Alpha Company. He was transferred to Headquarters Company, First Division, as staff officer in the G1, located in a series of bunkers on the very secure east slope of Hill 327 in Da Nang.

Sean sat alone at a corner table in the division officer's club, a large, one-room, screened-in facility jutting ten feet off the ground that abutted the lower slope of Hill 327. Stirring the ice in his glass, he nodded as Chaplain Flynn slid into a chair. "Sean, really sorry to hear about your girl. That's terrible. I can only imagine your pain. I prayed—"

"Want a drink, Chaplain?" Sean stirred his ice. Flynn nodded in silence. Sean raised two fingers, signaling to the waitress standing behind the makeshift bar across the room. "Two scotches, Mai Lin. Make 'em doubles."

"How did it happen, Sean?"

"I really don't know what happened. She was at a party and someone killed her. That's all I know. Got a half-dozen letters. Everybody is sorry as hell, but nobody knows who did it or why. Until I find out who and why, I really don't want to talk about it."

After a long silence, Flynn asked, "What do they have you doing in the G1?"

"Pushing a lot of paper, keeping track of unit manning levels, making sure replacements get to the most depleted units, R&R quotas, all kinds of important stuff," Sean replied with a half-grin.

"It's important you keep busy. I know it'll be difficult. Time tends to heal. Perhaps they'll let you go back to your battalion in a few weeks."

"Maybe so. Like I told the division shrink, don't care where they want me, as long as I get home, find out who killed Sandy, and kill 'em."

"That must have gone over well on your psych evaluation," Flynn said.

"Don't really give a shit about how I am evaluated, Padre."

Later that week, Sean received a letter from Sal, the first since the one that had told of Sandy's death. Sitting at his gray steel desk in the crammed, plywood-walled G1 office, Sean set aside his paperwork and opened the letter. The four pages covered a brief but touching description of Sandy's funeral at Washington Jewish Cemetery. Sal told how people were reacting to Sandy's death and how all the guys were trying to support Sean's mother and Rosa, both of whom had become very close with Sandy. Describing Rosa as almost inconsolable, Sal added that, except to attend the funeral, she'd not left her house since the incident, not even to attend Mass.

Sean was numbed by the first few pages but was stunned and enraged when he read the last two.

There is something I was told to keep quiet about but decided you should know. We think we got a lead on Sandy's killer. Actually, I had a hand in it.

Your uncle and I were in the Wrong Number when Jimmy Nap paid a visit last week. Seems he wanted to keep Frank updated on the investigation. He said they found out Sandy had a run-in with a guy at college several months ago, a guy named Jay Delfano. I told Jimmy I was there when it happened. I don't know if Sandy ever told you about the incident. Anyway, I told Jimmy what I remembered and mentioned this Delfano guy runs around campus with a big peace symbol on the back of an

Army fatigue jacket. Jimmy gets all excited and says that checks with a guy that was acting strange the night of the murder.

They picked up Delfano for questioning. Turns out they had him for less than an hour when his old man, who's a judge, gets him sprung. Jimmy didn't get much of a chance to grill the guy but said he had a feeling. Jimmy said Delfano was picked up once for having some high-grade weed in his possession. His daddy, the judge, got that rap squashed. The judge told the cops that his son was home all night, so he couldn't have been involved with any murder. We hear that the cops can't get a positive ID on anybody, because everybody at the party was wearing a mask. Good chance this guy might walk.

Lost in thought, Sean was interrupted by Master Sergeant Al Patterson. "Excuse me, Lieutenant, begging your pardon, but we gotta get these reports to the chief for signature this morning."

"Okay, Top, what have we got?" Sean said, stuffing the letter in his pocket.

"Next month's R&R orders gotta be reviewed and processed. We have four to five flights going out most days, about six thousand Marines a month getting seven days, plus travel time, to garden spots in the Pacific." The crusty sergeant grinned. "Married types generally go to Hawaii to hook up with wives. Bachelors hit Bangkok, Hong Kong, Manila, KL, or Sydney—every last one of them looking to get laid! Don't want to screw that up, do we, Lieutenant?"

"I thought that paperwork and quota-assignment processing was done at battalion level. Why the hell do we get involved at division?"

"We gotta coordinate, sir, especially the no-shows," the master sergeant replied. "Location quotas are made three to four months in advance. Flight and seat assignments are made sixty days in advance. Everything is set—that is, if a guy doesn't wind up KIA or WIA in the meantime. Then we wind up with unfilled quotas and empty seats. Try to stay on top of that. It's a bitch." He shuffled a pile of paper in frustration. "We lose about 10 percent, sometimes 15 percent, of the original quota assignees on any given flight. If we stay on top of the situation and backfill properly, we generally see that most flights are fully booked."

Patterson picked up a multipage listing and tossed it to Sean. "Here's the names, ranks, and serial numbers of everybody assigned to go to Hawaii for the next two months. Every week we review casualty reports to flag KIAs and medically evacuated WIAs, then work with the units on reassignments. It's important the names are removed from the final personnel manifest we provide the R&R center just before departure."

Sean leafed through the pages. Several names had been lined out in red. On the draft manifest for a flight departing for Hawaii on January 22, 1968, one redlined name caught his eye:

Slattery, Michael, 2nd Lt., 0100488, 2nd Bn., Fifth Marines … KIA.

★   ★   ★

Early that evening, after much thought about the role played by his section in the R&R process, Sean returned to the privacy of the now-empty office, sat behind an old Olivetti typewriter, and composed a letter.

20 November 1967

Dear Sal,

Thanks for your letter. I know it must be difficult for you to chronicle what's going on. I find it tough to read, but I guess it has to be done. I do want to know what's happening. It helps. I'm coming to realize I'm not the only one who lost Sandy. I'm really concerned about her parents. I haven't written them yet. I haven't answered any of my mail in the last couple of weeks. I'll get to it soon enough. I don't know what I'll say to Rosa and my mom. Maybe you can tell them I'm okay and safe as a rear-echelon paper-shuffler. Might put their minds at ease.

You mentioned a suspect, a guy named Delfano. Never heard of him, but if Nap has a feeling, I want to meet him. If he's the one who killed Sandy—I want him.

I think I'll be able to make a trip back to the States in late January. If I do, I'll make a side trip and spend at least three days in Brooklyn. Please don't tell anyone except Frankie. Not even the Marines will know about this. What I need from you and Frankie is to confirm Delfano is the one. If he is, then I want you to set him up for me.

We have about two months to figure it out. I know I am asking a lot, but it's all about Sandy. I'll write soon.

Sean

Chapter 29

Frankie Ryan sat alone in the rear of the bar. He'd received word from Frank Cercone that the cops were coming up empty on finding Sandy's killer. Jimmy Nap still believed Delfano a prime suspect but had little to prove it. Delfano's story—backed by his father, a sitting federal judge—that he was home all evening was holding. It was likely the leader of the Brooklyn College antiwar movement would not be charged in the murder of the social worker from Gravesend.

"Looks like more snow. Man, it's cold out there," Sal said, joining Frankie in the dimly lit lounge.

"Never mind the snow. Did you find anything on college guy?"

"Yeah, lots. It seems that Delfano—"

Frankie raised his hand. "Hold it. Don't use his name."

"Okay, okay," Sal continued. "Seems college guy is into weed big time. Just as you thought, he gets his stuff out of Coney Island. His source is a small-time pusher named Rocco the Rabbit, part of Joe-Joe Spike's mob. Got permission from Spike to talk with the Rabbit. Used your name and Spike was very accommodating." Sal lowered his head and whispered, "Caught up with Rocco yesterday. He told me college guy is one of his biggest customers, maybe four hundred dollars, sometimes five hundred dollars a week. He's probably reselling down in Brighton, maybe on the Brooklyn campus. Haven't had time to check it out." He hesitated. "Think we should pass this on to Jimmy Nap?"

Frankie smiled. "So, college guy gets a drop once a week. Where?"

"When I asked Rocco that very question, he clammed up. Said it was privileged information."

"I know fuckin' Rocco," Frankie snarled. "He's been a pothead and small-time pusher since high school. I'll give that little prick some privileged information. Let's go down to Coney Island and grab some knishes at Nathan's. Then let's stop in and visit that asshole. Think he lives in Trump Village, behind Lincoln."

Rocco the Rabbit was home alone when Frankie and Sal knocked on the door of apartment 18C. They entered the one-bedroom sparsely furnished co-op, ostensibly to negotiate a purchase. Once inside, Frankie smacked the skinny pothead, sending him tumbling across the tile floor. He picked the dazed Rocco off the floor, forcing him out onto a terrace that fronted each apartment. Sal held him against the four-foot steel guard railing, and Frankie pushed his head over the side. "Wanna ask you a few questions, Rabbit. And I want straight answers." With a quick heaving motion, they had Rocco half over the railing, each man clutching a leg, hanging the terrified pusher's upper torso eighteen stories above the ground.

Back in the apartment, Frankie addressed the ghost-white, trembling drug pusher. "Okay, Rocco, that was wise of you to let us know your drop-off schedule. Now here's the deal. When you meet Delfano next week, I'm coming along. You'll introduce me as a temporary contact. I'll be taking your place for a few weeks while you are down in Florida on vacation. Oh, by the way, I'll need three weeks' worth of good stuff to feed this guy while you're away."

Rocco blubbered about not being able to afford to go to Florida. Frankie motioned to Sal, who walked across the room and slowly opened the door to the terrace.

Rocco's eyes widened in terror. "I'll do it. I'll go to Florida. I'll stay a month—whatever you say."

★ ★ ★

"Think you can pull this off and get close to our college guy?" Sal asked, driving his Chevy Nova under the elevated Brighton Line subway station onto Ocean Parkway.

Frankie fidgeted with his ponytail. "We'll find out next week. I'll pay a call on Joe Spikes and get this all cleared. I'm sure it's gonna cost me. The big thing is that I get to work three or four drops with college guy. Wanna get him talking to me in confidence. Wanna make sure he is the one before I set him up for Sean."

"I gotta tell you, Frankie, I'm not good with this. Sean is over his head wanting to whack this guy. That's a murder rap. Not sure he's thinking straight. If we do our part, that means we can be in some serious shit—like accessories to murder." Sal raised his eyebrows and flashed an anguished look. "If we find out college guy is the one who killed Sandy, let's just go to the older guys. I'm sure we can get him hit for nothing. And how the hell is Sean going to be back here for three days next month without the Marines or anybody else knowing?"

"Hell if I know how," Frankie said. "If Sean says he's gonna be here, he'll be here. Our job is to set things up. Far as what he's gonna do, that's up to him. You read the last letter. Guess he's done some killing. Maybe he feels he's got a right to do this. I'm not judging him." Frankie grunted. "Matter of fact, I think he's got the right. Far as our involvement, I'm working on that. We're not gonna be around. We're goin' dancing. Maybe roust some spics."

"Hope you're right, Frankie." Sal made a left off the parkway onto Avenue T. He nodded when they passed Sandy's house on the way to the bar. "Wonder how the Golds are doing. They seemed out of it at the funeral."

"What did ya expect?" Frankie said. "Suppose it was your daughter. What we're doing, we're doing for Sam and Juliana. They didn't deserve this. Maybe we can give them some justice, maybe some closure. That's something you might want to think about, case ya have any second thoughts or moral qualms about what we're doing."

As they approached McDonald Avenue, Sal replied over the roar of the passing F train, "Let's get it done and let's do it right."

Chapter 30

DA NANG
CHRISTMAS EVE

Sean decided to make a recon of the R&R center on the north end of the Marine airbase just outside of Da Nang. He spent several hours in the huge, warehouse-like hanger that served as the processing point for incoming and outgoing R&R flights. He wanted to make sure of the procedures, especially how each Marine identified himself before boarding.

He found the process simple. Officers and staff noncommissioned officers had their own line. They queued up behind a table for their destinations and presented their orders. A single clerk behind each desk checked off the name against the flight manifest and handed out a boarding card with a seat number. That was it. There was no identification check, because, except for dog tags, few Marines carried any form of official identification.

Back at his office, Sean drafted a set of orders made out to Lieutenant Michael Slattery for an R&R flight to Hawaii on January 22. He placed them in his desk drawer on top of another set of orders that had been issued to Lieutenant Sean Cercone for an R&R flight to Bangkok leaving that same day.

He would be traveling east across the international dateline to Hawaii, landing early in the morning the day he left. With luck, he could catch a midmorning flight to San Francisco with a connection to New York late that afternoon, allowing himself three days and three nights in Brooklyn before reversing his course. He would have at least one day to spare in Hawaii before catching his flight back to Vietnam on January 30.

Sean had already sent Frankie nine hundred dollars to purchase round-trip tickets from Hawaii to JFK under the name of Peter Ambrose. The name matched a false ID, complete with a college picture of Sean that he had acquired a few years back in order to barhop at the Jersey Shore prior to his twenty-first birthday.

After working on the plan for his clandestine trip to the States, Sean stopped by the O Club. He was surprised to find only a handful of occupants. "Hey, Mai Lin, where's everybody? You chase them all away?"

The shapely Vietnamese barmaid smiled, revealing a slight space between her front teeth. "They at church for round-eye baby's birthday. Your friend, that priest major, looking for you to go church. Don't know where he now."

"Probably looking for an altar boy to help with the service." Sean snickered, realizing he had forgotten it was Christmas Eve. "Glad I wasn't around, Mai. How about a double scotch for the round-eye baby's birthday?"

By the time Mai Lin brought Sean's drink, the club had begun filling up with the recent churchgoers. Most of the bamboo-topped tables were quickly occupied, and someone started playing Christmas carols on a harmonica.

Chaplain Flynn appeared, carrying two drinks. He sat down and pushed a drink to Sean. "Merry Christmas, Sean. It's a beautiful night—look at those stars."

"Merry Christmas to you, Padre." Sean raised his glass. "Yeah, it's a beautiful night, except for Third Recon. Message-traffic reports they lost an eight-man patrol twenty clicks west of Phu Bai."

"The war is certainly terrible, Sean, but the birth of Christ gives us all hope."

Sean took a deep breath. "I haven't had a real good year, Padre, but I actually buy that. Maybe it's my crazy faith, courtesy of my Irish mother, but I do believe in Jesus and his message of peace and hope. Problem is those Buddhist bastards aren't on the same page. So things can get kind of complicated for those of us in the peace-on-earth crowd."

Flynn frowned. "As usual, Sean, you have a way with words. But there've been many dark Christmas Eves. Think about Bastogne in Europe; go way back to Washington and his men freezing at Morristown.

Not all Christmas Eves are merry, Sean. But all Christmas Eves give hope." Flynn paused, raising his glass. "Here's to you, Sean. May God help you find peace and hope."

"Thanks, Padre. I'd welcome some peace in my life. Know for sure I'll need some hope for what I'll be doing in the New Year."

Chapter 31

The D'Angelos' Christmas party was less upbeat than previous years. Frankie sat down to join the group: Joe Senior and his wife, their son Joey, Grandma Rosa, Sal Lente, Ann, her brother-in-law Frank, and several neighbors. The food was the same as always, with wonderful aromas of spicy sauces and cheeses filling the room. But the conversation was stilted. Laughter was rare and muted.

The tone for the gathering was set by the old woman from Palermo sitting at the head of the table. Off to her right was an empty chair. At Rosa's insistence, the unoccupied chair was to remind everyone people were missing. The old lady sat stoically, dressed entirely in black except for an out-of-place multicolored summer bracelet, a birthday gift from Sandy.

Frankie understood Rosa's thinking. *Sandy recently murdered, Sean in Vietnam. Christmas or not, these aren't happy times.* He tried addressing part of the problem. "Mrs. C, great to hear Sean was transferred to a rear echelon unit. Said his location is safer than walking down Avenue U. You gotta be happy about that Christmas news."

"I won't be happy till Sean and all those boys are home from that war," Ann replied, her voice cracking.

Nodding, Rosa raised her frail hands. "It's not a time for much happiness. Remember we lost a young woman who sat with us at this very table. Don't know why God let that happen, but I'm sure he can figure out why we're not so happy on his son's birthday."

Rosa's almost blasphemous remarks cast a pall over the group.

Frankie fidgeted with his ponytail and broke the silence. "But Rosa, with respect, bad things happen even around Christmas. Look at the first Christmas. Remember that sick madman, Herod. Wanted to get Jesus, so he killed all those innocent babies. That's why we have the Feast of the Holy Innocents."

Rosa nodded, and Frankie continued, "Maybe God wanted us to remember that bad things can happen, even when his own son came into the world. Christmas doesn't mean all the mad men will go away. It means, least I think it means, there's hope for better times. Guess because of that hope, we should be happy."

Rosa smiled faintly. "For a washed-up altar boy, that's pretty good, Brain. Maybe we should call you Father Frankie." Her face tightened, her dark eyes opened, and her shoulders bent back. "You're right, Frankie. On this day, we should be happy, even if we carry a stone in our hearts. It's just that I loved Sandy so, like my own daughter. She was so lovely to me, and now she is gone. Murdered! Taken away!" Lowering her gray head into her hands, she leaned her face down on the table and began sobbing.

Frankie and Joey moved quickly to lift Rosa gently from the table, guiding her toward the basement stairs leading to the first floor.

Arm-in-arm with the two young men, Rosa stopped and turned back to the table. "I'm tired. I'm too old to be happy tonight. It's up to me to grieve. It's up to you to celebrate, enjoy Christmas. Frankie's right. Eat, drink, and thank God for his son. Buon Natale."

The D'Angelos' first-floor living room was small. Along one wall was a light-green Italian provincial-style couch encased in clear plastic flanked by two pole lamps with dark pleated shades. Along the opposite wall, a single gray, pillowed, oversized chair, also encased in clear plastic, faced a Motorola TV, its screen protruding from a dark wooden cabinet.

Frankie made Rosa comfortable in the chair. Joey left, returning in a few moments with a stemmed glass filled with grappa. "This will make you feel better, Grandma."

Sipping the dark liqueur, Rosa eyed her grandson. "Come here and give your grandma, who loves you so, a kiss. Then go down and tell your mother to make me some coffee with a little anisette. Small piece of cannoli would be nice too."

Joey left to do Rosa's bidding.

She turned to Frankie, whispering in a stern tone, "Tell me what's being done about the one who killed Sandy."

Frankie pushed his hand through his wavy hair and tugged on his ponytail. "Well, Grandma, the cops don't have much, but Jimmy Napoli says—"

"I don't want to know about the cops or what that Jimmy Nap thinks. I want to know about what you're doing."

Frankie looked into her dark eyes, which glared as if they belonged on the face of a scorned woman. *She's gonna press me till I tell her something.*

"Known you since you were a little boy. I know that look. You're up to something, Frankie."

He lowered his head and then raised it slowly to meet Rosa's eyes. "Justice will be done soon. Very soon, Rosa. That's all I can say."

"That's good, Frankie. That's all I wanna hear. I pray to Jesus every night that the one who did this is made to pay, that justice gets done. I'll never have peace until it's done. Make that one pay, Frankie! Get him good—blood for blood!"

"It'll be done, Rosa. But I'm not sure Jesus would approve."

The old woman stiffened and gave her catlike smile. "He probably won't. Jesus wasn't Sicilian. I'll pray to him anyway, ask him not to interfere."

Chapter 32

SEA BEACH SUBWAY STATION
GRAVESEND, BROOKLYN
MID-JANUARY 1968

Frankie passed through the street-level entrance of the subway station and spotted Sal huddling against the far wall. The damp, fortresslike, gray brick station afforded complete privacy, which was lacking in the Wrong Number Lounge only a few doors away.

"How's it going?" Sal said, rubbing his hands against the cold.

"Going good." Frankie pulled up the collar of his black leather jacket. "Getting him to trust me. Met with him three times now. He's starting to open up. A smart prick though, keeps changing the drop-off points and meeting times. One good thing—got him to agree to have the Manhattan Beach parking lot as an emergency drop. That's the place I want to set him up."

"What about Sandy? Did he say anything?"

"Tested him a little," Frankie said with a half-smile. "Mentioned I'd seen his name in the paper as someone the cops questioned. He got all uptight, said it was all a misunderstanding. Told him I know a guy who goes to Brooklyn College who knew the Gold broad. Said she was a bitch who couldn't keep her mouth shut. I told him she probably got what she deserved."

"Did he buy your attitude?"

"Don't know. I didn't press. Just dropped the subject." Frankie raised his hand and clenched his fist. "Tonight, I'm gonna squeeze him, plan to get him uptight. Gonna show up with no stuff and tell him we'll be getting some high-grade stuff next week."

Sal grimaced. "Better move him along fast. We only have two weeks before Sean arrives. Got the motel room reserved for three nights, like he asked. I hope he knows what he's doing. Hope we know what we're doing."

★   ★   ★

A few days had passed since Frankie met Delfano without any pot. He drove his red Bonneville onto a narrow side street off Brighton Beach Avenue, parking in front of a four-story prewar apartment building. Before he could turn off the ignition, Delfano rushed out of a doorway, pulled open the door, and jumped into the front seat.

"Hey, you're getting pretty good at that," Frankie said, turning onto Brighton Beach Avenue under the elevated train line. The roar of a Coney Island–bound train prevented any conversation.

Once the screeching elevated train had passed, Delfano spoke in a nervous, almost pleading tone. "You got the stuff? How much ya have?"

Frankie glanced in his rearview mirror and moaned. "Oh shit, it's them again."

"What? Who is it? We being followed?"

"We're 'bout to find out." Frankie made a sharp left onto Surf Avenue, a major thoroughfare that ran the length of Coney Island. "Okay, it's okay—they didn't follow. Damned cops from the Six Two in one of their unmarked cars. Assholes haven't changed the car in years." Frankie let out a sigh. "Them and their friends from downtown been all over the neighborhood for the last two weeks. Word has it they got some new leads on that broad's murder. That's why we can't pass any stuff."

"What leads? What do you mean, can't pass any stuff? What the hell's going on?" Jay screamed. "This is the second time this month. I need that stuff. My people need it."

His uptight passenger was a lot more dependent on the weed than Frankie had suspected. "Shut the fuck up and I'll explain!" Frankie shouted. "Couldn't bring anything today. We got a double shipment in, good stuff. Saw it myself. Too risky to move today. Cops are pulling cars over, rousting everybody. My Bonneville is a little too well-known. Couldn't take the chance. I'll get it to you next Tuesday night. We'll do the drop in the Manhattan Beach site, and I'll use different wheels. Might have to use one of my guys. If I do, he'll use the normal hand signals."

Delfano slumped in the seat. "I need that stuff, Frankie."

"You'll get it," Frankie said. Casually, he added, "They say the cops got some partial prints or something. You didn't touch that loudmouth broad—you know, when you were at that party you told me about? They think the guy grabbed her hair, smashed her head on the wall; maybe he left some prints."

Jay stiffened. "I didn't touch her at the party. I didn't—"

"Look, I don't give a shit. Maybe you did, maybe you didn't. Just gotta know the story, case we ever get picked up together."

"Picked up? What do ya mean, picked up?"

Frankie responded in a staccato cadence. "Hey, say you're a suspect and I'm with you. You don't think the cops are gonna grill me if we ever get busted together? Taking a big chance working with you. Don't care what you did. Just gotta know your story will hold, or I might find myself as an accessory." Pounding the wheel, Frankie screamed at Delfano. "Did you grab her hair? What the fuck did ya do? If you did the hair, we're okay!"

"I just grabbed her hair when she went for me. Swung her around, never touched anything," Delfano blurted. He grew quiet. "I didn't mean to—"

"Don't worry about it. It's done." Frankie continued in a calm, melodic voice, "Let me drop you off at Stillwell Avenue. You catch a train to the Bay. Don't worry about it. I'll get you the stuff. Plan on Tuesday night, Manhattan Beach lot, about ten. I'll call."

After dropping off a very uptight Jay Delfano, Frankie continued driving on Stillwell Avenue out of Coney Island back to Gravesend. An image of Delfano smashing Sandy into a brick wall flashed in his mind. His jaw tightened. *Jay Delfano murdered Sandy. That bastard. We'll kill him. Rosa was right—blood for blood.*

Chapter 33

DA NANG R&R CENTER
MID-JANUARY 1968

Sean left the division dining hall on Hill 327 and heard the teasing voice of Top Patterson. "Hey, Lieutenant, make sure you don't bring back anything from Bangkok. Watch where you dip your wick, sir!"

Sean waved back, pushed through the screen door, and jumped into a waiting jeep. Arriving at the processing center two hours before his R&R flight, he sauntered across the wide concrete floor toward a bored-looking sergeant standing behind a desk for the morning R&R flight to Bangkok.

"Morning, Sergeant. Got a revised manifest from the G1 for your flight to Bangkok. Two names deleted. Should make a couple of wait-list guys happy. I'll need the old manifest for the G1 records."

"Thanks, Lieutenant. That'll be fine." The sergeant exchanged manifests, never noticing one of the deleted names was Lieutenant Sean Cercone. "Won't have any trouble getting two more bodies on this flight."

An hour later, Sean appeared before another sergeant behind a desk marked Hawaii. Smiling behind his aviator sunglasses, Sean handed his orders to the sergeant, who glanced at the paper, stamped an endorsement, removed a copy, and returned the original along with a boarding card. "Have a good R&R, Lieutenant Slattery."

"Will do. Thanks." Sean nodded. He passed into a room filled with Marines anxiously waiting for the flight that would deposit them on Oahu. He had studied the names on the manifest and was reasonably certain he didn't know any Marines on the flight. A glance around the room confirmed his good luck.

★   ★   ★

Awakened from a restless sleep by the clamoring of those on the port side sighting their destination, Sean stretched as the medium-body jet descended slowly over the Hawaiian Islands. During the ten-hour flight, he had reflected over the past several months, remembering young men laughing, cursing, crying; black canvas body bags; the smell of burning flesh and bloated bodies. He recalled long, boring days punctuated by minutes, sometime hours, of terror. Faces of Marines flashed in his mind: Captain Lee, Sergeant Boomer, Sergeant Murphy, Hollywood Olsen, Private Alan, and his close friend Mike Slattery—all gone. Images of Sandy came often, pushing all else away. The pain and the constant emptiness stoked his rage. He hardly felt the plane touching down to the cheers of the Marines on board.

"Have a great R&R, Marines," the captain announced as the he guided the lumbering jet toward the off-ramp. Sean walked through the brightly decorated corridor and smiled at a trio of Hawaiian girls in native garb offering flower leis. All around him, Marines dashed into the arms of young women, many in their late teens, who had traveled from all over the States to rendezvous with their warrior husbands for seven days and six nights.

Val and John would have fit perfectly into this scene, had he not been cut to pieces in the Que Son Valley. They should be here, not me.

★   ★   ★

In a men's room stall at the far corner of the terminal, Sean changed from his service uniform into brown khaki pants, a blue button-down shirt, and a light golf jacket, all purchased a few days before in the Da Nang PX. The clothes were wrinkled after being in his pack for almost two days. His shirt carried a slight odor of cleaning oil, having been packed next to a disassembled, recently cleaned .45-caliber pistol. He carefully repacked the weapon in a green towel along with two fully loaded magazine clips, stuffing all in the bottom of his Valpak.

Minutes later, Sean stood in front of the United Airlines ticket counter.

"Hi. Where we off to today?" a smiling ground agent of Hawaiian descent asked.

Placing his ticket and fake driver's license on the counter, Sean replied, "Frisco, with a connecting flight to New York—JFK."

"San Francisco. Yes, here it is, Mr. Ambrose. UA746, leaving today at ten thirty, arriving SFO for transfer to UA917 to JFK. You'll arrive at JFK early morning on the twenty-fourth. Let's see ... you're returning—boy, that's a quick trip—next Friday, the twenty-eighth."

Sean nodded. "Yeah, quick trip to see my folks."

He spent the next hours in the remotest section of the lounge, using a newspaper to shield himself from view. He smiled. The paper he had found was a week-old *LA Times*. His smile faded when he read the bold headline:

McCarthy Calls War Morally Indefensible in UCLA Speech

Eight thousand cheering UCLA students—a larger audience than turned out to hear Adam Clayton Powell earlier in the week—heard Minnesota Democratic Senator Eugene McCarthy describe the Vietnam War as morally and realistically indefensible. McCarthy criticized as inexcusable the indictment of Dr. Benjamin Spock for counseling evasion of the draft. McCarthy went on to state the war in Vietnam lacked the historical qualifications to be an American policy. "There is no traditionally American policy that gives justification to using military strength against backward people or against primitive people in any part of the world," McCarthy said.

What an ass. Wonder what the good senator thought about the morality of Korea. It cost of over thirty-five thousand American lives, kept South Korea from Communist takeover. He gripes about military force against backward, primitive people. How does he think our country was settled? Dumb shit should ask a few American Indians.

He tossed the paper. *Hate the war too, Senator. 'Cause in the end, a lot of guys are gonna die, lots more busted up for life.* He wasn't sure if the county cared.

Sean boarded UA746 bound for San Francisco and arrived on the west coast late that afternoon with a three-hour layover before his night flight to JFK. He passed the time sitting in the crowded terminal thinking about Sandy. He pulled out a letter from his wallet, a letter he'd read many times.

Twenty hours after leaving Da Nang, he boarded the sparsely filled UA917, lapsing into an exhausted sleep minutes after takeoff. Six hours later, awakened by a flight attendant, he looked out at the bright sun rising over Jamaica Bay as the plane made its landing at JFK.

Chapter 34

The taxi made the run from JFK to the Golden Gate Motor Inn just off the Knapp Street exit of the Belt Parkway in twenty minutes. Clad in his light golf jacket, Sean shivered in the early-morning cold and ran from the cab into the worn-looking two-story motel. Walking slowly across the garish lobby with its brass furniture and matted, deep purple rug, he approached the desk clerk. "Name is Ambrose, Tom Ambrose. Got a reservation for three nights."

"Mr. Ambrose—yeah, you're the guy up from Florida for your folks' anniversary. I was here when your cousin booked the room. Don't get many prepays for three nights during the week," the clerk said, adding with smile, "Get lots of one-nighters. Lots of actions by the hour. Know what I mean."

"That's good to know. Not looking for anything by the hour. I'm tired. Just want to get to my room."

★   ★   ★

Sean threw his pack on the bed, plopped down on the small sofa peppered with stains, and surveyed the shabby room. He shook his head, noting the graffiti-filled wall on the building behind the motel that formed the view from the room's only window. He was tired—very tired. He resisted the urge to close his eyes and instead reached for his wallet and the letter, Sandy's last.

October 31, 1967

Dearest Sean,

Miss you desperately. I'm keeping busy, spending lots of time with Rosa. Never had a grandmother, but I've got one now. She's wonderful, and one smart woman. She told me all about you. Not all good, I'm afraid.

I finally got to meet your friend Beth this week. Guess what? She's going to be working a few blocks from our settlement house. Never met a stronger, more focused woman. We'll be meeting again when Beth gets back from DC in a few weeks. We have a lot in common. I think we'll be good friends.

After working in the settlement house for the last few months and meeting someone like Beth, I now realize what I want to do with my life. Teaching is fine down the road, but for now I want to be involved in social work. I want to work right here in Bed-Stuy. I know I can have an impact. Maybe it's only a couple of girls at a time, but I know I can do it and do it well. Mom and Dad can't really understand. They keep carping about the dangerous neighborhood. I hope you can understand—you're working in a tough place yourself. The only other thing I want in my life is you. Hopefully, that part of my life will be complete next June. Please be careful. I love you.

Sandy

PS: Should have some fun tonight. Going to my tennis team's Halloween party over in Manhattan Beach. It should be a blast.

Sean's hand trembled as he vowed, *I'll get him, Sandy. He stole your life. I'll make him pay.*

★   ★   ★

"Good to see ya, Marine," Frankie said, hugging Sean as he entered the small, boxlike motel room.

"You look great, Sean. Man, you dropped some weight," Sal said. *Jesus, he looks different. Got that tired, faraway look in his eyes. Guess that's the war.*

"Yeah, well, guess it's my lifestyle." Sean laughed. "You guys took the back stairs, I hope. That front-desk guy seems weird."

"Yeah, came up the back stairs," Sal said, placing a brown paper bag on the only table in the room. "Meatball heroes from Joe's, the Sicilian place on Avenue U. Nothing but the best for our guys in uniform."

"God, can't believe how good this smells." Sean tore open the bag.

After a few bites, Sal wiped sauce from his chin with a paper napkin, placing his hero on the nightstand. "Sean, everybody is really sorry about Sandy. It was terrible. I don't know what to say." Face contorted, eyes welling, Sal looked at his boyhood friend and fell speechless.

"Real sorry too, Sean," Frankie said, staring at the floor.

Sean put his sandwich on the top of the bag. "She was all I could ever want—beautiful, gentle, and full of life. She cared about everybody. I think of her every day, every night. Can't get her out of my mind." His face hardened. "I just want to kill that fuck Delfano. That's why I'm here! I want him. I want him dead."

Frankie held up his hands. "Whoa, Sean, take it easy. That why we're here."

"He should be hit, Sean, no doubt about that, especially since he'll probably never be charged," Sal pleaded, "but you don't have to do it! Why risk it? It would be easy to—"

"Forget it, Sal. I have to do this. I want to do this. What the fuck, been killing for a while now. I don't like it. Hate it. But it's all legal, even moral, 'cause it's a war." He motioned as if pleading to a moot court jury. "Guess I have a right to kill. So now I'm declaring war on Jay Delfano. That'll give me a right to kill him. Got more right to kill him than those poor bastards over there."

The three men ate in silence. Sal had known Sean would be upset. It was clear from his letters that Sandy's murder had consumed him. But he hadn't been prepared for Sean's intensity and focus to the exclusion of all else. Sean didn't even ask about his mother, Rosa, or anyone.

Sean finally spoke. "Let's see the map of that parking lot, Frankie. I know the place but haven't been there in years. I'll want to be there before he gets there. Whose car am I gonna use?"

"Sal will leave his car in this lot tomorrow. Take a run over there tomorrow night, give the place a look," Frankie said. "Get familiar with the place at night. Figure out how you're gonna drive in and out of that neighborhood. Don't come back here after the hit. Make sure you get rid of the piece. Get on the parkway as soon as possible. You're going out of JFK on Thursday morning, right?"

Sean nodded. "Have a flight out at eight o'clock for San Francisco. Why don't I leave Sal's car at Bernie's Diner? I'll grab a cab for the airport and just wait for my flight."

Frankie shook his head. "No good! You want out of this area as soon as possible. Don't want to be lurking around a terminal all night either. Go out to JFK right away, get a motel room. Pay cash. Use your fake ID. Get up and go the next morning. Just call Sal and let him know where you parked the car."

Sal Lente sat in silence and watched his two friends cover details as if they were discussing a football game plan. Sean was leaner, his face more taut than Sal remembered. His eyes seemed different, darker and more focused yet somehow tired. Sean didn't smile either; his devilish grin was gone. He sounded the same, but his speech was rapid and commanding. Months of war had physically changed him. Now, with the trauma of Sandy's loss, Sal wondered what else had changed in Sean as he listened to him calmly plan to murder Jay Delfano.

★   ★   ★

Wednesday night, Sean waited in Sal's Chevy Nova at the far end of the deserted Manhattan Beach parking lot. Bushes and trees ran across the front of the lot and masked the car from the street. Had it not been a bitterly cold weeknight, some young lovers might have been parked in the same spot.

The lot wasn't large. It held a few hundred cars in four rows separated by three lanes. The entrance led to a double lane intersecting the parking spots, cutting the place in half. Opposite the street side, a narrow cement walk separated the parking area from the beach. Both sides of the lot were flanked by large homes; none showed any activity.

Sean put on thin leather gloves, jammed the clip into his .45-caliber pistol, chambered a round, and flipped the safety catch. Ironic that while he carried the .45 at all times, he'd never fired the weapon in combat, instead using an M-16 rifle whenever a firefight arose. He placed the weapon in his jacket pocket. Next to him was a brown paper grocery bag, neatly folded to allow half the bag to be filled with several packets of high-grade cannabis.

His body tensed the same way it had whenever he set his Marines in a nighttime ambush. A car moved, slowing, through the entrance of the lot. Sean turned on his lights, blinking them twice. The car hesitated and then inched forward, turning down the middle lane toward him. The car pulled into a space two car lanes away, the driver looking over. Sean waved twice over the driver-side window and watched for the prearranged return wave from the driver.

Heart pounding, Sean grabbed the paper bag, opened his door, and jogged toward the car. One hand in his pocket clutching the .45, the other holding the bag, he stopped a foot from the driver's door and stood motionless. The faceless figure peered out. The window slid down a few inches. "Is that all the stuff? I said, is that all the stuff?"

Sean took his hand from his jacket and pointed to his ear, as if he had trouble hearing.

Delfano lowered the window almost all the way and shouted, "Is that all of it? Is that—"

Sean pointed the .45 at Delfano's face. He slowly lowered the weapon, pointing it at Delfano's lap, and tossed the bag into the car.

Delfano froze, eyes wide in a look of absolute terror. "No, no! Please no!"

Sean tightly gripped the .45 with both hands and squeezed off six shots, fighting the weapon's recall after each ear-piercing crack.

The gun's roar, the animallike screams, and the blood splashing from Delfano's body like crimson star clusters in a fireworks show startled Sean. He ran back to his car, where he fumbled with the keys but managed to open his door. He drove out of the lot toward Sheepshead Bay, cautiously coming to a complete stop at each of four intersections before parking along the street that ran parallel to the seawall of the bay. Hands trembling, he disassembled the .45, placing the pieces in his jacket pocket. He left his car and walked along the waist-high concrete embankment that edged Sheepshead Bay. Every few feet, he tossed a piece of the weapon into the bay, constantly looking about to see if anyone was in the area.

He drove around the bay, making a right turn onto Emmons Avenue. Despite the hour, the avenue was alive with people moving in and out of restaurants and bars. His hands gripped the wheel, heart pounding, head throbbing, and mouth cotton-ball dry. Stopping for the light at Ocean Avenue, he heard sirens wail. A cop car passed, racing to the other side of the bay. Turning to watch a second cop car speed by, he noticed two well-dressed men coming out of Lundy's clam bar, one of them staring in his direction.

Shit. Sandy's brother. He looked away—quickly enough, he hoped—before Assistant District Attorney Robert Gold could fully register his face.

Chapter 35

After receiving a call just after midnight from the duty officer at Brooklyn South, Napoli arrived at the Manhattan Beach parking lot at 1:00 a.m. Jay Delfano's remains were still in the blood-drenched front seat of his blue sixty-seven Impala. NYPD crime scene people milled about. Napoli called the mayor's office and then dispatched one of his lieutenants to inform Judge Delfano and his wife that their son, Jay, had been found shot to death in his car four blocks from their home. No mention to be made of the bag of high-grade weed.

Detective Max Kline stamped his feet to ward off the damp cold. "Wasn't a pro hit, that's for sure. Doesn't look like an amateur either. We're not certain, but we've got some spent casings. Look like military-issue .45 caliber. Badass thing to kill with." He grimaced. "Somebody wanted this guy in a lot of pain. Six rounds—looks like three rounds in the lower stomach, one in the genitals, one in the upper thigh, and one missed. Coulda been a drug thing; the bag was definitely packaged for sale. Just doesn't look right."

Napoli shook his head. "Max, don't you remember? The deceased was a person of interest—real interest—in the murder of that Gold girl back in November."

"Yeah, but he had a tight alibi courtesy of his dad, the judge," Max said, cleaning his glasses. "Funny thing, just last week I was talking with my friend Abe Paser. You remember Abe, the guy who owns the luncheonette where the college kids hang out. Visited him just after the

Gold murder. Turned out he's a pretty good friend of Sandra Gold's old man. Every time I see him, he wants to know about how we're doing on the case." Kline pulled off his gloves. "Delfano's name came up. Abe said Delfano hangs out in his joint. Gave me a spiel about how he could never be involved with the Gold girl's murder. But did say he thought Delfano was acting strange lately, palling around with a guy Abe had never seen before."

Later that morning, Kline and Napoli sat at a counter in Abe's Brighton Beach luncheonette waiting for the old man to finish making two egg creams. The place was really an expanded candy store, with pretzels, bagels, and tuna sandwiches the main fare. Several booths and a few tables made it a popular spot for college kids, especially on cold nights.

"Strange looking guy, Max. What's the story with those scars on his head?" Napoli asked.

Before Kline could reply, Abe presented the detectives with the white-foamed chocolate drinks. "And vat can I do for New York finest?" He grinned, running a rag over the counter.

Without mentioning the killing, Kline probed his old friend about Delfano. Napoli said nothing, just sipped his egg cream and studied Abe.

"Jay's in here couple of time a veek. Just saw him a few days ago. Him and his new friend. Sat right over there in the corner booth."

"New friend—what did he look like, Abe?" Kline asked.

"Only seen him a couple of times. Tall, handsome guy," Abe said, laughing, "He vears his hair tied in the back like an Indian. You know, in one of those ponytails."

"This guy thin, about six-one with black hair?" Napoli snapped, easing off his stool.

"Yes, yes, zat's him," Abe replied.

Napoli nodded with a slight smile. *Now I'm gonna get that bastard.* Within the hour, Napoli had dispatched detectives to locate and pick up Francis Xavier Ryan.

★   ★   ★

Two days later, Napoli met at police headquarters with Commissioner Tim Murphy and several young lawyers from the district attorney's office. He sat at a long conference table in the well-appointed room with large windows overlooking the Brooklyn Bridge. He slumped, staring in disbelief at the report he had received minutes before.

"Shit! Seems Frankie Ryan, his friend Sal Lente, and two others were, of all places, in our custody Wednesday night! Apparently there was an altercation between Ryan's little group and some gentlemen from Puerto Rico during a Latin dance night at the Taft hotel. They were all arrested and taken to night court at approximately 9:00 p.m., appeared before the judge at twelve thirty, and were released at 2:00 a.m."

"I think that's what you call a locked alibi," the commissioner barked. "Better start looking someplace else, Jimmy. His honor, the judge, has already called the mayor wanting to know what we're doing to find the killer of his son."

As the meeting ended, Assistant District Attorney Robert Gold, Sandy's brother, approached Napoli. He had been in regular contact with Napoli since his sister's murder. "Jimmy, think this Delfano killing has anything to do with Sandy's murder?"

"Truth be told, Counselor, Delfano was my prime unofficial suspect in Sandy's death."

"I take it you thought those guys you mentioned to the chief may have been involved in the hit on Delfano. Who are they?"

"Neighborhood guys, real close friends of your sister's boyfriend, Sean Cercone," Napoli replied. "If they thought Delfano was the one responsible for Sandy's murder, I've no doubt they could be involved in his demise. Unfortunately, it appears they have a locked alibi."

Gold's eyes widened. "Sean Cercone! Of course, that's who he looked like—Sean."

"Who you talking about?"

"I was leaving Lundy's clam bar the other night. Caught a look at a guy stopped at a light maybe thirty feet away. Was sure I knew him, just couldn't place him," Gold said. "Now that I think about it, he could have been a double of Sean. I met Sean a couple of times at St. John's and once, very briefly, at my parents' house. He's still in Vietnam, isn't he?"

"Far as I know," Napoli said. "What time ya see this guy?"

"Wednesday night about ten thirty, maybe ten forty-five."

Napoli grunted. "Gotta make some calls, counselor. I'll be in touch."

Napoli left the conference room, his mind racing. If Sean, by chance, wasn't still in Vietnam, he certainly wanted to know about it. Especially with him maybe having been spotted in Sheepshead Bay at about the same time Delfano got hit with a .45—standard issue for Marine officers.

★ ★ ★

"See ya next Friday. Glad to hear everything's going well with Sean. He's a tough kid. I'm sure he'll make it back okay. Take care, Frank. Regards to Ann." Napoli put down the phone, feeling guilty about probing his best friend about Sean. He reached into his desk for a thin, silver-plated whiskey flask. After two long sips, he called his cousin, Major Phil Menetti of the Manpower Plans and Policy section at the Marine Corps headquarters in Washington, DC.

"Hey, cousin, how them Marines treating you? We missed you this year at Grandma's party. I'm doing great, Phil. Yeah, that was a laugh about the mayor. We always knew he was full of shit. Listen, I need a favor. Got a murder case. Think one of your guys, a young Marine officer, might know something. Somebody thinks they saw him down in Sheepshead Bay the night of the murder. Problem is, as far as we know, he is supposed to be in Vietnam."

"Even a Marine can't be in two places at one time." Major Menetti laughed.

"Yeah, right, Phil. Is there any way a guy could come back home, say for a quick visit, and then go back, maybe some kind of special leave."

Menetti coughed, clearing his throat. "Emergency leave, usually a death in the immediate family. Maybe an R&R to Hawaii, but travel to the US mainland is prohibited. Some guys, especially from the West Coast, do it anyway. But they do it on the sly. So yeah, it's possible."

"Okay, here's the favor. Can you let me know if a Lieutenant Sean Cercone took an emergency leave or one of those R&R trips within the last two weeks? Don't know his unit, Phil. How many Lieutenant Cercones can there be in the Corps? I'm not being a wiseass. It's a high-profile murder investigation. I need your help, Phil."

"Okay, Jimmy," Menetti replied. "I'll do some checking, maybe send out a message. Be back to you in a couple days."

"Couple of days. Thanks, Phil. Give my best to Rita and the kids. Yeah, okay. Spark's Steakhouse—it's a deal next time you're in town."

Napoli hung up and took another long sip from his flask. How could he face his lifelong buddy Frank Cercone and tell him he was going after his godson for murder? How could he charge young Sean, a Marine putting his life on the line for his country, with the murder of the scumbag that probably killed his girl? Hopefully, it was all a mistake. Maybe Sean wasn't involved—just a drug deal gone bad. His gut, and twenty years of experience, told him otherwise. He reached for the flask and drained it with one long swig.

Chapter 36

Sean watched the news report on an old black-and-white TV that sat on the three-drawer dresser in his cheap motel room less than a mile from the airport.

> There has been a dramatic rise in Americans who believe getting involved in Vietnam was a mistake, from 25 percent in 1965 to 45 percent today. The remaining 55 percent apparently want a tougher war policy focusing on the let's-win-or-get-out philosophy. Today we have 330,330 soldiers and 78,000 Marines in Vietnam.

The picture rolled, and static interfered with the commentator's voice. Sean turned off the TV in frustration. Last week had taken its toll. He was anxious and tired, feeling as if he'd been put through an emotional ringer. He wanted to take his mind somewhere else. He grabbed two pieces of faded stationery from the desk drawer, turned them to the clean side, and scratched a letter to his mother.

Crap—no envelopes. He would mail it when he got back to Da Nang. He'd been very lucky so far. The airport hotel off the parkway and travel from JFK to San Francisco had gone smoothly. His connecting flight from Hawaii had actually landed early. He had stayed in this motel room except for quick meals in a grimy diner two blocks away. He had even managed to iron his khaki uniform. Mr. Ambrose was no more.

It's Lieutenant Slattery for a little while longer. Just have to report into the departure lounge for the return flight. If luck holds, be in Da Nang tomorrow afternoon. A few hours later, back in the G1 office after a great R&R in Bangkok.

★   ★   ★

The long line of stone-faced Marines snaked from the terminal to the commercial aircraft that would bring them back to war. Among them was Lieutenant Slattery and, toward the rear of the line, a hulking sergeant major who looked like a professional football player moving to the field on game day.

Sean tossed and turned as the packed jet flew over the Pacific bound for Da Nang, his restlessness caused by the recurring image of Delfano's face and his animallike cry as bullets tore into his body. Any sensation of guilt faded as images of Sandy emerged. Still, the empty feeling persisted; he missed her desperately. The death of her killer didn't make a difference. Maybe justice had been served, but the hurt was still there, and she was still gone.

Four hours into the flight, the groaning comments of his seatmate, a sergeant reading a San Francisco paper, roused Sean from a restless sleep. "It looks like the NVA's stirring the pot. Says here they have three divisions assaulting Khe Sanh Combat Base up on the end of Route 9, not far from the Laotian boarder. What do you think they're up to, Lieutenant?"

"Don't know the area," Sean said. "Been down south with First Mar. Div. I know we moved several battalions up to Quang Tri right before I left. Whatever is going on is gonna be big!"

While he and the sergeant were exchanging views, the jet crossed the international date line, adding another day to the trip. Hours later, they landed at the sprawling Marine airfield in Da Nang at midday on January 31, 1968, the first day of the lunar New Year.

The sergeant peered out the window as the plane taxied across the airstrip. "Hell of a lot going on—strip must have been rocketed. Smoke still coming from a couple of those revetments. Looks like they hit a couple jets."

The captain's voice came on. "Heads up, Marines. You're back in Dodge. Just got news. The bad guys have apparently launched a major offensive, hitting several cities. Seem to have raised a lot of hell down in Saigon. Let's make sure you deplane quickly. Get your tails through that R&R center; might want to get a flak vest and helmet if you can find them. Get back to your units as soon as possible. Good luck, gentlemen."

Sean moved through the confusion at the processing center and found the jeep driver who had been sent to pick him up. "Afternoon, sir," snapped the private, who was wearing a flak jacket and a camouflaged helmet with its chin strap buckled. "Much shit going on, sir. Couple of bad rocket attacks. Some sappers got through the wire last night. Hit the comm bunker on the reverse side of Hill 327, killed three guys."

Sean wrestled to put on a flack vest. "Damn, that bunker is less than three hundred meters from my hooch on 327! Supposed to be one of the most secure spots in Da Nang!"

Chapter 37

"How bad is it?" Sean asked, rushing into his office a few hours after his return.

"Bad enough," Master Sergeant Patterson replied. "Got a big fight going on in Hue City. NVA are pressing hard on Khe Sanh, and we got heavy contact reported all over I Corps. Everyone asking for more troops. Don't have too much slack in the pipeline. We're trying to move units around, but it's gonna be rough for while."

"What's the intelligence scoop, Top?"

"Here's the latest intel brief, big-picture stuff. See for yourself! They're calling it the Tet Offensive."

Sean studied the terse assessment:

The North Vietnamese attacks on Khe Sanh and the Central Highlands are the first stages of a plan to draw US forces away from the coastal population centers. The NVA are calling for a general offensive, general uprising. They believe the South Vietnamese government so unpopular, that a countrywide attack will spark a spontaneous uprising of the population and unhinge the American forces from any semblance of popular support. Attacks are now underway in all major Corps areas.

"Where's Fifth Marines, Top?"

"The regiment is split up. I know they have a battalion out close to Hoi An with one battalion up at Phu Bai. Think the G3 is moving that battalion up to Hue. NVA is holding part of the city."

Sean helped Patterson sort through messages traffic, trying to update unit manning levels against steadily growing casualty reports. A heavyset, ruddy-faced sergeant major entered the office. "Watch out, Patterson—you can cut yourself shuffling all that paper."

Patterson grinned. "Hey, Buck, how ya doing? Just in time for the big fight."

"Hope so. Supposed to hitch up with the First Marines, as their sergeant major. Understand they're up north at Phu Bai."

"Lieutenant, say hello to Sergeant Major Buck Nelson, a good friend, and the oldest NCO in the Corps."

Nelson scowled. "Screw you, Patterson. I'm young enough to kick your ass." He extended his hand to Sean. "Good to meet you, sir. Hey, you look familiar—yeah, of course, weren't you were on my flight from Hawaii?"

"Don't think so, Sergeant Major. Just in from R&R in Bangkok," Sean said.

"Really." The sergeant major smiled. "Musta been your twin sitting a couple of rows in front of me on my flight from Hawaii."

"Guess so. Good to meet you, Sergeant Major," Sean murmured, leaving the office. *Don't want to jog this guy's memory.* "Be back in a few minutes, Top."

★   ★   ★

Sean had several restless nights. He had one of the safest jobs in the division but felt guilty about not being with his unit battling the NVA in Hue City. Taking him out of the field after Sandy's death had been the right thing to do. He had been in no condition to lead anybody at that time. But now was different. He had done what he had to do about Sandy's murder, and maybe because of that, Sean wanted to finish his tour of duty with Alpha Company.

Late that week, he approached Patterson before the master sergeant started sifting through the mountain of message traffic. "Listen, Top, been doing some thinking. With all that's going on, I wanna get back to the Fifth Marines. Get back to Alpha Company up in Hue City."

Patterson stood, folded his tattooed arms, and frowned. "Miss your men, Lieutenant? Wanna get back in the fight? Don't think that's a smart idea, sir." His frown broke into a broad grin. "But it's the Marine thing to do. And nobody ever accused a lieutenant of being smart. Problem is, if you request a transfer, the old man is gonna nix the request. He's gonna say you're needed here."

"But, Top!"

"Hang on, Lieutenant. The way to do it is to cut you temporary orders attaching you to the First Marines. They've got control of all units fighting around Hue city. I'll tell the boss we needed you to unsnarl the replacement system and that you'll be back in a few days. Once you are up there, you work your own bolt, if you get my drift. Just make sure you get back here when they finish kicking the shit out of the NVA. When they take back Hue, you get back here."

The leather-faced sergeant unfolded his arms in a palm-up gesture. "Sure you want to do this, Lieutenant? You seen those casualty reports; you been in the field. You know what it's gonna be like up there."

"I want it, Top. Make it happen."

That afternoon, Sean boarded a CH-46 helicopter heading for Phu Bai, a combat base twenty kilometers south of Hue City. A few hours after Sean's departure, Master Sergeant Patterson received a nonoperational priority message from the office of the assistant chief of staff, G1, Headquarters, Marine Corps, Washington, DC.

4 February 1968
From: CMC/ACSG1/AO1C28
To: CG First MarDiv/ACS G1
Copy to: CG FMF PAC & CG III MAF

Subject: Information concerning Lieutenant Sean Cercone, 0100488, last reported assigned to Headquarters Company, HQ Battalion, First MarDiv.

(1) HQ New York Police Department requests info on SNM (subject-named Marine) in connection with an active murder investigation. Please provide:

   (a) Details on any emergency leave to CONUS by SNM in past thirty days,

(b) Details on any R&R fight to Hawaii taken by SNM in past thirty days,

(c) Details on current assignment/location of SNM.

(2) Response requested not later than forty-eight hours after message receipt.

Chapter 38

Napoli sat at his messy desk as Detective Pierce rushed in his office. "Good morning, Jimmy. Looks like we got some interesting scoop from that kooky desk clerk at the Golden Gate Motel," Pierce said, reading from a field report. "He said there was a guy came in from Florida. Guy checked in on January twenty-fifth, left on the twenty-seventh. Said the guy's name was Ambrose. A young guy, midtwenties, 'bout six foot, kinda thin. We checked the passenger list at Kennedy like you suggested, boss. We got a hit. Guess what?" Pierce raised his fist in triumph. "Looks like Mr. Ambrose didn't come in from Florida. He came in from San Francisco! He flew out on the twenty-eighth back to San Francisco. Get this—with a connecting flight to Hawaii!"

Napoli motioned for the report and waved Pierce to leave. He sat back and put his hands behind his head. Why was he not surprised? Sean was a smart kid. Had balls too. He hoped it wasn't so.

Napoli's phone rang.

"You finally got a reply. Somebody labeled it routine. That's why it took so long. Forget it."

"What does it say?" said Napoli. "Read it to me, Phil!"

6 February 1968
From: CG First MarDiv/ACS G1
To: CMC/ACSG1/AO1C28
Copy: CG III MAF; CG FMF PAC
Ref. (a): CMC G1 ltr. of 020368
Subject: Information concerning Lieutenant Sean Cercone, 0100488

(1) The purpose of this correspondence is to respond to ref. (a).
(2) Detail review of R&R orders from this command and flight manifests from Da Nang R&R center for past thirty days indicates no record of travel to Hawaii by SNM.
(3) Detail review of all emergency leave orders from this command indicate no record of any emergency leave orders issued to SNM.
(4) SNM assigned to First Marine Regiment now in heavy contact with NVA forces vicinity of Hue City. Situation fluid, casualty rate among company-grade officers high. Precise billet of SNM unknown at this time.
(5) Should NYPD rep. wish to visit SNM, this command will assist in transporting NYPD rep. to specific unit within vicinity of Hue City.
(6) Please contact Master Sergeant J. L. Patterson, G1, First MarDiv., III MAF, FMF PAC, for more details.

Napoli grunted thanks after Major Phil Menetti ended his narration with, *"Capiche, paisano?"* He put down the receiver and looked over the boxes and paper files cluttering his office. On one level, he was ashamed of investigating Sean and embarrassed by the timing of his inquiry to the Marine Corps. On another, he was relieved his best friend's godson was apparently not involved in the murder. His investigation of Delfano's homicide, however, was going south, and the mayor and Commissioner Murphy were feeling the heat. On top of it all, Sandra Gold's murder was still unsolved. Adding to his troubles, an ADA had called that morning wanting to know if he had uncovered anything on the Ex-Lax caper.

Jimmy reached into his top drawer. Touching his flask, he remembered that he had failed to refill it. He wanted to be anywhere but his office. He called Frank Cercone, and they agreed to meet at the Wrong Number. After a drink, they planned to go to the Spumoni Gardens, pick up some Sicilian pizza, and bring it to Ann's house.

★   ★   ★

"Great to see you, Jimmy. It's been a while," Ann said, serving square pieces of thick pizza to Frank and Jimmy, who were sitting in the kitchen alcove.

"Well, our chief of detectives is a busy man, Ann," Frank said, pouring a beer into Napoli's glass.

"Sorry, Ann. Your brother-in-law is right for once. Got a lot on my plate. How's Sean doing?"

Ann took her place at the table. "From what I read this morning in the *Daily News*, things are going badly. Battles all over the country. Those poor boys …" Her voice trailed to a whisper. "Did get a letter just yesterday from Sean, and he sounded good." She motioned to her brother-in-law. "Frank, get that packet of letters on top of the fridge."

Frank retrieved the letters bound with a thick green ribbon and placed them in front of Ann. Most were on flimsy, government-issued stationery; a few were on lined notebook paper. The letter on top of the pack appeared out of place. It was on faded commercial stationary.

Ann carefully untied the ribbon, unfolded the top two-page letter, and read it aloud. The two men listened. Jimmy nodded, and his eye caught a single printed line on the back side of the stationery that looked like an address.

Frank smiled. "Sounds like he still has that admin job, which should keep him out of trouble, Ann. Should be thankful about that."

"Let's hope so, dear God. Jimmy, can I get you another piece?" Ann said, turning the pack of letters toward Jimmy and replacing the one she had read.

"No thanks, Ann," he said, stealing a glance at the pack of letters now facing him. The line on the lower edge on the back of the faded stationary was barely visible:

1622 Airport Blvd., Oahu, Hawaii 22331.

Chapter 39

Sean sprinted off the chopper as it made a hasty landing at Phu Bai Combat Base. He approached the two-man landing support team huddled in a shallow hole just off the landing zone. "You Marines know where I can find First Marine headquarters?"

One of the Marines took off his helmet and ran a towel over his face. "Sure, Lieutenant. Up about five hundred meters, that's Route 1. Make a right turn. Go 'bout ten miles till you hit Hue City." He closed one eye and smirked. "They left yesterday, sir. Sorry 'bout that."

Sean needed more information on what was going on. He sought out a buddy from his Basic School class, Lionel Kemp, who he knew was at the combat base. Lieutenant Kemp was assistant S-2, an intelligence officer charged with maintaining an assessment of enemy activity.

"Sean, let me give you the big picture first," Kemp said, pointing to a map on the bunker wall. "During the first two weeks of February, NVA and VC generated major attacks all over the country—down in the delta; Saigon; Central Highlands; Two Corps; Da Nang; and up here in the northern provinces, Quang Ngai and Quang Tri. We took some big hits. Bottom line, though, after two weeks, it's now apparent the NVA/VC general offensive has been a military disaster. There's been no uprising, and lots of bad guys are dead." Kemp shrugged and grinned. "They planned well but executed poorly. Launched over 150 attacks across the country, maybe seventy to eight thousand VC and NVA. Destroyed facilities and killed lots of civilians. But we kicked a lot of ass. Even the ARVN units, especially those with close support from us, did damn well. Vietnamese did better than most people thought they would. And as a result of heavy losses, the local VC infrastructure is in shambles."

"You'd never know that from the press accounts," Sean said.

"Yeah, well, the press is the press." Kemp smirked. "Tet is big news back home and a real political headache for Johnson. But I'm talking pure military outcome. But it's far from over, especially for us Marines. We still have a big fight on our hands in Hue City, the old imperial capital. Khe Sanh Combat Base up in the western part of the DMZ is virtually surrounded. That's a real problem."

★ ★ ★

Sean spent two more days in Phu Bai before hitching a ride to Hue City, where house-to-house fighting raged. Two battalions of Marines and two South Vietnamese battalions battled the entrenched NVA. A few hours after arriving, he stumbled into a narrow, white-bricked building.

Sean handed his orders to a major sitting behind a small field desk in the bomb-shattered building. The tired-looking S-1 of the First Marines laughed. "You gotta be shitting me, Lieutenant. These temp orders say you're here from the Division G1 to coordinate the flow of manpower! Tell those fuckers at division to keep the flow coming this way, and we'll do our best to keep down the flow of dead and wounded going back that way."

"Actually, sir, truth be told, that's not why I'm here," Sean said, gripping his M-16 in one hand. "I'm here to get back to my company. Was the XO of Alpha Five/Five before I got transferred to the G1. Getting temp orders was the quickest way to get here." He gave his sideways smile. "Far as my mission, pretty much determined the best way to coordinate the flow of manpower is to work as a platoon commander or an XO in one of the rifle companies—on a temp basis, of course. That is, if the regiment needs any company-grade officers."

The major stood and extended his hand. "Welcome aboard, Cercone—on a temp basis, of course." His face broke into a broad grin. "Soon as I can, I'll have you meet with Colonel Hughes. Then I'll send you down to Five/Five. They're at about 50 percent of their company-grade strength. Working down by the river 'bout two clicks away. Thanks for showing up, Cercone, and good luck."

When Sean reported into the Fifth Battalion, he was met by a familiar smiling face. "Well, I'll be damned." Gunny Katamana laughed. "Last time I saw you, you were blowing some bunker down around Tam Ky. Then I heard you got hit the same day as me."

"Just a scratch, Gunny K. Heard you were evacuated back to Hawaii."

"I was. Recovered real fast too." He frowned. "Then I found out my bitch of a third wife was running around with a sailor while I was in rehab. Of course I was working on one of them nurses, so I didn't get all broken up about it. Figured rather than get stuck with a fourth one, I'd volunteer to come back. Got in-country about three weeks ago, been back here as S-3 ops chief for last two weeks."

"Makes sense to me, Gunny. Where is Alpha Company?"

"Just up the street about five hundred meters. We got most of the company standing down. They've had a rough couple of weeks, but they're getting in shape."

"I'll leave my pack and stuff here, Gunny. Want to see how they're doing."

"Suit yourself, LT. The old man won't be back for a couple of hours. Alpha's two blocks up, one street from the river. Stay off the street that runs along the river—lot of sniper fire still coming from the other side."

★ ★ ★

Hue had a surreal quietness, with a gray-black layer of clouds blanketing the city as if someone wanted to keep light out of the old provincial capital. Sean trotted through the almost-deserted streets, changing course several times to avoid the smell of decaying bodies that seeped from piles of rubble. Approaching an intersection, he spotted two Marines in the doorway of a half-destroyed two-story building.

"You Marines know where I can find Staff Sergeant Lynch?" Sean hollered.

"And who wants him?" a familiar voice cried from the rear of the building.

Sean cried back, "The British do, for being a bad boy."

"And who the fook is this?" Finbar said, poking his shaved head around the wall. "For the grace of God, if it isn't Mr. Cercone, and looking very well, I might say. Looks as if you're prospering up at division. You working with any of them generals, Lieutenant?"

"Not really, Finbar. Just looking for some honest work. Thought I'd try to get hooked up with my old company."

Sean and Finbar spent the next half-hour sitting in the rubble behind the two remaining walls at the rear of the building. Finbar covered the action of the past two weeks. Sean listened, saying little to the man who had taken over his platoon three short months ago. The twenty-three-year-old staff sergeant had the gaunt look of a tired man in his midthirties. His already lean frame had shed so much weight he could only be described as skinny. Dark shadows ringed his soft blue eyes, one of which appeared permanently bloodshot. Finbar's almost perpetual grin had been replaced by a fierce look accentuated by dirt-crusted frown lines across his forehead and cheeks.

"It's a different kind of a fight, sir," Finbar said, flipping open a civilian map of Hue City. "Street by street, house by house. And you gotta take every room of every bloody house. Passing by a window or a door can mean taking a hit. Alleyways are just another kind of fuckin' shooting gallery. High ground still a big deal, just like out in the bush. But here it means rooftops. It's a whole different ball game. We're learning fast but lost quite a few lads in the process."

Sean gave an understanding nod. Finbar relit a half-smoked cigar. "First couple days were a real cluster fuck. Nobody knew what in hell was going on. Goddamned HQ said we couldn't destroy certain buildings. That bullshit order got pulled quick." He motioned to the map. "We got lucky, 'cause the zips didn't blow this major bridge. We got a company across the river. That was the turning point."

Sean listened intently. In a matter of hours, he would be trying to apply everything Finbar was passing on.

"Just remember—set good rally points, get a high observation point when you're gonna assault. Watch them low windows and them sewers."

A Marine poked his head around the wall. "Staff Sergeant, better come quick. Second squad's got a bad scene in that yellow house up the street."

Lynch and Sean jogged after the Marine, who led them to a French colonial building that had been spared major damage. The pastel-yellow two-story house faced a wide avenue, providing excellent observation for several blocks, and was being used by a forward observer team attached to the second squad.

Rushing through the rear door on the second floor, they encountered a Marine crouched against the wall and murmuring, "Told her to stay away from the window! Told her twice! That fuckin' sniper got her. Now look at her. Look at that kid. What are we gonna do with the kid?"

A slender woman clad in a white ao dai lay perfectly still on the floor. Her high-cheekboned face appeared startled, with dark eyes open wide below a black hole in her forehead. Behind her head, blood gushed through thick, long black hair. A boy of about five clad in black shorts and a pajama-like brown shirt clutched one of the woman's arms, trying to raise her as dark streams of blood flowed around his bare feet.

"Spider, get a body bag!" Sean cried to the Marine in the doorway. "Wasn't your fault, Lenzeni. Can't help her now. We might help the kid. Let's get him down to the medical tent. Maybe they can get him evacuated out of this hellhole."

Finbar growled, "Welcome to Hue City, Lieutenant."

Sean nodded and slowly walked across the room. He knelt down on one knee, prying the hands of the little boy from the woman's arm. Gently picking him up, he wiped the blood from the boy's tiny feet as the child screeched and cried.

"See you in a while, Finbar. Come on, Lenzeni," Sean said. "I'll help you with the kid. Let's get him back to the medical people."

Sean held the sobbing boy against his flack vest, and he and Private Lenzeni moved through the devastated streets of the once-beautiful neighborhood. They tried calming the child, but nothing worked. Arriving at a battalion medical tent, they were greeted by a Navy corpsman who looked as if he hadn't slept in a week. "Is the kid hit?"

Sean shook his head. "No. But he just saw his mother get one in the head. Guess he's kind of all alone now. Can you guys get him some help?"

"Don't know, Lieutenant, but we'll try." The corpsman took the screeching child from Sean.

The two Marines stood motionless, watching tears flow from the boy's black, beady eyes.

"What's gonna happen to him, sir?"

"Don't know," Sean said. "Maybe he'll get to grow up. Guess that's kind of up to us. Know for sure he's not gonna forget today. Neither will I. God, I hate this fuckin' war."

★ ★ ★

"Welcome aboard, Lieutenant." Lieutenant Colonel Grimes, battalion commander of Five/Five, smiled. "I'll get some flak from the G1, but I'll go along with that bullshit manpower-flow story. We'll get you some temp duty down with Alpha Company. First I need you to do something." The colonel's smile turned into a frown. "There's been a report of some big-time atrocity. The ARVN uncovered a mass grave. Regiment wants us to check it out. Got a reporter, pretty good guy, who also wants to check it out. Find Lieutenant Lam, our liaison officer. Tell him to get you out to wherever the hell this site is. Report back here; let me know what's going on."

Sean, Lieutenant Lam, and the reporter drove through what once had been a well-to-do suburb of Hue where several destroyed chateaux marred the otherwise tranquil streets. Approaching a school building that had been spared major damage, they were overwhelmed by a putrid odor. It was a smell Sean had experienced before, but now it seemed to engulf the very air he was breathing. They parked their jeep and went to the rear of the school and up a slight incline toward an oversized white medical tent. The stench of death washed over them.

A trench cut across the well-kept back lawn of the school like a terrible scar on a beautiful face. Three feet wide and over fifty yards long, it was stuffed with bloated bodies being exhumed from the firmly packed dirt.

"My God, what have they done? How could they do this?" Sean's voice fell to a whisper.

The reporter went down on one knee, tied a green hankie over his nose and mouth, and began taking notes. Lieutenant Lam stood in silence, watching two nurses who had their faces covered in green surgical masks move about the corpses exhumed from the trench. One nurse removed wire that bound the hands of the disfigured bodies. The other washed the horror-stricken, lifeless faces of men and women who had incurred the wrath of the liberating North Vietnamese.

Sean's head pounded. He felt queasy. He just wanted to get away from the gruesome scene. After a few agonizing minutes, they drove back into Hue City. Now he really understood the NVA and what this war was all about. Now he knew why he was there.

Chapter 40

"Let's hit the Wrong Number before we go down to the bay for dinner," Frank said, pulling onto the Belt Parkway, already crowded with rush-hour traffic.

"Okay," Napoli said, "but I'm not so popular in that joint since I rousted your nephew's pals in connection with that Delfano murder."

"Hell, they been rousted before. No big deal. Actually, you proved they weren't involved." Frank laughed. "Got any leads on the case?"

"Not a one. Nor do we have anything on the Sandy Gold murder." Jimmy sighed. "But I'm fairly certain Delfano was her killer. He had motive. He was at the scene, despite what his old man the judge claimed. Speaking of the judge, last week he tried to get the Feds involved. The commissioner cut him off by informing his honor about the bag of hash we found in his son's car and the sworn testimony implicating his little peace-activist boy as a major pusher on the Brooklyn campus."

"Think the hit was drug related?"

Napoli moved his head from side to side and pursed his lips. "Yeah, maybe … probably so." *Unless Sean somehow came back home from Vietnam via Hawaii and blew away Sandy's killer.* "So what do you hear from Sean?"

"Just got a letter yesterday," Frank said. "Seems they're moving him out of his rifle company to a slot on the regimental staff. That's the good news. The bad news is Sean thinks his regiment, the First Marines, is getting ready to deploy to Khe Sanh."

"Christ, Khe Sanh. That's been all over the news. Place is surrounded by thousands of gooks. Being defended by a couple of thousand Marines. Sean sure has a knack for getting himself in tough places."

Frank sighed. "Tell me about it!"

★ ★ ★

Early evening, and the bar was already two deep, patrons coming in waves each time the Sea Beach subway disgorged rush-hour commuters onto the Avenue-T station a few doors from the Wrong Number lounge. Frankie and Joey had started their weekend drinking a few hours earlier and sat at a rear table awaiting Sal.

"Sal, over here," Frankie hollered as Sal passed through the crowded entrance.

"Hi, guys." Sal smiled. "Pull up another couple chairs. Frank is just parking his car. Jimmy Nap's with him."

Frankie cringed. *Just what I need to start my weekend—having a drink with the chief of detectives.* "No offense, Joey. It's not like I dislike cops, but Nap is a real pain in my ass."

Frank Cercone and Jimmy joined the trio, huddling around a small cocktail table covered with drink glasses. After exchanging small talk, they fell into an embarrassing silence. Jimmy rose to leave.

"Have another drink, Nap," Frankie said. "Sal's got a letter from Sean last week. You should hear it."

Sal pulled out two sheets of flimsy, dirt-stained military stationery and began reading Sean's letter, which was dated 4 March 1968:

Hi Sal,

The last time I wrote I was still in Da Nang trying to find some way to get back to my old company. I succeeded and rejoined Alpha Company last week. We're in Hue City. I think it's making the press back there. Hue is the old imperial capital of Vietnam. The NVA captured most of the city at the start of the Tet Offensive early last month.

I got my old job back—XO of Alpha Company. Before I took the job, I was assigned to investigate a mass murder of civilians. It was the most horrible thing I've witnessed in this war. I accompanied a reporter and our Vietnamese liaison officer to a high school playground on the edge of the city. We arrived in time to see them unearth about 170 civilian corpses: men and women, hands tied behind their backs, rags stuffed in their months, bullet-riddled bodies, some with a single shot in the head. A few had contorted bodies but no surface wounds, probably buried alive. Our liaison officer, Lt. Lam, said the dead were government officials, their family members, students, ARVN soldiers, policemen, and two priests. The trench was about fifty yards long and stuffed with bodies. The stench was unbelievable; I don't know how they could process the remains.

When I got back to Alpha Company, I had no problem going after the NVA. We had a tough week moving through the Citadel, kind of a walled city within the city. We took the place house by house. I really just caught the tail end of this fight but saw enough to know how much we paid to take this place back.

I told you I hated this war and had doubts about us being involved. Maybe I was wrong. I'm not in love with the South Vietnamese, but they're decent people and our allies. They deserve better than to be butchered by Communists. If the Commies win, what happened at Gai Hoi High School is going to take place all over this country. It's tough losing a lot of good Marines to prevent that, but maybe that's the way it has to be. That's the way it was in Korea, where my uncle Frank fought. That's the way it was in the Pacific, where my dad gave his life.

I'm glad I'm here.

Frankie watched in silence as Sean's godfather, the tough Korean War vet, fought back tears. Napoli placed his arm around his friend's shoulder and looked at the stone-faced trio. "Get us another round, Mr. Ryan. We'll drink to Lieutenant Cercone."

Frankie nodded. "Good idea, Chief Napoli. Real good idea."

Chapter 41

A major, two captains, and recently promoted First Lieutenant Sean Cercone waited anxiously for a helo lift. They were an advance party being sent to Khe Sanh to coordinate the relief of the Twenty-Sixth Marine Regiment, under siege at the combat base since January. The base, a mile long and a quarter-mile wide, sat on a plateau in the northwestern corner of South Vietnam, ten miles east of Laos and four miles below the DMZ. It was twenty miles from Sean's location at Dong Ha. The base and its small airfield served as a major staging and logistical area for Marine forces trying to interdict NVA infiltration into the South from the Ho Chi Minh trail.

Sean leaned back on his full pack, clutched his M-16 upright, and listened to the major brief the advance party.

"We've held Khe Sanh for the past fifty-five days. Four thousand guys, mostly from the Twenty-Sixth Marines, are in the base and on key Hills 881 and 861." He stopped his briefing and looked up. He jumped to his feet at the sight of a CH-46 breaking through the early-morning fog. The major slipped on his pack, stared back at the trio, and barked, "Saddle up, gents—here comes our ride! Better part of two NVA divisions still around Khe Sanh. They hit the base with over a thousand rocket and mortar attacks. We took over four hundred killed, triple that wounded. NVA dead in the thousands. Now it's our turn to hold Khe Sanh."

After a choppy, twenty-minute ride, the CH-46 circled high above Khe Sanh Combat Base and made a rapid descent. Sean looked out a portside window. He was mesmerized by the lush terrain north and west of the base—mashed into a cratered moonscape by hundreds of Marine artillery strikes and tons of bombs delivered by B-52s. The chopper made a hard landing on the steel-matted strip, startling Sean. He followed the others down the helicopter's ramp, sprinting toward a series of bunkers and trenches all covered in a thin layer of red dust.

★   ★   ★

Sergeant Major "Buck" Nelson of the First Marines greeted the four officers as they entered the underground bunker that served as the regiment's command and control center. After introductions, he pulled Sean aside. "Welcome aboard, Lieutenant!" Nelson grinned. "This bunker is the safest place in this hellhole. Them 122 rockets can't get you in here."

Sean tried to recall where they'd met. "Oh, Top Patterson's buddy. Now I remember—the G1 office at division. How you doing, Sergeant Major? Say, maybe you can tell me about why I was transferred to a staff job. Just getting back to form as a company XO. Then I get transferred back to battalion. Two days later, I'm transferred from Fifth Marines to First Marines."

Nelson shuffled, wiping red dust from his sweat-stained utility jacket. "We needed an experienced guy to be an assistant ops officer up here with First Marines. As you know, I got a friend in the G1." Nelson smiled. "The rest is just between us staff NCOs. We thought your time in the field, your promotion, and your ability to be in two places at one time made you the man for the job."

Sean gasped. *Jesus, does he know about Hawaii?*

"Look, kid—sorry, I mean, sir. Don't give a shit about what you did in Hawaii, or points east. Top Patterson gave me the scoop on you. You done well down south as a platoon commander—Bronze Star and two Hearts." Nelson glanced down as if speaking to the bunker floor. "Told me about your girl too. Fuckin' shame." He looked up at Sean. His lips quivered. "Said your dad was killed on Iwo and your mom raised you real good. I was on Iwo too. Let's just say I'm taking care of the son of an Iwo Marine who didn't make it back."

"Thanks, Sergeant Major. I'm sure my mom would appreciate that. Guess my dad would too. Not sure I do, but thanks anyway. Guess I better get settled in." Sean moved to the far end of the dimly lit, foul-smelling bunker, passing several radio operators working their transmitters and frantically scribbling messages on little yellow pads. The place looked like a bookie shop after the last race. He caught sight of familiar figure—his old roommate huddled over a map board.

"Hey, Farnsworth, good to see you! How'd a smart mustang like you get hooked up in this dive?"

Standing to greet his old roommate, Lieutenant B. W. Farnsworth grinned. "Somebody said they needed help coordinating fire support. Division volunteered me! Been in this hellhole for two months. Say, thought you were up at the G1 in Da Nang." He paused and frowned. "Sorry to hear about your girl."

Sean stared at the wall-mounted maps surrounding the field desk. "Yeah, well, that's all over now; nothing anybody can do. What the hell is going on in this place?"

BW motioned Sean to sit on his cot. "It looks as if you guys in the First Marines and your Army Airborne friends are about to break the siege and rescue us from the clutches of the NVA." He pointed to one of the maps with red circles denoting Marine positions on hilltops northwest of the base. "We had it bad down here, but the rifle companies on the hills had it a hell of a lot worse. They deserve the credit. They should be the first to get out of Khe Sanh. Right after them, I wanna be next to go. Gonna break three hundred days next week. Want to spend my short-time back at a safe job at division."

"Get orders for your next duty station?" Sean asked.

"Got a great deal—got orders for the bootstrap program. Seems the green machine thinks I should finish college. They're gonna send me to finish my degree. Probably take about three years. I'll owe them a hell of a lot of time, but I think it's worth it."

"Yeah, that is a good deal. You deserve it after two tours in this place," Sean said. "Now all you gotta do is make it through the next three months."

"Roger that. Still lots of NVA around. We're still getting plenty of incoming rockets from that Co Rock ridgeline just over the Laotian boarder."

★　★　★

Sean spent most of his time in the underground COC bunker. He assisted the operations office in maintaining the situation map, plotting the movements of the four Marine battalions, two ARVN battalions, and an entire Army Airborne group, all operating in the Khe Sanh area. He enjoyed BW's company and especially that of Sergeant Major Nelson, who was becoming a father figure to the son of an Iwo Marine.

"Say, Sergeant Major, how come you're back in-country so soon? Heard you say you were down south a little over a year ago," said Sean. "You wave your overseas control date?"

"Yeah, I did. Crazy, I guess." Nelson rolled his eyes. "Couldn't stand all that paperwork and the headquarters bullshit at FMF PAC."

The ops officer, a major, overheard the conversation. "Jesus, Sergeant Major, my old lady woulda cut my balls off if I short-toured a stateside billet."

"Yep, mine woulda too—if I was still married." Nelson laughed. "Divorced *twice*. Been shot three times, blown up once. Goddamn Marine Corps—you gotta love it!"

"You can love the Corps," the major said, "but you can't go to bed with it."

Nelson flashed a smile. "Sir, you stay around the Corps long enough, you'll get fucked so many times you'll never want to bed down with anyone."

Sean nodded. "Maybe so, Sergeant Major, but nothing says you gotta push your luck!"

"Not trying to be a hero, if that's your drift, sir," Nelson retorted, opening his beefy hands. "Just trying to be with my Marines. Maybe help a couple of 'em get through this. Hell, if I even help one get back, it'll be a good tour. That's all I wanna do—by hook or crook, help some get back."

Chapter 42

After a week of his mole-like existence in the musty bunker, Sean decided to chance a run across the base to Alpha Company. His old unit was manning a perimeter position on the other side of the narrow airstrip.

"Watch yourself, Lieutenant. Keep your ears open for that popping sound," Nelson snapped. "That's the sound of them rockets leaving the launcher. You got maybe five seconds to get your ass in a hole somewhere."

"Thanks, Sergeant Major. Will do," Sean said with a nod, respecting the advice of the veteran, now in his third war.

Sean dashed around antennas and mounds of debris and past the several bunkers, finding his way to the edge of the small airstrip that ran down the center of the base. The burned-out hulk of a C-130 transport sat on one side of the runway, a grim reminder of what it cost to resupply the base. He glanced skyward, scanning for incoming helicopters that were sure to bring a rocket attack. Seeing none, Sean put his hand on his helmet and sprinted across the steel-matted airstrip. Reaching the far side, he slid behind a bunker, panting. He looked over the bunker wall at a trench line that snaked along the edge of the base, thick rolls of razor-tipped barbed wire running parallel to it. Sandbagged bunkers jutted just above the trench line every few dozen meters. It looked like the Western Front of World War I.

Walking a short distance down the trench line, he caught whiff of the all-too-familiar smell of rotten eggs. "My God! Finbar, when are you gonna stop putting chili sauce in those ham and limas? Makes you fart like a sick mule," Sean said, stumbling into a narrow bunker with a piece of runway matting topped with sandbags serving as a roof.

Staff Sergeant Lynch grinned as he lounged on a makeshift cot eating C-rats. "That may be so, LT, but you don't see any of them little fat rats running around, do ya?"

Sean laughed. "When they're not trying to avoid the rats or being gassed, how's the platoon doing?"

"We're gettin' along. This place ain't as bad as Hue, long as you don't mind living underground like a bloody caveman. Then again, I'd rather be a fookin' caveman than a dead man." Lynch raised his arm and clenched his fist. "Got some good news. Doc Jackson got a letter from Murphy. He made it. Lost half his stomach and screwed up one arm, but he's gonna be okay. Says he'll be out of the hospital in a couple of months. Says he's going back to college."

"Jesus! Unbelievable!" Sean cried. "That's great news! Murph made it out. He made it. South Boston's finest, like a rock." He started to well up. *Thank God. I thought he was gone. Thank God.* Regaining his composure, Sean asked, "Talking about good news, heard Slink got his promotion to E-5. Gonna make him your platoon sergeant?"

"I was—I certainly was," Lynch growled, tossing his C-ration can at the bunker wall, "but he refused to take the job. Said he didn't want his promotion either. He's gone off the deep end ever since the news of that guy King getting killed last week. Ever since then, Mr. Jefferson A. Washington says he doesn't give a shit—not about the platoon, not about anything."

Removing his helmet and wiping the back of his neck, Sean turned to the flustered platoon commander. "Martin Luther King wasn't just any guy, Finbar. He was a real leader, maybe the biggest leader of the civil rights movement. For lots of colored people, he was a symbol of something few of us can really grasp. My girl Sandy"—Sean hesitated— "she told me Dr. King was the kind of man she'd follow anywhere. If she were alive, she'd be devastated by his assassination."

Sean put on his helmet and slid to the far end of the bunker. "Not surprised about Washington. He's a sensitive guy—smart too. Matter of fact, I helped him with an application to college just before I left the platoon. Said he wanted to be a teacher. I want to see him, Finbar. Where can I find him?"

Finbar gestured with his thumb. "Third bunker, about fifty meters down the line. What are you gonna do, LT, maybe give him an attitude adjustment?"

"No," Sean said, climbing out of the trench. "Just want to tell him I'm sorry about King. Don't think it'll change how he feels. Just want to let him know how I feel. How Sandy would have felt. Be back in a couple minutes." Leaving the protection of the slit trench, Sean jogged in the direction of Slink Washington's bunker.

With the screeching roar of a freight train, a rocket exploded twenty meters away. A split second later, Sean was tossed in the air, his body smashed against the sandbagged parapet of a nearby bunker. He couldn't hear anything. His body didn't respond. He lay dazed, gasping for breath. A Marine bent over him, and then another joined. They tried talking, but he couldn't hear. He closed his eyes and then opened them a moment later to see Finbar's face close to his. He took a breath, trying to clear his head.

He could barely hear Finbar yelling, "Hold on, LT. Just hold on." Lynch screamed, "Tie it off, Goddamn it. Use your belt—tie it off!"

He was hurt badly. Closing his eyes again, he slowly moved one arm and clutched his hand on his crotch, feeling for his manhood. His breath was short and rapid, but he could breath. He could feel his other arm. He started moving his fingers, then his toes inside his boots.

Everything is there; I'm gonna be good—it's all there.

The two Marines were still bent over his lower body. Lynch grabbed his hand. Sean couldn't understand what was going on. Another Marine stabbed his arm with a needle.

A shot. Putting me out. Gonna be okay. Closing his eyes, Sean felt his body being lifted and placed on a stretcher. His head fell to the side. His eyes opened as the stretcher was raised. He heard himself scream as he saw the bottom of his leg, bones protruding and awash in blood, still in his boot on the hard clay ground.

"No, my God, no, please, not my leg. God no—please. Finbar, don't let them. Finbar—"

Book III

Chapter 43

On the 334th day of his Vietnam tour, Sean was airlifted out of Khe Sanh directly to the hospital ship *Sanctuary* floating three miles off the coast in the South China Sea. Two days after surgery on his traumatically amputated lower leg, he was choppered to Da Nang, where, along with dozens of other wounded Marines, he was strapped in a canvas rack on a C-141 transport for the long ride to Triplet Army hospital in Hawaii. Three weeks and another surgery later, he was transported to St. Albans Naval Hospital in Queens, New York.

Throughout his painful ordeal, heavy sedation caused him to slip in and out of restless sleep. Images flashed in his mind day and night. New images now unfolded, as if someone had placed another reel in the camera: contorted, swollen bodies in a mass grave; a little Vietnamese boy standing in his mother's blood; a severed leg in a blood-splattered boot. Another image that occurred far too frequently was the anguished face of Jay Delfano and his awful screams as Sean put an end to his life. Could he ever escape what he'd seen, what he'd done, and what had been done to him over the past year? Today a new anxiety plagued him. How would his widowed mother react to seeing him as an amputee?

★ ★ ★

"Thanks for coming, Frank." Sean spoke in a raspy voice. "Just wanted to see you before my mom visited. She sounded out of it when I called from Hawaii. Anything you can do to prepare her? I mean, having her visit this place, seeing me like this and the rest of these guys—"

Standing with his back to a portable white screen that afforded some privacy, Frank grasped his godson's hand. "Certainly look a little beat up, but thank God you made it. I'm very proud of you. We all are." The old Marine sergeant turned his head and quickly brushed away a tear. He forced a grin. "Your mom took it bad. Now she's beginning to realize it coulda been a lot worse. Rosa screamed at her the other day. Said we all ought to be down on our knees, thanking God you made it back."

"Yeah, that's one way to look at it. Man, wish I could get some sleep. Unless they dope me up, this thing hurts like hell. Can't get any sleep."

"It'll take some time, Sean, but you'll make it. You'll be back in school in no time."

"Back in school—law school! I don't think so," Sean said, looking away. "After what I've been doing, don't think the law is for me."

"Whaddaya mean, what you been doing?" Frank raised his hands. "You were in a war, Sean. I know you had to do some terrible things. So did I. Just have to leave it be, forget it—don't bring it home."

Sean murmured, "Maybe I already did. Maybe I already brought it home, Frank."

★   ★   ★

Sean wondered how his mother would react to seeing him when Frank brought her to visit. He didn't have to wait long.

Later on the same day, Frank returned with his sister-in-law, Ann, along with Rosa and her daughter, Mary. He led them down the long corridor of the hospital's second floor. Paint pealed from the drab green walls, and the antiseptic smell of the ward was pronounced. They moved cautiously down the narrow hall as legless young men scooted by in wheelchairs. It was if they were moving down a busy street against traffic.

A tall blond boy on crutches, missing a leg, stood in a doorway. "Welcome to the ortho ward, folks."

Ann entered first. The cavernous room had a high ceiling; narrow, frosted-glass windows; and six widely separated beds occupied by young men, all missing one or more limbs.

"Mom! I'm over here."

Rushing to the bed, she threw herself into Sean's open arms. Hugging him, she wept softly. Rosa and her daughter, Mary stood at the other side of the bed, staring down at the flat sheet where Sean's leg would have been. Frank stood silently.

"Good to see you, Rosa, Mary. Thanks for coming," Sean said as his mother drew back from her embrace.

Mary spoke in a whisper. "My God, Sean. You lost a lot of weight."

Rosa placed her frail hands around Sean's face, kissing him on his forehead. "You know how many rosaries we had to say to get you back home? I'll bet the blessed mother is tired of hearing from us."

Sean laughed. "Well, it worked. You got me back—most of me, anyway."

"You're back, Sean! That's what's important," the old woman said with a frown. "And you're gonna start getting better right now. Show the Marine what we brought him, Ann."

Frank handed his sister-in-law a large, insulated picnic bag. "Looks like they're still warm," she said, reaching into the bag to produce a hero sandwich. "Sausage and peppers with my special sauce. We brought several. Do you think the other boys might like some?"

Sean beamed. "My God, thought I smelled something. This is great. Hey, guys! Anybody want one of the best sausage-and-pepper sandwiches ever to come out of Brooklyn?"

Sean's ward mates responded with enthusiastic cries. Rosa and Mary distributed the sauce-laden heroes. A Marine on the far side of the room shook his head and declined. Mary smiled and moved to the next bed.

The decline didn't go unnoticed. His mother whispered, "He looks Italian. How could he not want a hero?"

"He's Puerto Rican, Mom. He lost his hands. A fire in his tank. They were burned so badly they had to amputate. His mom and little sister come every weekend. Don't think he has a dad. Think he's embarrassed about having to be fed. The nurses usually—"

His mother stood, never taking her gaze off the bed across the ward, her face stonelike.

"Mom, you okay?"

"Rosa, bring a sandwich and get that plastic plate, those cloth napkins, and the utensils. They're in the bottom of the bag."

She walked slowly to the bedside of the dark-skinned Marine, his sheet neatly tucked above his elbows. "I'm Ann Cercone, Sean's mom. What's your name, Marine?"

"Thomas Alvarez Rivera, Mrs. Cercone. My friends call me Tommy."

"My husband's name was Tom. He was a Marine too." She smiled.

"Well, the apple doesn't fall far from the tree." Rivera's grin turned to a frown. "Sean told me his dad was killed on Iwo Jima. I'm real sorry, Mrs. Cercone. My mom's a widow too."

Ann motioned to Rosa, who was setting the sandwich on the bedside utility tray. "Rosa, this is Tommy Rivera."

Nodding at the Marine with her mischievous smile, Rosa removed the tinfoil wrapping. "Nice to meet you, Tommy. Got you some sausages and peppers."

"I don't know. It's a little difficult right now. No disrespect, but—"

"Tommy, they tell me you Marines on this ward are very close," Ann said. "You'd do anything for one another. I think it's called being tight."

"Yes, ma'am. We're a tight group of Marines in this ward."

She smiled faintly. "Maybe you didn't get the word, Tommy. The moms of the Marines are pretty tight too. They'd do anything for each other and for their boys. Since your mom isn't here, Tommy, would you let me help you eat? I think your mom would want that. I'd want her to do it for Sean."

Corporal Rivera gazed up and nodded.

Sean watched his mom take a spoon at a time from Rosa, carefully feeding Tommy small slices of peppers and sausages. He looked away and began to cry. Frank passed a handkerchief. "She's a lot tougher than anybody thinks. That's what you're made of, Sean. That's why you're going to get through this."

Chapter 44

"God, I hate this place. All those young guys in that ward missing arms and legs—it just tears you up," Sal said as they pulled into the parking lot of St. Albans Naval Hospital, a half-hour's drive from their Brooklyn neighborhood.

"Yeah, well, I'm sure Sean doesn't like being in the place either," Frankie said. "Hell, been almost two months, and what, two surgeries. The fragments screwed the knee up so bad they had to reconstruct the thing. That's a bad deal, man—a real bad deal."

"When is he gonna get fitted for one of those legs?" Sal asked.

"Couple of months, maybe longer," Frankie said, flipping his ponytail as the two walked through the scrubbed courtyard. "It ain't the leg that's the problem; it's his head I'm worrying about. We've been coming here two, three times a week. Rosa has half the neighborhood on a schedule, somebody here almost every day. And he's still down. Nobody can get through to him. Says he wants to take it one day at a time, doesn't want to think about the future. He doesn't want to get back to the world."

Sal sighed. "Yeah, one of the docs told me that's common. Those guys in that ortho ward support one another, joke around, and kid each other. They get accustomed to the other wounded guys and helping each other out. The doc said none of them will admit it, but most are afraid of getting back to the world where they stand out, where they're pitied rather than accepted." Sal shook his head. "Maybe that's the way it is for

Sean. Add to all that losing Sandy, and I guess he feels there's not much to look forward to."

"Maybe you're right. Could be more than that," Frankie said. "Think he's got some real guilt about knocking off that prick who killed Sandy. Either way, we gotta think about getting him out of here so he can clear his head."

★   ★   ★

Sean beamed when he saw his two buddies. Frankie shouted, "Hey, Marine, what's going on? Been up on those crutches?"

"Yeah, Sean," Sal added, "you gotta get going on those things so you can get out of this place for a couple hours."

"So where am I going?" Sean said, raising himself to a sitting position. "Maybe hobble around the neighborhood? Maybe sit around drinking in the Wrong Number, listening to everybody tell me how sorry they are? Bad enough they come here and—"

"Could take you down to Brighton Beach," Frankie said, extending his palms upward. "Hey, you could sit on the boardwalk, get some sun, smell the ocean, and watch the broads go by. Anything's better than hanging out here. You think they'll let you out for a few hours?"

"Not a bad idea," Sean said. "I'll check with the doc and let you know."

"Sean, you shoulda seen the doll we just passed on the stairs," Sal said. "Incredible—tall, great legs. Didn't catch her rack, but what a face! Right, Frankie?"

Sean smiled. "She had light blue eyes and long black hair."

Sal's eyes widened. "Yeah, Sean, that's her. Did you see her?"

"She was visiting me. Name is Beth." Sean grinned. "Met her at a friend's house down in Woodbridge, Virginia, when I was at Quantico." His grin faded. "She's a widow. Husband was an Army lieutenant, got himself killed in the Ashau Valley in '66. Her best girlfriend married my buddy John Slattery. He was KIA last November. Tough visit."

Frankie raised his eyebrows, and he broke into a slow smile. "All the way up from Virginia to visit you! Hey, maybe we got something going here."

"No, she didn't come up just to visit me. She works for Senator Kennedy. Actually, think it's the Kennedy family," Sean said in a matter-of-fact voice. "Spends a lot time doing legal work at a settlement house in Bed-Stuy run by the family foundation. She met with Sandy a couple of times before … before Sandy was murdered. Guess that's where she got my home address. Mom told her I was here."

Frankie glanced at Sal, who said, "Sure don't like her choice of an employer but can overlook that. Matter of fact, I'd overlook anything for a woman like that. She gonna visit again? Think you have a shot?"

"A shot, a shot at what?" Sean snapped. "She already lost one guy. I'm fairly certain she doesn't want a one-legged vet as the next. No, I don't have a shot." He hesitated. "Not much of a shot, at least—maybe a long shot. I don't know. Doesn't matter."

They don't have to know she'd been here twice. And she's coming back Friday afternoon.

★ ★ ★

Early that evening, Sean received a letter typed on military stationery. *Son of a gun, Buck Nelson. Wonder what the old sergeant major has to say.*

> Lieutenant,
> Real sorry you got hit. We heard you made it and got evaced back to the States. Lt. Farnsworth gave me your address. Thought I'd wait a few weeks before sending this letter. I reckon those were rough weeks. Hope you're getting along now
>
> Guess my plan to take care of the son of an Iwo Marine backfired. Then again, if I didn't get you transferred out of that rifle company, who knows what might have happened. Maybe a lot worse.
>
> All I wanted to do on this tour is get as many Marines as possible through this war, get 'em home safe. Kind of jumped the gun a little on you. Thought you'd been through enough. Still do. Thought you'd be pretty safe as an ops officer. Guess nobody was real safe at Khe Sanh. Like they say, only bad things happen when you stay on defense too long.
>
> The brass finally got it right. We closed Khe Sanh, leveled the whole damn base. Regiment HQ is now in Cau Viet, me with them. Battalions are in maneuver mode. Moving and shooting, going after the NVA. Still not going into Laos—not yet anyway.

This scoop probably isn't doing you much good. It's rough losing a leg. Know several guys in your situation. Some never really recover. Don't think that'll happen to you. You're too smart, got too much going for you. Reckon you have some shit days. Just remember you're a Marine officer, even on one leg. Act like one and take charge. You know the drill—accomplish the mission and take care of your people. First thing you do is to take charge of your rehab and get that done. Then you'll be able to take care of your people. Don't know who they might be, but I'm sure your mom is one. Then move on to the next mission. For men like you, Lieutenant, there's always going to be more missions. My gut tells me there'll be some big ones.

Speaking for another Iwo Marine, I'm sure if your dad was around he'd be real proud of you. Think he would say what I said.

Enough of my bilge. Longest letter I've typed in years. Hope it was worth it. Certainly was far as I'm concerned.

Good luck, son. Semper fi.

Sean read the letter a second time and smiled. *Thanks, Buck. Guess Dad would have been just like you. Semper fi, Sergeant Major.*

Chapter 45

Beth decided to travel back to New York by train rather than an eastern shuttle flight, allowing her to stop in Philadelphia to have lunch with Val.

"How's my little sister doing?" Beth smiled and entered the stately Bryn Mawr mansion.

"Thanks for stopping in, Beth," Val said, kissing her cheek. She led her to a comfortable drawing room off the ornate marbled foyer and spoke before Beth had a chance to sit. "Getting by, one day at a time. Teaching helps. Third graders have a way of taking your mind off things. It's the nights I hate."

Beth sat in a multicolored wingback chair, crossed her legs, and stared out a bay window. "Know the feeling, Val. How 'bout a glass of wine for a weary traveler?"

After a light lunch with Val's mother, the two women returned to the drawing room. "Met a guy at school, an eighth-grade teacher," Val said, adding in a defensive tone, "Just coffee a couple of times. He seems nice. Felt guilty as hell. It's only been six months."

Beth pushed her hand through her flowing black hair. "You could use someone in your life right now. Just be careful of moving too fast. Maybe treat it as a friendship. See where it goes."

"That's what Mother said. At least he'll be around for a while. He's got a deferment, teaching full-time. No more military guys. With the war and all, it's just not fair."

Beth took a deep breath. "No, it's not fair. But sometimes you don't get to choose."

Val frowned. "Beth, it's been almost two years. You don't seem to have a social life. It's all work."

"You mean no social life and no man in my life? All true—till just recently."

Val gushed, "Who is he? Tell me about him; where'd you meet?"

"Too early to talk, little sister." Beth grinned. "Let you know in a couple of weeks if it's going anywhere."

"Geez, hope it does," Val said.

"Me too! Hey, don't want to be late for the four o'clock. I'll have to run."

★ ★ ★

Beth peered out at the dilapidated factories and shabby wood-frame houses that flew past as the New York–bound metro liner sped through the factory towns of north central Jersey. It could have been a scene out of a forties movie in the rural South.

Not much better than Bed-Stuy. So much poverty out there. Hard to think anyone can make a dent. Guess I'll find out. Her thoughts changed to another part of her life. How did he feel about her? Maybe she was just a rebound from his trauma—just filling a void. Maybe he was just a sexual attraction for her. She wished she could understand him better.

"New York—Penn Station, Thirty-Fourth Street next stop. New York, next stop."

She glanced at her watch. Too late to visit St. Albans. Plenty of time for that later—neither of them were going anywhere.

★ ★ ★

During the following weeks, Beth Wilenski became a frequent visitor to St. Albans. Sean had a hard time keeping her off his mind.

Boy, she was something. A hell of a lot different from anyone else, and not simply because she was a knockout—it was that air about her, the confident way she carried herself; nothing rattled her. Strong and precise, but not cold. Listened well and grasped just about any subject. Smart as hell. Except for a polite inquiry now and again, no pity or concern about this amputation. Almost as if they weren't in a hospital ward.

"How was the trip to DC?" Sean asked as she sat down at his bedside.

"It went well. We're making some good progress getting instructors hired for the center. Want to have at least a dozen by the fall." She opened her bag and passed Sean a multipage report.

He glanced at the document. "Impressive. Looks like a Marine operations order."

"Slightly different mission." Beth raised an eyebrow.

"Yeah, a lot more important mission than the ones I got involved in."

"Glad you feel that way, Sean. Appreciate that."

"And I really appreciate you visiting, Beth. This isn't the most pleasant place to spend your evenings." He maneuvered his crutches to lift himself off his bedside.

"Maybe I like the company." Beth laughed. "Even with your primitive political views and bush-league references to us Democrats, I sense there's a social conscience beyond that hard-ass Marine veneer."

Sean smiled. "That's good to know." He went quiet; his smile faded. "Sandy once said much the same thing." It was the first time he had mentioned Sandy during any of Beth's visits.

Both fell silent.

"Jim was a lot like you, Sean—maybe even a bit more conservative. I guess opposites do attract."

"How long did it take to get over Jim?"

"Don't think I'll ever get over Jim. I've come to accept I'll never be with him again. He'll always be there, in a special place ..." Her blue eyes moistened. "I'm sure it's the same for you and Sandy."

"Yeah, it's the same."

Chapter 46

Over the next several visits, Sean became more comfortable sharing his feelings with Beth. Most of them.

"Goddarned, can't believe they lost again." Sean tossed the *Daily News* across his bed. "Probably Mantle's last year, and the Yanks are barely above five hundred. Fifteen games behind Detroit!"

"Good thing you're not a Phillies fan like me." Beth laughed. "Reaching five hundred would be a major milestone. Apart from your passion for the Yanks, what else is new?"

"Well, let's see, just got a letter from my former platoon sergeant, one Finbar Lynch. My old platoon took a bad hit. He was wounded, got evacuated out. He's going home. That's the good news. One of my sergeants, a black kid named Slink, took over the platoon and was shot up pretty bad. Finbar doesn't think he made it out." Sean exhaled. His face hardened. "Really liked Slink. Now I have to tuck him away in my mind with all the others." He shook his head slowly. "Just have no more room, Beth. I'm sick of tucking people away."

Beth grasped his hand. "Maybe it'll end soon. They began peace talks in Paris a few months back."

"Yeah, let's hope so. Maybe if Nixon gets in, things might change."

"McCarthy or Humphrey would seem a better choice," Beth teased.

"Sure thing, if you're rooting for the other team."

"You're impossible," Beth said in mock disgust. "I've no idea why I keep coming here."

"Well, Beth, not sure we have much in common." Sean laughed as she rose to leave. "You're a liberal, dovish Democrat and a Philly fan. I'm a conservative, hawkish Republican and a Yankee fan."

"Is that right—nothing in common?" Beth said, moving closer to stand at Sean's bedside. Reaching over him to fill a glass on the other side of the bed, she slipped her free hand under the sheet and ran it across Sean's bare lower stomach. "I think we can find some common ground one of these days. Don't you think so?" She rose quickly, barely putting a few drops of water in the glass. "See you in a few days." Raising an eyebrow, she gave Sean a sheepish look. "Maybe we'll talk more about finding some common ground."

Sean gave one of his sideways smiles. "Yeah, Beth, love to find some common ground. Don't think we could do it here. Maybe we could—"

"Find someplace else?" Beth teased, turning her head as she ambled toward the door. "We'll have to work on that one, Sean."

Once she left the ward, Sean realized he was physically aroused. He grinned. *It's been a long time.* Thoughts of making love to Beth flashed in his mind. But how could he betray Sandy's memory so soon?

Chapter 47

"God, it's great to get out of that place, if only for a few hours," Sean said as Sal drove his Nova out of the hospital's cobblestone parking lot.

"Where to today, Sean? Wanna hit the Spumoni Garden, get a few slices of pizza? Maybe just go to Nathan's, then down to Brighton."

"Let's go to the Garden and get a large Sicilian pie. We'll have a couple of pieces and bring the rest back to the guys in the ward. There's a stop I want to make along the way."

"Sure thing. Where?"

Sean stared out at the passing traffic.

"I said, where you wanna stop?"

Sean turned to his old friend. "Sandy's house."

Sean made his way up the stairs and leaned awkwardly on his crutches at the Gold's front door. They lost Sandy too. What could he say to them?

Mr. Gold opened the door, and both men stood in silence.

Sean forced a smile. "Hi. Was in the area and wanted to say hello. Wanted to say thanks for—"

"Come on in, son," Mr. Gold said. "Come on over here to the den. Let me give you a hand."

"I'm okay. I can make it," Sean said, positioning his crutches to negotiate the step into the foyer. "That leather chair would be fine. May need a little help getting up." He laughed and glided passed Sam into the den.

Mrs. Gold sat on the twin sofa next to her husband. Both looked to Sean's missing lower leg as he tried to position himself in the high-backed leather chair. Mrs. Gold stood abruptly. "Sean, can I offer you something? Coffee, soda? Have you had lunch?"

"No thanks. Sal is picking me up in a few minutes. We're gonna grab some pizza." He let out a deep breath. The couple appeared quite different. Mr. Gold seemed bloated and tired. Mrs. Gold's face had thinned. Her hair had lost its shine; it was beginning to gray. "Just wanted to say thanks for visiting at the hospital. Afraid I was out of it. Remember you being there but not much else. Pain pills kinda blank things out."

Mr. Gold gave an understanding nod. "You've been through a lot, Sean. I guess we all have."

Mrs. Gold sat down and reached for her husband's hand.

Sean's lips tightened. His green eyes welled with tears. He clasped his hands, looked at the couple, and tried to speak. Tears streaming down his face, he almost screamed, "I'm sorry about Sandy! If I were here, if I'd only been here, it never would have happened. I'm so sorry. I …" He dropped his head into his hands, sobbing with the same loss of control he had experienced when he first learned of Sandy's death.

"Juliana, make some coffee," Mr. Gold said, crossing the room. He placed his trembling hand on Sean's shoulder and knelt by his side. "Wasn't your fault, Sean. Don't blame yourself. A sick individual did this. He'll pay, and he'll rot in hell for what he's done."

Sean raised his face from his hands. "He's already paid—trust me, he's paid. But that's not going to bring Sandy back."

"No, it's not going to bring her back. She's never coming back," Mr. Gold said in a tone of hopeless resignation. He grasped Sean's hand. "But you're back. And there's something you should hear." He hesitated. "When you went over, I had an awful feeling you might not come back. Spent nights preparing what I was going say to my daughter if the worst happened."

He stood and grasped the library shelf with one hand as if he needed support to continue. "I guess the worst has happened. I think my little girl would want me to tell the guy she loved what I was gonna tell her. Terrible things happen, Sean. Life can be cruel. We can't change that. I know you loved her—maybe as much as we did. And you won't forget her. It just wasn't meant to be." His face contorted, dark eyes welling. "That doesn't mean some good can't come of it all. You have to move on, live your life. Sandy would want that. You would have wanted that for her, wouldn't you?"

Sean looked up. "Yes."

Mr. Gold went on as Mrs. Gold came back into the room. "Because of Sandy, you know how to love and be loved. You know the kind of person you want to spend your life with. Maybe very soon, maybe in a few years, you're gonna meet that person. When that happens, open your heart. Love her the way—the way you loved my daughter."

"Sandy would want that for you, Sean. So do we," Juliana said, embracing the sad, wounded young man who their daughter had so loved.

Chapter 48

Beth had spent the entire week in the heat and humidity of Washington, DC. It was the longest she'd been away from Brooklyn since becoming a regular visitor to St. Albans. She was anxious to see Sean and caught up with him sitting on a tiny bench in a small garden off the front entrance of the hospital.

"Hey, mister, that Brighton Beach tan has you lookin' pretty good." Beth squeezed next to him on the bench.

"Must be doing okay if I can attract a beautiful woman to join me on this humble excuse for a seat." Sean reached for her hand. "Really missed you, Beth."

She brushed her long, straight hair aside and smiled. "Missed you too. Never realized how much I enjoyed bantering with a guy from Brooklyn."

"Bantering, is it?" Sean gave a sideways grin. "Didn't know I was good at bantering. Have to remember that. Right now, looks like we're gonna get some rain; better banter ourselves back to the ward."

They walked through the rock garden path back to the hospital entrance and the industrial-sized first-floor elevator. Watching his determined gait, his strong arms pushing down on his crutches, Beth realized the depth of her feelings toward this brash Marine. He was strong and sure of himself but sensitive in a strange way. She was especially pleased how supportive he was of her work in the settlement house. Despite his conservative political views, he shared her commitment and passion for the civil rights movement. Until she had started visiting Sean, her work had been her life. She had resisted getting involved with anyone. Now she wanted Sean and was excited by her feelings. But something didn't seem right.

On reaching Sean's room, it hit her. At first she had thought it was latent guilt over the deaths of Sandy and her husband. Now the issue was clear. Despite all the time they had spent together over the past several weeks, Sean never had spoken about what he wanted to do with his life. Whenever the obvious subject of returning to law school arose, he managed to take the conversation in another direction. She tried once again. "So, Sean, what's the future hold? Thinking about going back to law school?"

Sean picked up a *Time* magazine from his dresser top. "Can't seem to focus on that right now. Say, how's the senator doing? RFK being shot—it's unbelievable. Two brothers assassinated. Says here the family is devastated. They want Teddy out of politics."

She grimaced, frustrated over his evasion. "Haven't met many family members. I did meet with Bobby's wife, Ethel, twice. She's very interested in the settlement house. Met a couple of times with the senator's brother-in-law, Sergeant Shriver. He's on our board. They're tough, committed people, just like the senator. They lived through some great tragedies. I think they'll make it through this one." Beth shook her head. "No, I think the senator will be around for a while, if for nothing else than to get us out of Vietnam."

"Lots of luck to him on that one." Sean smirked. "Especially since his big brother got us into Vietnam in the first place."

"Sean, it was Johnson who escalated the war."

"I said got us into Vietnam, not escalating the mess. When JFK took office, we had virtually no military presence in South Vietnam. Maybe a couple hundred advisors. Three years later, when Johnson took over, there were more than fifteen thousand men, including thousands of Green Berets running their own little war."

Beth looked away and locked her jaw. Clearly annoyed, but not wanting to get embroiled in a debate about the war, she changed the subject to domestic political issues and the forthcoming presidential election.

Sean ticked off a number of things wrong with the country, the economy, the civil rights movement, and several other issues, on each of which he was decidedly pessimistic.

"You seem awfully negative about a lot of things. If you feel that strongly, why don't you plan to do something about them?" Beth nodded, eyebrows raised in a hint of sarcasm.

"Did my thing, Beth. I can have an opinion without leading the charge. Kinda hard to charge on one leg."

Beth stood, adjusted her slim-fitting skirt, and glared. "There are lots you can do! The first of which is to get rid of that self-pity. Take a look around this room, Sean. You're not the only one to take a bad hit. You're not the only one who lost someone." She pushed her hair to the side. "Tell you what, when you decide to stop being a wounded spectator and figure out what you're going to do with your life, give me a call."

She walked out of the ortho ward.

Chapter 49

BRIGHTON BEACH, BROOKLYN
MID-AUGUST

"Appreciate you picking me up," Sean said as Frankie drove in heavy traffic past JFK airport en route to Brighton Beach. "You guys have been unbelievable. Don't think I could make it without you being around. Same for my mom, Frank, and Rosa. The guys in the ward can't believe how lucky I am to have all of you." He turned toward Frankie and wrinkled his brow. "Couple of the guys say vets aren't being treated so well in some parts of the country. Think nobody gives a shit about us. They say some antiwar groups are actually hostile to the guys coming home."

"Yeah, I heard some of that," Frankie said, raising his chin. "That's something you don't have to worry about. You're from Gravesend. We know what you guys went through. We ain't forgetting anytime soon. None of that shit is ever gonna go on in our neighborhood."

Sean replied almost under his breath, "You don't know how much that helps, Frankie. Thanks."

"How's Beth? She's been a fixture in that ward, but I haven't seen her all week. Thought you two were, you know, kind of hitting it off."

"We were." Sean frowned. "Guess I screwed that up. Last week she beat me up pretty good. Told me to call her when I decide what I'm gonna do with my life. She's probably right. Just gotta get through this thing first."

| 218 |

"Yeah. We all wanna see you get through this thing. Which poses a question, Sean. What is this thing and when the hell are you gonna get through it?"

"What do you mean, Frankie? I'm doing okay. I'm being fitted next month. I'm gonna—"

"It's not the leg, Sean. It's your head. Sometimes you're up, looks as if you're getting back to normal. Then bang, you hit a wall. It's like you're not letting go, holding something back." He shot a quick glance, raising one hand from the wheel in a gesture of understanding. "I know it was rough over there, Sandy getting killed, losing your leg. It's a lousy deal. But it's the hand you got dealt. You gotta play it and get on with your life."

Sean rolled his eyes and threw his hands up. "You sound like my Navy shrink. But you know something he doesn't. It's not what happened over there. It's not my leg. I did what I had to do and paid a price. I can accept that. Someday I may even get past Sandy's death." He raised his voice, almost shouting. "It's what I did over here, Frankie. I murdered him."

"Killed him, Sean," Frankie shot back. "And you had the right to do it! Maybe not a legal right under our system. So what! The damn system fails people all the time. Every once in a while, someone has to screw the system to get justice."

Sean went quiet for a few moments. "Yeah, Brain, maybe you're right. Maybe it's about justice. But there's the moral side."

"Hold it! The moral side is gonna lead to religion." Frankie snickered, changing lanes to approach the Ocean Parkway exit. "And us having been all-star altar boys, we know a little something about religion and how God is all forgiving. And we know how this forgiveness thing works. You remember?"

Stopping for the light at Ocean Parkway, Frankie waved his hand in the gesture of a blessing. "First, you confess your sin, which you just did to me. Are you sorry about nailing that murdering pothead peace activist? Just nod your head. Okay, you sorry about offending God? Of course you are. Promise to amend your life and never kill again? Good, you're almost there."

Sean shook his head as Frankie made a left onto Ocean Parkway.

"Now, all you have to do is penance for your sins. I'll leave you to come up with that one." After a moment of silence Frankie grinned. "Just remember you already paid some of your penance bill with your leg. That should take any prison time off the table. When you perform your penance, go in peace, my son, and sin no more."

"You're unbelievable." Sean laughed. "Unbelievable! Okay, Father Frankie, just park over there in front of the entrance to the boardwalk."

Frankie pulled into the space, and Sean opened the door. He closed it abruptly, sliding back in his seat. "You know, Frankie, can't figure you out. What do you want out of life? What is it you actually believe in?"

"Not much. Life is a series of transactions. Just want to come out on top of most of 'em. Far as believing—guess I believe in me, maybe a few friends. Guys like you, Sean. If there's anything else out there, it'll just be another transaction."

"Thanks. That really clears it up for me. Pick me up in an hour or so."

Frankie rolled down his window. "On the serious side, if you're really concerned about guilt and getting past this thing, maybe the first person you have to forgive is yourself."

Dressed in a blue polo shirt and khaki slacks with one leg hemmed to accommodate his missing limb, Sean approached the benches just behind the iron guard rail that lined the seaward side of the wide boardwalk. He was uneasy with Frankie's mocking the elements of confession. True to form, though, Frankie had come up with something to think about: forgiving oneself.

A soft morning breeze brought more people than usual, mostly elderly, to the boardwalk. Sean found an empty bench. As the crowd grew, a short, thin man with sloping shoulders sat on the other end of the bench. Sean had seen the man several times over the last few weeks, but they had never conversed.

"Mind if I sit?" the man asked, nodding his dark, bald head. It seemed misshapen, with scars forming two thick, white lines on one side. His short-sleeved white shirt and light gray pants hung awkwardly over his thin frame, giving him a scarecrow-like appearance.

"Sure," Sean said, not failing to notice the man's pale blue eyes, which seemed oversized and out of place for his face.

"I've zeen you quite recently on these benches, my friend. You new to this neighborhood?" the man said in the heavy accent of a European Jew.

"Grew up a couple miles away in Gravesend off Avenue U. Kind of rehabbing down here. Really like Brighton Beach. As a kid, I spent practically every summer day right out there on Bay Seven."

"Vell, my boy, velcome home. My name is Abe—Abel Paser."

"Nice to meet you, Abe. I'm Sean."

Abe leaned over in his seat. "So, Mr. Sean, looks like you had a bad accident."

"Suppose you could call it that. Lost my leg in the war a few months ago. I'm a Marine."

"I'm sorry. Zat's terrible. Do you have a wife, a family?"

"Just my mother."

"A handsome Marine like you, you must have a voman friend. I'll bet you have several."

Sean looked at old man for a long moment. "I had a girl. She's dead. She was murdered. Don't think you would understand something like that. So no more questions about my love life, okay, Abe?"

Abe raised his sticklike arms in a gesture of surrender. "No more questions, Mr. Sean, but I might understand. I had a girl too, a little girl. She was murdered too. So was my wife."

Sean caught a glimpse of the faded purple numbers on the inside of Abe's forearm. "You were in the camps!"

"Just one camp." Abe's large blue eyes blinked rapidly as if stimulated by an unseen force. "Bergen-Belsen, with my wife and my little girl. Zey separated us on the first day. Never saw them again."

"I'm sorry, Abe." Sean fell silent, embarrassed by his comment to a Holocaust survivor about not understanding loss. He recalled television documentaries about the camps—the naked corpses bulldozed into mass graves, the haunted faces of human skeletons staring up from the crude wooden stalls, massive cement crematoriums, and the somber voice of a commentator detailing the horrors inflicted on the Jews. He vividly remembered the scene of young children behind a barbed-wire fence holding up their arms to display tattooed numbers.

The two men, generations apart but joined in deep loss, sat in silence. Abe began to speak as if he were narrating a story. "I spent three years in that camp. They vorked us like animals, vhipped us, kicked us, choked us, and pissed on us. Then they starved those too weak to vork. Some survived. I survived. I wanted to live to see my wife and my little girl, Lana. I never did."

Abe moved his frail body toward Sean. "And who murdered your girl? Did zey get the one who did it?"

Sean's face tightened in anguish. He shook his head slowly, looking out to the ocean, a soft breeze blowing in his face. "No, they didn't get him. I got him."

"Hey, Sean. Sean, over here!" Frankie called from across the boardwalk. "Come on, I'm just out front. Had to double-park."

Sean rose quickly, positioned his crutches, and glanced over his shoulder. "I'll see you around, Abe."

The old man turned to look across the boardwalk. It was the one with the ponytail. The one he'd seen with Jay Delfano before his murder.

Chapter 50

Sean again sat on his bench. Abe approached and sat at the far end without comment.

"Morning, Abe."

Abe smiled. "Good morning, Sean. Looks like your friend got you here early today."

"Yeah, Frankie runs a limo company. His schedule varies a bit."

Abe glared, his huge blue eyes fixed on Sean. "I've seen your friend in my luncheonette a couple of times several months ago. Difficult to forget someone with zat ponytail. Always with a boy named Jay Delfano." Abe hesitated and drew back against the bench. "Delfano was killed last January, murdered in his car. The police suspected him in the murder of a beautiful girl—my friend Sam Gold's daughter." He stared at Sean. "Her name was Sandy. Was she your—"

"Yeah, Abe, she was."

Abe whispered, "Vere you involved?"

"I killed the one who murdered my Sandy. That's all that matters. I'll live with it," Sean shot back, his eyes closing.

"I understand that feeling, Sean. I killed someone too. The day before zey liberated the camp in '45. Most of the guards had left. One of them, a big Hungarian, came back looking for something. He thought we vere too veak to do him harm. He was wrong."

Sean turned to face the old man, and Abe's voice grew stronger. "Four of us jumped him in the yard. My friend Josh led us. He always

| 223 |

talked of vanting to die with some dignity. The big bastard tossed three of us off him like rag dolls. Josh vas burning with fever and had little strength, but he latched onto one of the pig's legs. Vouldn't let go. Others joined in. They came running in those filthy prison rags. Looked like an angry horde of gray-striped volves." Abe stiffened. His pale eyes grew large. "Zey grabbed his feet, clutched at his arms, and brought him down on his back. Must have been ten of them pinning him on the ground. He was screaming and cursing, the same vay he did when he beat us." The old man paused. "I managed to get back on my feet and picked up a brick. Smashed it in his face. Smashed it again and again. I remember the crunching sound and the vetness. Then I passed out."

Sean's face tightened. *This old guy has been through hell.*

Sitting back on the bench and taking a deep breath, Abe folded his hands on his lap. "The next thing I remembered vaking up on a cot, a British medic vashing my face with a rag. Some of the others vere with me. I asked about Josh. They said he died holding on to that guard's leg. They couldn't get Josh's arms free from his death grip on that pig. They had had to throw him and the guard in a big pit with the other dead. He was one of the few Jews who got his vish. He died with dignity, he died fighting. I was happy for Josh. I felt good about killing zat pig bastard—for a while, at least."

Sean faced the old man, who had lowered his head. "I guess you and your friend Josh had the right to kill, Abe. I'm not so sure I did."

"The right to kill—I don't know. Maybe, maybe not." Abe raised his anguished face to Sean. "Is that vhat's bothering you? Are you questioning your right to kill the one who killed your woman?"

Sean nodded in silence.

"Don't know the answer," Abe said, "but I know it's the wrong question. The question isn't your right to kill. The question now is your right to live. The camp and vhat it did to me, my wife, my daughter, and the guard I killed is the past. Your war, vhat it did to you, your woman, and the murderer you killed is the past."

Abe moved closer and placed his frail hand on Sean's shoulder. "Take it from an old Jew. The past never leaves us. It does grow over time, and you can grow it in a good way. What you do today, this veek, this month, will soon be part of your past. Yesterday may be recent and horrible. You can't change it. But you can make its memory more bearable by living today to grow better memories for your tomorrows."

Abe's voice softened, his huge blue eyes still fixed on Sean. "So go, Mr. Sean, start creating a life zat will soon be part of your past. Find a voman to love, plant your seed, produce new life, and vork hard at something. Vork with passion, trust friends, and help people." He reached and touched Sean's hand. "Your past will change, slowly at first, but the years will fly. Time will weave you a different past. When you look back, you will see far more light than darkness—and you'll have some peace."

Sean covered his face with his hands and pondered Abe's words. *Maybe the guy was right.* He looked into the watery blue eyes of the camp survivor. "Tell me, Abe, are you at peace?"

The old man smiled. "Yes, my boy, I am at peace—most nights."

Chapter 51

Driving alone in his Fairlane coup for the first time since coming home, Sean glanced out over Gravesend Bay. The majestic Verrazano Bridge connecting Brooklyn and Staten Island dominated the skyline. The bay washed up against a rocky shoreline that was separated from the densely populated neighborhoods of Brooklyn by the Belt Parkway. Tucked off the parkway, Dyker Park was a small oasis of green housing Brooklyn's only golf course along with several acres of baseball and football fields.

He exited the parkway, driving to the eastern end of Dyker Park to a lonely cement field designed for softball. On Sunday mornings in the fall, however, no softball was played. Instead, teams of tough men in their twenties, some in their early thirties, did battle in the John F. Kennedy Touch Tackle League. Sean was excited about seeing his team, the Gravesend Gremlins, play their longtime rival, the Red Hook Stomper.

The end zone abutted an eighteen-foot-high cyclone fence that ran across the entire park, leaving no room to cross to the far sideline without actually being on the field of play. Sean did his best to push his crutches as quickly as possible but glided at a slow pace across the end zone. At midfield, play came to a halt. The Gremlins stood at their positions, watching their former teammate hobble across the field to their sideline. The Stompers turned and watched as well. No one said a word.

Frankie raised his arm with clenched fist and screamed, "Sean!" Sal was quick to follow. In a moment all the Gremlins were screaming the solidarity chant, "Sean! Sean!" In a show of respect for an old rival who would never plague them again, virtually all of the Stompers picked up the salute. First one sideline and then the other joined the chorus, which now had a rhythm of its own: "Sean! Sean! Sean!"

When he reached the far sideline, his heart pounded, partly from pushing himself across the field but mostly from being overwhelmed by the chanting gesture. The roaring died down, replaced by individual greetings as he made his way up the Gremlins' sideline.

"Welcome home, Sean!" "Way to go, Marine!" "Welcome back!" "Good to see ya, man." Familiar faces extended their hands to touch him and pat his back. He glided along, flashing his smile. His garrison cap hung on his web belt, silver lieutenant bars on the collar of his neatly creased shirt, and three rows of multicolored ribbons above his left breast pocket. One leg of his dark green trousers pinned neatly back behind his knee.

Coach Franco, in his familiar leather All-Star jacket, and Tony Numbers, the local bookmaker, pushed through the sideline crowd. "One of my ball players!" Franco cried, his faced flushed, voice cracking. "First Tommy, now you. Sean, I'm sorry. I'm so sorry."

"Real sad about Tommy, Coach, but I was lucky. I'll be fine." He grabbed Franco's hand. "Hey, better watch out—I'm gonna get in the coaching business now."

The skinny bookmaker gave a thumbs-up and laughed. "Sean, you beat the odds. Maybe you ain't gonna play anymore halfback, but I'll lay anybody four to one whatever you do, you're gonna come up big."

"Thanks, Numbers. Hope I can get a vig on all that action."

At the midfield sideline, Sean spotted his uncle Frank sanding with Jimmy Napoli. He shouted, "How they doing, Frank? Any score?"

"Nothing, nothing—they can't get anything going!" Frank cried.

Sean drew closer. Frank smiled warmly at his godson. "Welcome home, Marine."

Napoli approached Sean as he repositioned his crutches. He reached behind Sean's neck, drawing their heads together in an awkward hug. He spoke in a solemn voice. "Welcome home, Sean. You did what you had to do. It's over."

"Hey, Jimmy, you make that sound official."

The chief of detectives of Brooklyn South smiled. "Yeah, it's over."

"Cercone! Cercone, get your ass over here. Help me call plays," Nicky Chico, the Gremlins' coach, cried. "We gotta get these guys moving."

Unlocking their embrace, Sean nodded. "Thanks, Jimmy. Glad to be home."

Sean hobbled toward the excited coach Nicky and barked, "Strong right, fake power sweep right, X fly, hit Frankie long."

Turning toward the field and slanting his crutches forward for support, Sean screamed, "Hit somebody! Let's go, Sal. Come on, Frankie. Let's go, Gremlins."

Epilogue

A heavy morning shower dampened the wooden benches lining the boardwalk. Sean wished he'd thought to bring a slicker. He placed his stump on the wet bench, carefully put his book next to him, and glanced down the boardwalk.

The wide wooden thoroughfare was coming alive, the sun peaking through fading clouds. In the distance, Sean could see a hallmark of Coney Island, a narrow steel structure rising more than three hundred feet. What looked like white sheets were drawn skyward, and below them hung narrow canvas chairs occupied by one or two thrill seekers. When each sheet touched the circular grating on top of the structure, as if by magic, a parachute blossomed. Guided by thin cables, the parachutes floated swiftly earthward to a jarring landing, all in about eight seconds.

Sean laughed, recalling the many times he and his friends had ridden the relic of the 1939 World's Fair: uncertainty and fear about getting on, an anxious slow climb, a panoramic view, a sudden jolt, and a quick fall back to the world. *Just like a lot of other things in life.* Lost in thought, he didn't sense anyone's presence until a soft hand touched the side of his neck.

"Good morning, Marine. They told me this is where you hang out. Well, look at this, a book on Constitutional law. Guess you've decided on what you are going to be doing for the next couple of years."

"I guess so," Sean said, reaching up to grasp her hand. "Good to see you, Beth. Thanks for coming."

"What then, Sean, after law school?"

"Not sure just yet. Maybe law, maybe politics. Got a problem though. Whatever it is I'll be doing, I don't want to do it alone."

Slipping her arm around Sean's chest and drawing her cheek next to his, Beth whispered, "I think we can work on that problem."

Once he saw the sun come out, Abe left his store and began his midmorning visit to the boardwalk. He sat on his normal bench and noticed Sean sitting a few benches away. He hadn't seen his young friend in a week and was anxious to hear if he'd gotten back into law school.

Abe rose and was walking toward Sean when he saw a woman approach his bench. She stood erect. She was on the thin side but somehow looked very strong. He watched for a moment and smiled as she bent over, placing her arms around Sean. Nodding his head slowly, blue eyes watering and twinkling in the glare of the sun, Abe cried,. "Shalom, Mr. Sean. Shalom!"